PRAIS

Roll the Sun Across the Sky

"A spellbinding story of a complex woman and her imperfect choices, and how those choices resonate from mother to child and beyond. Probst's latest is a treasure—her nuanced portrait of tragedy and renewal is profound and moving, and impossible to put down."
—**Fiona Davis**, *New York Times* bestselling author of
The Stolen Queen

"Probst has created an unflinchingly gritty, sexy anti-heroine you can't look away from. I gritted my teeth and hoped for the best as I raced toward the conclusion."
—**Alka Joshi**, *New York Times* best-selling author of
The Henna Artist and the Jaipur Trilogy

"*Roll the Sun Across the Sky* mesmerizes from the first pages. How can one be good and still exist in a complicated world? Barbara Linn Probst deftly handles this question via her complex characters in this multi-generational novel. Stunningly written, compelling, and suspenseful, this is an unforgettable read."
—**Julie Maloney**, author of *A Matter of Chance* and
director of *Women Reading Aloud*

"With vivid intensity, from the fading glamour of the Orient Express to the elite enclaves of Manhattan, Barbara Linn Probst delves into a woman's decades-long journey through love, loss, and wisdom— an exploration of growth and self-discovery that is raw and profound."
—**Randy Susan Meyers**,
author of *The Many Lives of Ivy Puddingstone*

"If the devil is in the details, Probst is diabolically good. . . . Characters are richly drawn, exotic locations are artfully described, and the language is fresh and sometimes poetic. . . Much to chew over, including explorations of the role of motherhood, the need for forgiveness, and the power of memory. Thought-provoking, textured, and touching."

—*Kirkus Reviews*

"Probst masterfully succeeds in bringing out the nuances of mother-daughter relations, as well as the complicated nature of grief."

—*BookLife Reviews* (Editor's Pick)

PRAISE FOR BARBARA LINN PROBST

Queen of the Owls

"A nuanced, insightful, culturally relevant investigation of a woman's personal and artistic awakening."
—**Christina Baker Kline**, *New York Times* #1 best-selling author of *Orphan Train* and *A Piece of the World*

"A stunner about the true cost of creativity, and about what it means to be really seen. Gorgeously written and so, so smart. . . . Probst's novel is a work of art in itself."
—**Caroline Leavitt**, *New York Times* best-selling author of *Pictures of You* and *Days of Wonder*

"Probst plumbs the depths of Elizabeth's desperation with a delicacy that underlines the brutal truths her protagonist must face . . . . A thought-provoking, introspective examination of self and sexuality."

—*Booklist*

"A 'must-read' for fans of Georgia O'Keeffe and any woman who struggles to find her true self hidden under the roles of sister, mother, wife, and colleague."

—**Barbara Claypole White**, author of *The Perfect Son* and
The Promise Between Us

The Sound Between the Notes

"A tour de force steeped in suspense . . . a sensitive, astute exploration of artistic passion, family, and perseverance."

—*Kirkus Reviews*, starred review

"Barbara Linn Probst delivers yet another powerful story, balancing lyrical language with a skillfully paced plot, and offering a deep exploration of the search for identity and connection."

—**Julie Cantrell**, *New York Times* best-selling author
of *Perennials*

"A beautifully-written, engrossing, and emotional journey through a woman's search for her own identity."

—*Midwest Book Review*

"A story of tragedy and triumph, of the push and pull of family, of the responsibility we feel to ourselves and those we love. Once I started the book, I couldn't put it down until I reached the last, gorgeously written note."

—**Loretta Nyhan**, Amazon best-selling author of *Digging In* and
The Other Family

The Color of Ice

"Exquisite . . . a passionate tale of love, loss, redemption, and healing as seen through the power of glass and ice."

—**Lisa Barr**, *New York Times* best-selling author of *Woman on Fire*
and *The Goddess of Warsaw*

"Seamlessly portrayed, tenderly sculpted, *The Color of Ice* is an alluring, stunning literary vision that will stay in your mind long after you finish it."

—**Weina Dai Randel**, *Wall Street Journal* best-selling author of
The Last Rose of Shanghai

"A brilliant novel of art and passion set against a stunning Icelandic backdrop. Through vivid descriptions and a keen insight, Probst creates a seamless journey of self-discovery culminating in acceptance, healing, and ultimately, unconditional love."

—**Rochelle Weinstein**, author of *This Is Not How It Ends* and
When We Let Go

"A vivid travelogue, an ode to art, and a compelling journey of self-discovery—all in one remarkable, utterly engrossing novel."

—**Katherine Gray**, award-winning glass artist and
resident evaluator on the Netflix multi-year series *Blown*

ROLL
THE SUN
ACROSS
THE SKY

ROLL
THE SUN
ACROSS
THE SKY

A Novel

BARBARA LINN PROBST

SHE WRITES PRESS

Published 2025
Printed in the United States of America
Print ISBN 978-1-64742-899-0
E-ISBN 978-1-64742-901-0
Library of Congress Control Number: 2025900941

For information, address:
She Writes Press
1569 Solano Ave #546
Berkeley, CA 94707

Interior design by Stacey Aaronson

She Writes Press is a division of SparkPoint Studio, LLC.

. . . the daily miracle of dawn when, for a brief moment, time feels suspended and everything seems possible.

—THIERRY GUILLEMIN, painter
from his 2024 show: *The Promise of Dawn*

PART ONE

———⊰⊱———

ENROUTE

THE LAST DAYS OF THE ORIENT EXPRESS

1977

The summer before I ruin his life, Robert and I travel across Europe—from Amsterdam to Paris and Milan, through Yugoslavia and Bulgaria, all the way to Istanbul, on what turns out to be one of the last crossings of the once-glamorous Orient Express. We fly home at the end of August, and by October everything Robert thinks he knows has been shattered. I don't mean that the trip to Europe caused the ruin of Robert's life. It's simply the order that things happened back then.

The three-day train ride from Venice to Istanbul is my idea; everything is my idea, including the trip itself. I like my job, teaching English at a girls' school in Brooklyn, but all year, ever since the September morning when I handed out freshly-mimeographed copies of the syllabus, I've been dreaming of a summer in Europe. I imagined myself tossing bright new coins into the Trevi Fountain, sipping espresso at the Café de Flore in Paris, licking chocolate and whipped cream from my fingers in Vienna. At eighteen, I would have been happy wandering from place to place with a backpack, Eurail pass, and two or three girlfriends. At twenty-four, I want to go with a man. Not Robert, necessarily. But he happens to be the person I'm dating and, like me, is on a schoolteacher's schedule.

I work out an itinerary and convince Robert to join me. He questions the logic of some of my plans, but mostly he is easy to persuade. He even agrees to the Orient Express. As it happens, we've both seen the film of the Agatha Christie novel and have similar, equally incorrect, visions of what the train will be like— forgetting, or wanting to forget, that Christie's novel was written decades before we were born and intended, even then, as fiction.

We arrive at Santa Lucia Station early in the morning, lugging suitcases and paper bags filled with grapes, peaches, bread, cheese. The Orient Express we board in Venice is, of course, nothing like my image of "the world's most luxurious train." There are no Russian princesses, chandeliers, or gleaming mahogany. Still, the very fact of the journey is thrilling. We find an empty compartment in one of the cars idling on Binario Quatro, and Robert hoists our suitcases onto the overhead rack. There is a faded photo of Hagia Sophia pinned above the seat.

For a while, we have the compartment to ourselves. We sit by the window and watch the scenery roll past: scalloped hills, rows of olive trees, houses made of orange stucco with dark green shutters folded over tall windows, geraniums in clay pots. Women bend in their gardens or stretch to pin big white sheets to clotheslines that loop from tree to tree. Workmen with dark caps and rolled shirtsleeves wait for the train at the local stations. Our fellow passengers lean out the windows to buy cold drinks from the women and boys who rush toward the cars, waving bottles and shouting in Turkish and Italian.

At Trieste, Yugoslavian workers crowd onto the train, heading home for the weekend. One of them makes his way into our compartment. He is tall, scowling, with a striped tee shirt stretched tightly across his chest. He sits down next to Robert and helps himself to one of Robert's cigarettes. Then his features shift. Grinning, he raises a finger to signal *wait a moment*, pulls a pair of stiff new blue jeans from the bag between his feet, and points to Robert's suitcase. Robert leans toward me and whispers, "I think he's smuggling jeans across the border and wants us to pretend they're ours. Otherwise, he has to pay duty."

I wonder how Robert knows this, but it's exactly the sort of thing he knows. Import duties, exchange rates. "No, *nyet*," I tell the Slav. His grin turns insolent and he edges closer, puts his hand on my arm. I jerk away. I can't believe Robert is sitting there, letting the man into our space. "Get rid of him," I hiss.

Robert winces but doesn't move; his lips are fixed in a sheepish smile. I hear the clack of the train wheels, the echo of voices. I can't stand how long it's taking Robert to respond. Why is this so difficult? The Slav waits, as if he already knows that Robert will give in.

After a moment Robert extends his hand and accepts two pairs of jeans. The Slav looks pleased. He claps Robert on the back, puts another cigarette behind his ear, and slips out the door.

I inhale, preparing words to convey my displeasure. Before I can speak, three people push into our compartment, right behind the departing Slav. A German family: husband, wife, and teenage son. They pile coats and parcels onto the empty seat. A loaf of bread juts from the open end of a paper bag.

There are five of us in the compartment now. I assume that someone will take the remaining seat, despite the mound of coats, since the corridor is packed with workers squatting on bundles or standing near the open doorway, smoking. But whenever one of them presses his face to the glass, trying to peer inside, the German waves his hands and shouts, "*Occupato,*

occupato!" He turns to Robert and me with a distasteful look. "*Arbeiter*," he explains, the German word for worker, meaning lower class, not one of us.

At the Yugoslavian border we doze while the train crew is changed. It's dark outside, quiet except for the high-pitched barking of a dog. A two-story building with boarded windows marks the border. Men in uniforms with red stars on their caps prowl the corridors. Every so often, one of them yanks open our door and glares at us.

One of the soldiers demands to see our passports. Robert and I hand him our documents, and he frowns. The German translates into French, a language I can more-or-less speak. It seems that our visas are lacking a particular stamp. I understand the words, but not the reason for the problem. More sentences in German, French, another language I don't recognize. The German says we have to take our passports to the police station, the building with the boarded windows, and have them authorized. "*Une personne*," he says. "*Eine person. Der Mann.*"

He means husband. I try to explain that we're not married. Robert Altschuler, Arden Rice. *Pas marié.* The soldier doesn't understand or doesn't care.

Robert says that he'll go. I need to guard our seats, the peaches and the grapes. He takes the passports and follows the soldier. I lean against the cracked leather, folding my arms. The German woman offers me some bread, but I shake my head. I'm already having crazy thoughts. Guns, a Communist prison. The train leaving without Robert, who now has my passport. I hear the grinding of the engine, a strain of discordant music. Just as the whistle trills, Robert appears in the doorway. The German woman pats my hand. The train begins to move, and the man in the striped tee shirt returns to claim his jeans, no longer smiling. We don't see him again.

4

We pass the first night in our cramped compartment, legs stretched between the legs of the German family across from us. As the sky grows light, we sit up, stretch, and peer out the window at the Yugoslavian countryside. There are fields of tall yellow corn, haystacks built against poles, red-roofed villages. Peasants swinging shovels and scythes. Women in headscarves, men leading horse-drawn carts piled with straw. Many of the villages have no electric wires, though some have television antennas. All have churches. As we move eastward, the pointed steeples give way to Orthodox onion bulbs.

I take out my mirror and try to comb my hair. My mouth is dry, my skin slimy, and I can smell the others. It's no use trying to wash. The stench in the toilet at the end of the car is so bad that we go there only when we must. The Germans dab at their necks as the train speeds on to Belgrade.

At Belgrade we get out while cars are exchanged. A uniformed guard points to his watch and demonstrates that we have half an hour until the train departs. The station is dark, dirty. No color, only shades of black and grey. We buy some börek, the Turkish pastry stuffed with spinach and feta cheese. Bread, bottled water. I want to look around—it's my only chance to see Yugoslavia— but Robert is afraid to miss the train, so we elbow through the crowd and make our way back to our car, clutching our packages. The grease from the börek is already starting to leak through the brown paper. We fan ourselves with Italian magazines, too weary to read.

Later that afternoon, we arrive at the Bulgarian border. The guard takes a long time searching the Germans' luggage. The son leans close as the soldier studies his tee shirts —Pink Floyd, Fleetwood Mac—but the father motions for him to step back.

Finally, the guard indicates that he's finished, and the father hurries to fasten the straps. Robert starts to pull our suitcases from the rack, but the guard dismisses him with an impatient gesture. "America," he snaps. Apparently, he's not going to search our luggage. He asks for our passports and stamps them quickly. Then he says, in heavily-accented English, "You stay in Bulgaria?"

"No," I tell him. "We're going to Istanbul."

"Transit visa," the guard says. "Sixteen American dollars, each person."

I turn to Robert. "I thought you took care of that. When we stopped."

"I'm not sure this is legitimate." His words are slow, uncertain. "I think they're just trying to get money from us. Anyway, we don't have American dollars. Just Italian lire."

I start to vibrate with a weirdly thrilling oscillation between panic and rage. I'm furious at Robert and excited by my own fury. I want to shove him aside and take over. Then I want to clench my teeth and make him take charge, even if he fails.

Robert turns to the guard. "Will you take a traveler's check?"

I choke back a laugh, though the guard doesn't understand. Robert tries again. "I have about twenty dollars in Italian money," he says. "Is that enough for the two of us?"

"Twenty dollars?" The guard curls his lip and stamps our passports a second time before handing them back. Robert draws a wad of Italian lire from the pocket of his jeans. The man shakes his head. "American dollars," he repeats.

"I only have Italian lire," Robert says. "It's worth at least twenty dollars. I can work out the exact amount if you give me a minute."

The guard stares at him, as if he can hardly believe Robert's stupidity. Then he jerks the door open and slams it behind him as he leaves. Robert puts the lire back in his pocket.

"That was awesome," I tell him. He's done what I never expected. Proven himself, proven me wrong. Maybe he's someone I want after all. I put my hand on his. "You were amazing. You bluffed him like a pro."

Robert looks at me strangely. "I wasn't bluffing. I told you, that's all I had. I wouldn't play games with the Bulgarian police."

I let my hand drop. I'm disappointed. Relieved. I don't know what I feel.

The guard doesn't return. The German family eats the last of their bread and sausage. This time, they don't offer us any.

At Sofia, the Germans depart and their places are taken by three Poles and a skinny Italian student named Leonardo who has beautiful dark eyes and the hopeful beginnings of a beard. Leonardo carries all of Carlos Castaneda's books, in hardcover, in his backpack. "Do you know Mr. Castaneda?" he asks. "I have heard that he lives in California. In America."

"We live in New York," I tell him. I give Robert a quick private eyeroll that immediately makes me feel dirty and wrong. I send Leonardo a silent apology.

The Polish girl, Anya, speaks broken English and begins to flirt with Robert in a sweet, kindly way. The Polish boys—brothers, friends, it's impossible to tell—are huge and blond, stupid-looking. I stare at their enormous thighs, their pink cheeks. Skinny sincere Leonardo is crushed between them. Anya sits on Robert's other side, leaning across his lap to point out the passing sights.

After a while, she tires of the scenery and takes out her Polish-English and English-Turkish phrasebooks. We laugh at the unpronounceable syllables and exchange curses in Polish, French, Italian. I tell her that my father's family came to America from

Poland, between the wars. They were Ryżu then, before they became Rice. She gazes at me in delight. "We're sisters!"

She motions to the Polish boys. "Come, time to eat." Then she grabs me by the shoulders, burrowing her face in my neck. "We gobble you up, Arden Ryżu!"

At home, I would hate this. But I am not home, and Anya's delight is contagious. I wrap everyone in my laughter, even Robert.

After a while, the sky darkens. The little compartment feels cozy and intimate. Robert and I share our bread and cheese. The Poles share their fiery Bulgarian vodka. We pass the bottle around, applauding each other's toasts. The air is thick with cigarette smoke and the heat of bodies. One by one, we drift off to sleep, heads on each other's shoulders.

We reach the Turkish border at four in the morning. Groggy, greasy with sweat, we wait for the guards to make their way to us. The train is halted for two hours, three hours, as they examine each passenger's visa. Again, we Americans are passed over in the baggage check. Then there is a sudden, loud commotion. Apparently two Egyptians are being ousted from the train and sent back to Sofia, amid much shouting and cursing. At last, the train begins to move again.

Eight in the morning, and it's already hot and humid. It's our third day in the same clothes. We eat the rest of the börek, washing it down with warm water. Leonardo munches on a pear while Anya dozes against the chest of one of her companions. Robert gazes listlessly out the window.

I'm desperate to use the toilet. My trips to the latrine have been as infrequent as I could bear. The sink doesn't work, and there's no one to mop the floor or empty the metal can that's overflowing with soiled paper, crusts of food, and sanitary napkins wrapped in newspaper. I'm pretty sure, from their smug grins when they return, that the Polish boys have urinated off the side of the gangway between the cars.

The pressure from my bladder is excruciating now; there's no putting this off. I take a wad of tissues from my bag and stand, stepping over legs as I stumble into the corridor. When I get to the latrine, I'm relieved to see that it's free. I take a deep breath, bracing myself for the smell, and pull the door shut behind me.

It won't close. I pull harder, then realize that one of the hinges has broken free. The door is hanging crookedly from its remaining hinge, leaving a wedge-shaped gap. There's a rusted bolt, but it's too short to reach.

Damn it, I think. I'm not pulling my pants down in an unlocked toilet.

I push the door open and look around. A man is leaning against the inside of the car, smoking. He is heavyset, with hooded light-green eyes. It seems unlikely, but I ask anyway. "Speak English?"

He blinks, his face expressionless. "*Parli italiano?*" I ask.

This time, he lifts his chin. "*Sì.*"

"*La porta,*" I tell him. "Can you guard it for me?" I don't know how to say, "Make sure no one comes in." Then I remember a sign in Milan, when we got to La Scala too early. "*Chiuso,*" I say. I pantomime shutting the door. "*La porta* needs to stay *chiuso.*"

I know I should find a woman, but there are no women lounging near the toilet. I give the man a final look, somewhere between pleading and *don't mess with me*, and fling open the door. I close it as much as I can, roll down my jeans, and prop myself so my skin doesn't touch the rim of the bowl. Then I shut my eyes and surrender to the merciful release.

When I open them, I see another eye watching me through the crack between the door and the wall. Green, like the inside of a grape. Somehow, I'm not surprised. I'm not afraid, either. But I'm angry.

Fuck you, I think. You really want to watch, big guy?

I stand, wipe myself carefully, not even trying to hide what I'm doing. The man disgusts me, but I won't cower. I have nothing to apologize for.

When I'm done, I push the door open, hoping to hit him in the face, but he's gone. I make my way back to the compartment. Robert has fallen asleep.

We make our way across Turkey, and the landscape changes again. Instead of red brick houses and vegetable gardens, there are tents, dust. Men with tall staffs tend cattle and sheep. One man has a pole across his shoulders, a bucket swinging from either end; another guides an ox with a stick. The women, clustered around stone wells, wear pantaloons and head scarves. Children play in the dirt.

We take turns sitting by the window, for the fresh air. Leonardo has just begun his turn, leaning out so far that it's hard to believe he won't fall, when someone raps on the door. I start to get up, but Leonardo has already slid back inside. He raises a palm. "Please."

He steps across the Poles' outstretched legs and opens the door to our compartment. A small dark woman is framed in the doorway. She is gesturing angrily, hands opening and closing like beaks. "Bad men," she shouts. "You help."

"What's wrong?" Robert asks, sitting up.

"Turks." She turns her head and spits. Then she makes a gesture with her hands—her right index finger pumping in and out of her left fist—that can't possibly stand for anything except fucking.

Anya looks interested. *"Insieme?"* she asks in Italian. *"O con te?"*

Leonardo translates. "She wants to know if they're screwing each other or want to screw her. The woman."

I lean forward to hear the woman's reply. "You help," she repeats. She points at Robert, who is older than the others—and American, which means he has more authority. "You come."

I look at Robert and raise an eyebrow. He's going to single-handedly take on a group of sex-crazed Turks? To my astonishment, he actually seems to be considering her request.

"Quanti?" he asks. Then, as if remembering that the woman knows some English, he adds, "How many Turks?" He flushes. "I mean, how many men? Their nationality doesn't matter. I don't believe in stereotyping people."

It's obvious that he's lost her. Anya looks amused. She can't have followed all that English, but Robert's awkward, back-pedaling speech—explaining, instead of jumping up to help—needs no translation. She pokes one of the Polish boys and lifts her chin toward the woman in the doorway. *Go. You.*

The Poles stand and move toward the woman. She lets out a screech. "Bad men!" she screams. She backs away, slams the door in their faces. We hear her running down the corridor.

"She's crazy," I say. "I don't think there were any Turks bothering her."

"Or maybe she just wanted me to rescue her." Robert gives me a coy, smug look. "If she couldn't have me, she wasn't interested."

I can't believe he's serious—unless Anya's silly flirting has made him think he's some kind of stud? Anya flirts with everyone, even me.

I look away, finished with the conversation.

We arrive in Istanbul late in the afternoon of the third day. As soon as the brakes grind to a halt, everything bursts into a frenzy of movement, urgency, noise. A conductor runs through the car, flinging open doors. *"Arrive, arrive!"*

People spill into the corridor, shouting and passing suitcases overhead. Within seconds, our companions have grabbed their belongings and are pushing into the aisle, calling merrily, "Goodbye, goodbye! Arden and Robert, you have fun!"

Wait, I want to cry. Aren't we going to kiss each other's cheeks, exchange addresses?

There is a flash of scarlet from Anya's sweater, and then they are gone. There is only Robert now. And me.

We stumble off the train. I feel dizzy, lightheaded. Disoriented. I want to share my cleverness with Robert—"Disoriented, as in: no longer on the Orient Express?"—but it takes all I have to lift one foot after another. I try not to inhale the stench of bodies.

Robert and I are thrust forward. Elbows and parcels thwack against me, a sack of hazelnuts, a chicken squawking in a wire basket. Nausea rises in my throat. I lurch against Robert—and realize that I've made a mistake.

I thought the train was simply a way to get to our destination. Something to endure, a story to tell later, about what we went through to get to the glamor of the Blue Mosque and the Grand Bazaar. But we're at our destination, and it's no different. There are faces inches from mine, with pockmarked noses and gleaming teeth. Heat, flesh. The smells of diesel and cooked meat. A world as crowded and dirty as the train.

We make our way out of the station, onto the teeming street. People thrust food at me, donut-shaped rolls covered with sesame seed, cucumbers peeled and sliced lengthwise with a salted knife. Boys run through the street with trays of tea in painted glasses balanced on their heads. Tiny children sell cups of water. Old men sit by scales, a lira to weigh yourself. Younger men strut past, arms loaded with jackets, sweaters, shoes. Others lounge in front of cafés, smoking waterpipes. The women, linking arms, wear coats buttoned to the neck or dresses over loose trousers. A fat woman plays an accordion.

Robert has a piece of paper with the address of the tourist office; they'll get us a map, a room. I want a private bathroom. It's an extravagance, but I don't care. I don't want to squat on a porcelain square that someone has just used. I want my own shower, a door that locks.

We cross the street, dodging a minibus as it careens around a corner. People are hanging out the doors and windows, suspended by an elbow or fist. The minibus slows to a half-stop and, somehow, six more people get on. Robert and I are swept along by the crowd—in the wrong direction, away from the tourist office.

There's no air, no space between one person and another. It's worse than the train. As if there were no destination after all.

Finally, we break free, stumble into a doorway. Robert puts a hand on my shoulder. I want to slap it away. I want everyone to leave me alone, even him. Especially him.

I wanted to go to Europe with a boyfriend, but Robert is the wrong person. I was impressed with him at first—the way he organized our currency, with little packets for each country; at the Rijksmuseum, when he knew so much about the paintings. I thought he was deep because he took a long time answering my questions, sensuous because he made love slowly.

It's only later, in Egypt, that I realize I've made each thing into what I wanted it to be. And much later, back in America, that I learn how cruel my impatience can make me.

All this happens in 1977, when I am twenty-four and think that I understand everything important about life and people and myself. Of course, I understand nothing at all.

GLEN FIDDICH
2013

For as long as she could remember, Arden had been told that she was impatient, and she rarely denied it. First, because it was true, and second, because it seemed to her that there were worse things than being impatient—like being stingy or two-faced or pretending to be right when you knew very well that you weren't.

Or not texting when you said you would, which was what her husband Connor was doing right now. He'd promised to text and let her know that, yes, he and Leigh were on the early morning train to Manhattan, but it was eight-seventeen and he still hadn't. It wasn't like him, especially since it was her sixtieth birthday and not just any old day.

Connor and Leigh, her daughter, were coming into Manhattan together, full of secret birthday plans that Arden wasn't supposed to know about—and might, of course, be the reason for his distraction. Even so, the absence of a quick little message hurt more than she wanted to admit.

Connor had spent the night in Albany after an all-day conference and was meeting Leigh on the southbound train, as he sometimes did, since she lived in one of the towns on its route. He wasn't Leigh's father—Leigh's birth was years before they met—but he'd been more of a parent than any of her previous fathers, none of whom Arden wanted to think about and definitely not today.

Danielle, her ten-year-old granddaughter, was already in the city. Arden had wanted to do something special for her, so she'd picked Danielle up the day before and taken her to the costume exhibit at the Met, followed by an expensive lunch. Danielle had removed the mint leaves, goat cheese, and shaved radish circles from her salad, as Arden knew she would. That left only the lettuce and grated carrots. And the rolls, of course. Arden didn't care. She loved her granddaughter, though ten was a difficult age, even for someone with a mellow temperament and adaptable nature, neither of which Danielle had.

Arden knew that Danielle irritated her mother. When Danielle had to align the silverware *just so* or posed one of her quirky, out-of-the-blue questions, Leigh would give her a deadpan look and change the subject. The deadpan looks made Arden uncomfortable; surely a mother would find her child's idiosyncrasies charming, at least some of the time? Yet Leigh didn't seem to. Well, Arden would. That was one of the reasons for the visit to the costume exhibit and the extravagant lunch.

She checked her phone again. Eight twenty-four. Danielle was still asleep, burrowed under the wedding ring quilt in the guest room, but she'd have to wake her soon. Arden was certain that there would be a "surprise" brunch, probably at La Grande Boucherie, and Danielle moved slowly. She desperately hoped there wouldn't be sixty candles.

Sixty. Arden could hardly believe it. She'd outlived three Kennedys, two Beatles, seven crew members of the Challenger, and three thousand people trapped in the Twin Towers. She was a survivor, partly by luck and partly by something other than luck, a mixture of agility and bullishness that she'd honed over the years. She'd done what she needed to do, no matter what kind of rock slide was threatening to bury her. If that meant keeping her eyes straight ahead, ignoring the debris—well, so be it.

It was a trait that had won Connor when, supposedly, he wasn't winnable. Arden had been thirty-eight when they met, twice-divorced, with an adolescent daughter and a ridiculously oversized apartment on Riverside Drive. The official story of their meeting was that Leigh, who was doing a school project on sustainability, wanted to visit a place that actually practiced the principles she was studying. Arden found a farm two hours north of Manhattan, midway between Pine Plains and Red Hook, that did all the right things to preserve soil health, manage rainwater, and support a resilient ecosystem. She called and arranged a visit.

The McRae Farm had been in continuous use for three generations; Connor, the grandson, had taken it over when his father died. But Connor wasn't the affable farm-boy Arden had pictured. He had a graduate degree in crop sciences, an eye on the cash register, and an aloof edge. And, of course, he was breathtakingly handsome.

According to the official story, Leigh had wanted to see the barn where the horses were kept, tripped on a rock, and had to be taken to an urgent care center in Rhinebeck where she got five stitches on her left shin. Connor had been attentive and solicitous. He insisted on driving them to the clinic and, when they returned, cooking them a farm-to-table dinner. Arden had scanned the farmhouse for signs of a wife but there weren't any, just three college students who seemed to be living and working on the property. After dinner, he'd given them a basket of perfect red apples to take home.

Later, Arden turned it into a joke. "Call me Eve. He offered me an apple, and I couldn't refuse."

From there, however, the official and unofficial stories diverged. In the version that Arden related to those who asked, she and Connor began a friendship that eventually turned into a romance. In the real story, the Eve quip was more cringe-worthy than clever. While the mythic Eve wanted to cover her nakedness when she bit into the apple—Arden, in contrast, wanted nothing more than to throw the apples on the ground, rip off her clothes, and slide her arms around Connor's spectacular body. Her lust, blindsiding her, felt juvenile and embarrassing.

Just as they were about to leave, the basket of apples stowed in the back seat, one of the college students offered to take them to see the horses while it was still light. "I felt bad," the student said. "Your daughter wanted to see them so badly."

Arden could feel Leigh's surge of eagerness, her hope. "You go," she told her. "You're the horse fan. I'll wait here."

Connor waited with her, leaning against the side of the farmhouse as the student helped Leigh into a tractor and propped her bandaged leg on a crate. Arden watched the tractor disappear down the lane, acutely aware of the man next to her. The two-way buzz was unmistakable. Warning lights flashed in her brain. He was too young, too handsome. Plus, it had been a while. Deliberately. After two marriages and a string of stupid affairs, she'd sworn she was finished.

On the other hand: maybe not.

As if he'd read her mind, Connor gave her a long, thoughtful look. "You're a lovely woman," he said. "I'm sure you know that. But it's only fair to tell you that I'm celibate right now."

Reactions collided across Arden's astonished mind. Had she been that obvious?

And then: Who the hell was celibate, intentionally?

And then: We'll see about that.

Again, Connor seemed to have heard her thoughts. "It's not some kind of weird come-on. It's just something I need to do."

Arden couldn't help herself. "But why?"

"I've been screwing too many women, that's all." Connor dropped his eyes, and Arden couldn't tell if he was being reticent or showing off. "I need to redirect that energy toward my inner development."

The image of Connor screwing too many women seared itself into her flesh. Which women? How many? And what, exactly, was it they did?

Then, in the next instant, Arden wanted to roll her own eyes at his ridiculous New Age declaration—because, really, all those gurus had mistresses and illegitimate children, and it didn't seem to stunt their inner development one bit. Unless he was inventing a reason to reject her?

Well, fuck that. She'd been through too much to get rejected by some jargon-spouting fruit farmer. She lifted her chin and tried to salvage her pride by turning the conversation into the kind of banter she was good at. "Hey, that's my line. Works every time."

"Don't do that," he said.

"Do what?"

"Get all cold and brittle. It's just something I'm doing. It's not personal."

The hell it wasn't. Everything was personal to the people it affected. You could quote whatever cliché you wanted, but in the end the person standing in front of you felt what they felt. Only a callous or clueless person would claim otherwise, and she didn't think Connor McRae was either.

Arden folded her arms and studied the man who was leaning against the farmhouse and, clearly, studying her too. The buzz was still there. And something else, a kind of curiosity, like a thought bubble suspended over their heads: *Who are you, really?*

He intrigued her. And she was certain that she intrigued him too.

Oh, let him redirect his precious energy. Eventually he'd get tired of that lunacy and come to her—because no healthy man who wasn't an actual monk could keep that kind of pompous self-denial going forever.

"I was thinking of lunch," she said. "A nice platonic lunch. I owe you a meal after that wonderful dinner."

"It was my rock she tripped over. Dinner was the least I could do."

"Is that a yes or a no?"

Connor smiled. "It's a yes."

They made a plan to meet at a restaurant in Rhinebeck the following Tuesday—and then, as it turned out, every Tuesday after that. Connor was good company. He was full of ideas, interested in everything, and interested in what Arden thought, too—about Ram Dass, Robert Mapplethorpe, *The Tao of Physics.* Did she think industrialization made it impossible to have a direct relationship with nature? Did she think competition was part of our evolutionary DNA or an aberration?

By the third Tuesday, Arden found herself staying to help him deliver produce to a circuit of rural churches. One week it was apples; the next week, blueberries or tomatoes. She hoisted the heavy cartons into the back of his pickup and onto the stainless-steel counters of the church kitchens, surprised that she could do it—or was her own celibacy, begrudging as it was, making her strong?

Winter vegetables began to replace the fruit. Parsnips, squash, cauliflower. Sometimes Connor would include a few tiny pumpkins or late-ripening tomatoes. The autumn light, slanting through the high windows, turned the color of honey.

One afternoon, as they were setting crates of tomatoes onto a butcherblock table, a small girl appeared in the doorway. She had a gingham dress and thin blonde braids. "What are you doing?" she asked.

Connor turned to her and smiled. "We're the tomato elves. We give people tomatoes on their birthdays." He picked up a bright red tomato and held it out to her. "Here you go. For you."

She shook her head. "I can't. It's not my birthday."

"Every day is your birthday," Connor said. "It means everything is brand-new, like the day you were born. Every moment, really."

The girl grabbed the tomato and ran off. Despite herself, Arden was charmed. It struck her that she might be starting to appreciate Connor's experiment, improbable as it seemed. This intentional celibacy did seem to make things easier—lighter, freer of all that scheming and expectation and then, afterward, the endless analysis.

And yes, okay, she wanted credit for her open-mindedness and wondered if this was a test she had finally passed. A strange test, especially for someone with her complicated history.

Or else it was the perfect test. Tomatoes. Celibacy. Of course.

In a single head-smacking moment, right there in the sunlit kitchen, Arden felt everything come together. Her whole broken life, the pieces snapping into place.

Her heart began to pound so hard that she had to put a palm on her chest, as if to hold it in. She needed to tell Connor what she had understood. Right now, this very second, as if everything depended on telling him before the next thought came and turned it into a tidy little parable with a purpose and a plot—instead of what it really was, something nascent and huge.

And she would have told him, she was sure of it, but there was a rummage sale in the church parking lot, and then the truck wouldn't start and he had to borrow jumper cables, and by then it was late and he had to get back to the farm. She sat next to him in the truck, hugging her elbows as she watched the telephone poles click past.

She'd tell him at their next lunch. Speak. Let herself be known, at last.

They met the following Tuesday at a sushi place that Connor liked. Arden tried to quell her nervousness—half excitement, half dread—as she pulled her chopsticks across the table. "You know," she began, "I think I can see how your celibacy might be helping you."

To her surprise, Connor laughed. "Oh, I'm not doing that anymore." He lifted a dragon roll with a deft pinch.

Arden froze. He wasn't?

Was this it, finally, her reward for waiting? But why hadn't he told her, the moment he decided? "What do you mean?"

He shrugged. "I met this woman who's into polyamory, and it seemed like a better way to practice non-attachment."

Arden felt the chopsticks slip from her fingers. They fell onto the table in a symmetrical X, as if whatever she'd thought was going on between them had been marked incorrect. "Polyamory?"

"*Many* and *love*," he explained. "No limits on who you can love. Just giving and receiving, without preferring one person over another."

For a long humiliating moment, she couldn't speak. Then the words dropped from her lips like chips of ice. "And how is that different from *screwing too many women*—except that you don't have to lie or feel guilty or worry about anyone's feelings?"

"It's based on respect." His voice was calm, almost casual. "Both people agree to each thing that happens, moment by moment." He met her eyes. "Interested?"

Arden stared at him as he reached across the lacquered tabletop and drew his fingers along the skin above her wrist. Tendrils of sensation slid up her arm, like silk.

Then, like the flick of a switch, she felt her fury uncoil and rise up in a spear of white-hot rage. As much as she'd wanted him to touch her, all those Tuesdays, she had accepted his celibacy experiment so she could be with him. But this polyamory bullshit was nothing, nothing like that. She wasn't a member of someone's harem, no matter what kind of pretentious, self-serving name he gave to it.

Anger burned though her. She grabbed his hand and shoved it across the table, onto his plate. "Leave me alone," she hissed.

No limits on who you can love. He was a child. A thirty-eight-year-old woman with a child of her own had nothing in common with a thirty-three-year-old New Age wannabee.

She pushed away from the table and stormed out of the restaurant, flinging the door so hard that it bounced open again. She'd survived more than anything Connor McRae could do to her. Two husbands, a life stuffed into garbage bags, a clump of blood in the toilet that wasn't a baby after all. She'd done some shitty things, but she didn't share, compromise, or wait for someone to decide if she was worth desiring. It was the tripod of her identity and she wasn't going to change it now, not for a glib, self-righteous apple farmer who had no idea what he was talking about.

So much for Connor McRae. If she'd imagined there was something else between them—well, she'd been wrong. It wouldn't be the first time.

When he called three weeks later, asking if she would meet him for a drink, Arden was surprised. He'd drive all the way to Manhattan, he told her—because he had to see her, talk to her. The tremor in his voice startled her, even more than the call itself.

She hesitated, not trusting his motives or her own. Then the curiosity she'd felt, the first time she met him, made her push the hesitation aside. "All right," she said. "I'll meet you in Tarrytown."

They met at a pub by the river. A waiter took their order, then set their tumblers of Glen Fiddich on the little wooden table.

Connor gave a polite nod. Then he leaned forward, hands clasped, and began to speak. No prologue. Just his story.

It turned out that the woman who introduced him to polyamory was only using him to make her husband jealous. She wasn't committed to loving everyone equally; she just wanted to gain the upper hand with a man who was losing interest in her. And when she did, polyamory became irrelevant. So did Connor.

Arden stiffened. So that's what this was, a rebound drink, balm for his wounded pride. Yet there was something in his voice that made her stay, keep listening.

"I thought I'd be angry," he said. "So angry that I'd rush off to prove no one could treat me like that." His eyes were locked on hers. "What I really felt was ashamed. Because I realized that my interest in polyamory was just as dishonest as hers."

Arden felt the air sharpen between them. Every inch of her wanted to comment, maybe even gloat, but she willed herself not to move.

"It wasn't about love," he said. "It wasn't even about sex. It was about vanity. My endless need for the hit, the thrill, when I knew that someone couldn't resist me."

Again, Arden waited. She needed to listen to what he was saying and not add, even in her mind, what she wanted him to say. *I didn't appreciate you.* He hadn't said that. He was talking about himself, not her.

"There's a moment," he told her, "like the moment the addict sees the needle? That's what I wanted. Polyamory gave me a pretty theory to wrap it in, but underneath I was the same as I'd always been." His voice cracked. "I thought I was entitled to have that thrill, whenever I wanted it."

"Because you're so attractive."

"Because I'm so attractive."

She liked him for that. The way he just said it, a fact.

"Good looks might seem like a gift," he said, "but they're not. Not if they make you shallow and stupid, like me."

Arden remembered the Japanese restaurant, how she'd been ready to fall under his spell. It was a power he knew how to wield.

Because he could get away with it. That's what he was telling her. Trusting her with.

She understood, because she'd gotten away with things too. Different acts, the same damage.

Connor shook his head. "I can't believe how naïve I was. Vanity made me naïve, gullible, because I never questioned what I was doing."

Arden could feel the stillness inside her, and around her. It was like the place between heartbeats. The hinge between past and future, when everything could go one way or another.

It was up to her and what she wanted. There was a part of her that wanted to be right, to say, "I told you so." To make him suffer and apologize for humiliating her.

Yet there was something else too. A possibility.

There were things she had done and never paid for, far worse things than toying with someone in a Japanese restaurant. But she could pay it forward, right now. With him. Transform all those mistakes into something good.

She moved her glass of Glen Fiddich to the side and took Connor's hand. "Maybe gullibility is a prelude to trust. If we never dared to be gullible, we'd never have the experience of trusting someone who turned out to be worth trusting."

He laced his fingers through hers. "Are you worth trusting, Mary Arden Rice?"

I could be. I could be that person.

Arden thought of the people she had been mean to, or careless with, which ended up being the same thing. How selfish she had been, except with Leigh.

A yearning echoed in her mind, from long ago. *Let me be good.*

"Yes," she said. "I am."

They were married the following spring, even though Arden had sworn she wouldn't marry again. Connor volunteered to move into the Manhattan apartment: Leigh had a school, a life; she couldn't relocate to a farm three counties away. When Arden tried to thank him for being so gracious, he brushed away her gratitude. He liked Leigh. She was lively, curious; besides, it was the right thing to do.

Connor turned the McRae farm over to his brother, though he returned to help in the summers, except for the year he had the knee replacement. He still gave seminars on sustainability, attended meetings in Ithaca and Albany. That was where he'd been the day before, transferring from Amtrak to the commuter railroad so he could travel the rest of the way with Leigh. For Arden's birthday.

Arden looked at her phone again. Eight forty-one. Nothing.

Her impatience spiked. She thought of texting him first, then decided: No. It was her birthday, not his. She threw the phone on the couch, tired of its silence.

Danielle, her granddaughter, screamed in her sleep. An unearthly sound, like the screech of an owl or a crow.

Arden raced to the guest room and found Danielle writhing on top of the quilt. "Sweetheart, sweetheart." She gathered the girl into her arms. "A dream, darling. You had a bad dream."

Danielle pulled away. "I didn't," she whispered. "I saw."

At four-thirty that morning, the engineer assigned to operate the commuter train that Connor and Leigh would be on rose from his bed, showered, and drove to work. When he arrived at the railroad's northern terminus, he bought a cup of coffee and a roll, filled out the required paperwork, and attended a standard safety briefing. The train's equipment was tested and found to be in proper working condition. The doors opened seven minutes before the scheduled departure and the waiting passengers, including Connor McRae, boarded its six cars. Connor settled into a three-person seat in the front car, where he and Leigh had agreed to meet. The train departed on time for its route into New York.

Two stops and seventeen minutes later, it pulled into a local station along the river where eight new passengers got on, including Leigh. She spotted Connor and gave him a merry wave. "Hey there," she called. "Did you bring me a bagel?"

Connor turned to greet her. "I did." Leigh settled into the aisle seat as he extracted two items wrapped in waxed paper from the bag that he'd placed on the middle seat. He had promised to text Arden when he and Leigh met up, but his fingers were greasy with cream cheese and it was still early. Arden was probably asleep. He'd text later.

He and Leigh ate in companionable silence as the train made its way south. By Croton-Harmon, like many of the passengers, they had fallen asleep against the faux-leather seats. Connor awoke, briefly, when they stopped in Tarrytown. He gave a small private smile as he remembered the evening twenty-two years earlier and the glass of Glen Fiddich. Then he remembered, again, that he needed to text Arden, but dropped off to sleep a moment later.

As they neared the Bronx, the engineer was supposed to slow the train in anticipation of the sharp curve ahead. But he didn't, and the train entered the curve at nearly three times the posted speed.

Later, the engineer told investigators that he'd gone into a kind of daze, like the hypnosis that long-distance truck drivers can succumb to as they stare at the taillights in front of them. By the time he jolted awake and tried to apply the emergency brake, the train was already entering the curve, the front two cars tumbling off the track onto the cliff below.

Of the one hundred and twenty passengers on board, half were injured and five were killed. All five were in the front car. Among them were Connor and Leigh.

It was eventually found that the engineer had undiagnosed sleep apnea, exacerbated by a recent shift to an early-morning schedule.

The call came from someone named Officer Navarro. Bizarrely, Connor's driver's license in its plastic case was intact; that was how they determined his identity so quickly. Leigh, whose poor broken body had been hurled down the cliff, wasn't officially identified until later.

Arden, frozen with horror, could barely take in Navarro's condolences. They were just sounds, because consolation was irrelevant. He didn't understand, as she did, that the train had been moving toward her for years.

The punishment she always knew would come.

The price for all the acts she'd never had to pay for.

THE WRONG SEASON
FOR LUXOR
1977

After Istanbul, Robert and I go to Izmir to see the ruins of Ephesus, the ancient Aegean port that belonged, in turn, to the Greeks, Lydians, Persians, Macedonians, Egyptians, Romans, Ottomans, and modern-day Turks. I especially want to see the Temple of Artemis, one of the Seven Wonders of the World, and the cult statue of Artemis—a standing figure covered with little globes that, supposedly, represented dozens of breasts. Or else, as some claimed, the testicles of sacrificial bulls.

Artemis fascinates me. Goddess of the hunt and the moon—of the wilderness, chastity, fertility, and childbirth. An odd group of opposites. I'm crushed when Robert tells me that virtually nothing of her temple remains. I insist on going anyway, but Robert is right. There is nothing to see, only a single column and bits of stone.

I decide that we should go to Greece, a country full of temples. Greece isn't part of the itinerary, but there are three weeks until we have to be back at our jobs—Robert's, as librarian at an elite all-boys school; mine, teaching English to pampered middle-school girls. I'm tired of Turkey, where the women are hidden by trousers and coats while the men strut ahead. We have three weeks, and I want one more country.

Robert is reluctant, but concedes. We book a ferry from Izmir to Piraeus, near Athens. From Athens, any sensible tourist would go to the Greek islands, but we meet a Canadian at a kafenio who goes on and on about how cheaply you can get to Alexandria if you're willing to go deck passage and how crazy we'd be to miss the Pyramids. The Canadian is confident, charismatic, so I badger Robert yet again until he gives in. The Canadian claps Robert on the shoulder and gives us the address of an agent who can book us a last-minute passage.

The Canadian was right; deck passage is lovely. There is space, fresh air, and the quiet of the stars. In two days, we are in Alexandria. In three days, Cairo.

The first hours in Cairo are a shock, even after Istanbul. The teeming buses and packed sidewalks are the same, but this is a new continent, foreign in a way I didn't expect. Billboards are covered in a red script that reminds me of birds in flight; donkey carts weave between the buses and cars. There are men in turbans and burnooses, white robes, black robes, striped pajama-like garb. Gold earrings and gold teeth, Nubian skin. Saudi sheiks, in their immaculate galabeyas. For each sheik, there are a dozen filthy children who tug at my clothes and plead, "*Baksheesh, baksheesh?*"

On our second afternoon, Robert and I go to the Egyptian Museum. A trio of old men follows us. "*Baksheesh,*" they whisper through missing or rotten teeth, obsequious and aggressive at the same time, demanding payment for creeping along behind us and saying, "Ramses!" or switching on a light we don't need.

The Egyptian Museum is a refuge—cool, quiet galleries with

inlaid furniture and jewelry made of gold and lapis lazuli, pharaohs in their stone coffins. Away from its serene halls, Cairo stinks of garbage. A boy urinates in the street. Watermelon rinds buzz with flies, and there are flies crawling across a sleeping baby's open sores. Old men sprawl in the gutter, hands out. The flies crawl across them, too, even on their eyes.

We're warned by a woman in the tourist office that it's the wrong season for Egypt, and definitely the wrong season to head any further south. Sensible people visit in the winter; only idiots in August, when temperatures of forty-two Celsius—Robert does the conversion, looking pleased with himself—keep all but the hardiest natives in shuttered rooms from nine in the morning till nine at night.

There's no point explaining that we're prisoners of the academic calendar, trying to stretch our time and money. They assume that we're wealthy because we're American. The Egyptians like Jimmy Carter, and they love American television, especially *Little House on the Prairie*, but they aren't interested in the fine points of American social class. We have good teeth and the means to travel; that makes all Americans the same.

We take a day trip to Giza and the Pyramids, and I get to see one of the Seven Wonders of the World after all. The Great Pyramid, tomb of the Pharaoh Khufu, is still intact, even if the monument to Artemis is not. No surprise; everything here is focused on the men. That was clear when we booked our deck passage. The agent would only talk to Robert, not me, even though Robert kept turning to see what I thought.

Still, the Great Sphinx has inspired me, and now I want to go to Luxor, to see Karnak and the Valley of the Kings. Robert quotes the woman in the tourist office about the triple-digit heat. I hate having to nag, but it's the only way.

Robert adds up the time, the money. He records everything

in a spiral notebook that he keeps in his pocket. One baguette and eighty grams of cheese, twenty-four minutes from central Cairo to Giza. He's meticulous about checking ingredients so he can avoid foods that disagree with him: citrus, sesame, corn. I'm fairly certain that he keeps track of when we have sex.

Luxor is impractical, he tells me, but I want it. I sink my teeth into the idea, like a dog. Wear him down, get what I want. I learn that there is a train from Cairo to Luxor. After three days on the Orient Express, an eleven-hour train ride is now in the category of *no big deal*. I want to take the overnight sleeper, but it's more expensive. The day train is fine, Robert says, taking a stand. We can see the countryside.

We leave Giza Station at eight in the morning, hoist our bags onto the rack, and settle our tightly wrapped falafel between us on the seat. I watch as Cairo's squalor and filth give way to rolling fields of cotton, fava beans, alfalfa. Rows of date palms and mango trees line the river. It's mango season. In Cairo, I saw street vendors peel mangoes with the flick of a pocketknife, toss the pitted sections into the tumbler of a battery-operated blender, and sell mango smoothies for a piaster or two. Now I understand why the smoothies were so cheap. Soon, the fruit will rot and have to be thrown away.

We pass villages with mud walls and flat roofs piled with straw. Women kneel by the streams to fill clay jugs as the water buffalo wade past, stirring the mud. Children ride donkeys along the edge of the water. There are camels, too, with their slow swaying walk, sometimes mounted, sometimes roped together, laden with carpets or straw. After a while there are no more villages and fields, just an expanse of desert rimmed by barren cliffs.

By the time we arrive in Luxor, it's seven in the evening. We need a place to sleep, but everything is shuttered against the heat. Just as the woman in Cairo warned us, businesses are closed until eight thirty or nine o'clock. I wait for Robert to say, "You're right, we should have taken the sleeper train," but he doesn't. Maybe he doesn't think I was right. After all, we saved money.

I hate that I've even thought this. It's a Robert-thought, landing on me like a fly. I want to swat it away. I didn't travel halfway around the world to be someone who measures each experience before having it. Instead of having it.

I'm not that. Won't be that. I'm a woman who dances in the moonlight. Spends an extravagant amount of money on a scarf I don't need. Fucks against the side of a building because I can't wait a second longer.

I grab Robert's arm. "Let's forget those cheap hotels. Let's get a really incredible room, just this once." He gives me a dubious look, but I keep talking, more and more certain of the rightness of my vision. "I'm sick of counting pennies. We've been doing that all summer."

"Arden—" he begins, but there's no stopping me.

"I have a credit card," I tell him. "I'll pay for it."

I do have a credit card. My parents insisted on giving it to me before we left. They called it a safety net. They are like that. Ryżu, counting grains of rice, setting some aside. *You never know.*

When my mother was a girl, my grandmother made her sew a twenty-dollar bill into the hem of her skirt. A generation later, she presses a credit card into her daughter's hand.

I haven't told Robert about the credit card because I never intended to use it. But this one time, I will.

I'm giddy with excitement now, convinced that this is the answer. In a luxury hotel with good sheets fitted across a good mattress, Robert and I will shed the accountant-skin that's gotten stuck to our flesh. We'll be different, free and alive. *Luxor* and *luxury.* The connection seems obvious.

In fact, the high-end lodgings are open, even though the

shops and smaller hotels are not. I book a room for two nights at a hotel that looks like a sultan's palace, with fountains and tiled courtyards. Robert flinches as I put it on the credit card, but I pretend not to notice. The manager suggests that we have a drink in the garden while a porter takes our bags to the room. I think it's a wonderful idea. We'll sit by a fountain shaped like a fish and toast to a new possibility.

The waiter recommends Carcaday, a drink made from the petals of the red hibiscus. "Nowhere else will you find this drink," he tells us. "In it, the water of the Nile. There is a saying that once you have drunk from the Nile, you are obliged to return."

It's tourist nonsense, but I'm charmed anyway. "Carcaday," I agree.

The waiter looks at Robert, and I realize that I've violated the gendered rule. Robert is the one who is supposed to agree or decline, not me. The waiter tilts his head discreetly. "Carcaday," Robert echoes, and the waiter withdraws.

It's still early by Luxor time, so we have the terrace to ourselves. Soon four waiters have gathered around our table, offering advice and assistance. Each, it seems, has an uncle who owns a taxi cab and can show us tombs that ordinary tourists never see, or a cousin who makes unique Egyptian jewelry that he will only sell to special friends, like us. It's an upscale version of the street hustle we saw in Cairo, but it seems funny now, endearing. We thank them for the suggestions and agree that it's best to visit the tombs early in the morning, sleep all afternoon, and dine at night.

The manager tells us that our room is ready. We take the elevator to the fifth floor. The room, overlooking yet another patio with mosaic-tiled benches and birds-of-paradise in terracotta pots, is as beautiful as I imagined, but we're tired and there's no spark between us. We don't make love.

◄ ———— ►

We get up at five the next morning and take a taxi to the Valley of the Kings, burial ground of the pharaohs. Entranced, we wander through tombs carved from solid rock, with their long winding passages, side-chambers, and hidden entrances. Above Seti's tomb, there is a rounded ceiling covered with paintings. Incised figures line the underground walls.

Despite our similar enchantment, Robert and I can't seem to find a common tempo. He dawdles over hieroglyphics that don't interest me or hurries past murals when I want to linger. I'd rather separate, have my own experience, yet it doesn't seem right. That wasn't my plan, when I decided to splurge on a romantic visit to Luxor.

I can't remember my plan. I begin to panic as Robert disappears around a corner.

I feel a tap on my shoulder. I turn and see a boy with dark eyes and a dirty face. "*Baksheesh?*" he asks, holding out his hand. I shiver, then hurry to catch up with Robert.

After the Valley of the Kings, we go to Deir el-Medina, the Tombs of the Workers—the people who built the extravagant burial chambers of the pharaohs and then, in their free time, their own tombs.

Robert and I feel our way through the dark passageways. Each step, hewn from rock, is a different size, so we move cautiously, our palms grazing the damp walls. Our guide, a barefoot teenager, is a few steps ahead, holding a candle to light the way.

We turn a corner and reach the innermost chamber. The boy lifts his candle, and the room explodes in a riot of color. Clumps of purple grapes, twisting vines, sheaves of corn, serpents. Women with black, snakelike curls. Creatures with bird heads, jackal heads, cobra heads. Processions of baboons and white-robed maidens and slender golden youths carrying food and flowers, all crowded into the tiny underground room.

This isn't the homage to a dead king, designed to impress the gods and help him on his journey to immortality. It's a portrait of a real, human community. Vibrant, bursting with life.

The boy gestures and smiles, as if the paintings are his. "You like?"

I nod, unable to speak.

"*Baksheesh?*"

Yes, all right. *Baksheesh.*

By the time we leave Deir el-Medina, the heat is brutal. We return to the hotel to nap until dinner. Robert falls asleep right away but I lie on my back, wide-awake. I'm not thinking about dancing in the moonlight: a solitary figure, raising her alabaster arms to the sky. I'm thinking about the people whose world I've just glimpsed. How they celebrated their communal lives, adorned their communal grave.

Let it be for the good of all.

I don't know where the words come from or what they mean, but a new thought pulses in my brain. *Let me be good.*

I do want to be good. Patient, generous, kind. I don't know how long it will take to become this. I think of the mangoes. Of their ripeness, and how they will soon be useless.

I roll onto my side. There is something absurd about my longing. I am thinking impatiently about how to be patient.

I have booked the hotel for two nights. What do I expect, from two nights?

The hotel is a splurge, Luxor itself is a splurge. I don't know what else to spurge on, if this makes no difference.

It's after nine o'clock, though early for Luxor, when Robert and I set out to find a place for dinner. The air has grown balmy, with a soft breeze that stirs the palms. Lights glitter on the river as feluccas with their big white sails glide past.

I point to a sign by the water's edge. CHEZ FAROUK. Stone steps lead to an entrance strung with colored lights, a wooden deck. Robert nods. We make our way down a path lined with succulents and bamboo.

A waiter is arranging linens and carafes of water on the empty tables. He motions us toward the deck. "Please, welcome. Sit where you like. We open in a few minutes."

We settle ourselves at a table by the water. It's quiet, peaceful. I watch the pattern of red and blue light on the agave leaves, the jasmine. A flash of crisp white shirt catches my eye, and I turn to see a tall, slender figure striding across the deck.

The man, clearly Egyptian, approaches our table and extends his hand. "I hope you do not find me improper," he says. "I am here for the month working on my hotel—not *my* hotel, of course, I am merely the architect—and would be honored to speak with foreigners to learn what pleases them."

It's a charming speech, especially with the lilting formality of his accent. I can't tell if the man is sincere or the opposite— smarmy, a con artist—but Robert has already introduced himself and invited him to join us.

The Egyptian slides into an empty seat and tells us that his name is Nabil. Trained as an architectural engineer, he's part of the team hired to design and construct a new luxury hotel to accommodate the increasing number of tourists. He's older than us, perhaps in his mid-thirties. Next to his casual elegance, Robert looks like a boy.

Robert moves the carafe to the side. "Tell me," he says, "as an engineer, a businessman. What's your opinion of the Aswan Dam? Is it helping the country or not?'

"Ah, the Dam." Nabil folds his arms. "There are many answers to this question. Certainly, there is water for irrigation, and many villages have electricity for the first time. And yet, myself, I think it is not so good. As you know, it stops our yearly flood. You may think that floods are bad, but for thousands of years they have brought salt and minerals to replenish the soil. No doubt there are other ways to do that, but you cannot expect a whole people to change, *poof,* just because the government builds a dam. Plus, the project displaced tens of thousands of people and drowned many of our archeological sites. Was it worthwhile, nonetheless? I am not sure."

I hadn't expected so much passion in response to Robert's question. The question hadn't really interested me, but Nabil's response does.

Then Nabil shakes his head. "Please forgive me. I talk too much. That was not my intention."

"There's nothing to forgive," Robert says. "I asked, and you answered."

Nabil smiles. His teeth are white against his olive skin. His hair is dark and neatly trimmed, Western-style, but his beard is lush, incongruous for someone with such a modern profession. I thought only the devout had beards.

He spreads his hands. "What other questions can I answer for you?"

"Here's what I'd like to know." I angle my chair so I'm blocking Robert's view, as if we are vying for Nabil's attention and only one of us can have it. "Why do people pester the tourists all the time, trying to sell, sell, sell—when it's so irritating and hardly ever works?"

Nabil laughs. "It irritates you, yes. But why?"

"I don't want to buy anything. I haven't given any indication that I do."

"No, no, you misunderstand." He threads his fingers together, his voice earnest. "To us, you have unimaginable wealth. You fly here from the United States, so clearly you have money to buy whatever you like. The poor merchant only wants to be of service, to assist you in finding what you desire. If you don't buy what he offers, he is sad because it means he has failed you. He hasn't shown you anything good enough to satisfy your longing. And that is all he truly desires."

It's an extraordinary speech, a master class in seductive innuendo—if that's what it was. I am touched, flustered, turned on. I flick my hair and say, "It's not always about buying, owning. There was a man selling those carved boxes. I told him, just because I admire something, it doesn't mean I want to buy it. I admire the Pyramids, but I don't want to buy them."

"Well said." Nabil gives me another smile. "I'm sure the poor man was no match for you."

I've forgotten about Robert, but he is back in the conversation now. "You're right," he tells Nabil. "We come here for a few days, and we have no idea what anything really means."

His words deflate an atmosphere that has become too charged. I'm annoyed, maybe relieved. Then Robert puts his hands on the table and pushes to his feet. "I need to find a rest room. I'll be right back."

A moment later, he is gone. I look at Nabil and brush back my hair. More slowly this time, letting the strands fall between my fingers.

I study his face, the cheekbones and olive skin. The beard seems out of place, an affectation. "Why do you have a beard?" I ask him.

Seconds pass, achingly slow. Then he speaks. Each word burns into me.

"When I taste a woman, I stroke her with my beard. The smell remains, for me to savor after we part."

I have never heard words like these. They annihilate me.

When Robert returns, we order fava beans, grilled kofta wrapped in lamb fat, and salted fish. Robert has a long exchange with the waiter to make sure there's no citrus or sesame in the dishes. "I get hives," he explains. "Itchy eyes, congestion. It's not life-threatening, just unpleasant."

I close my eyes and hear Nabil's words again.

"No citrus," the waiter assures Robert. "No hives." It's not clear if he understands—I wonder if he thinks Robert is talking about bees—but Nabil confirms that the dishes we've ordered contain no citrus or sesame.

The waiter retreats, and I let Robert and Nabil talk. Robert asks Nabil what he thinks of Karnak, as an architect. Nabil's attention is focused on Robert, but I can feel that it's really on me, an invisible rope coiled around my body, pulling me toward him.

"It's an astonishing achievement," he tells Robert. "The Hypostyle Hall alone covers five thousand square meters. Your Notre Dame could fit easily into this one room. The enclosure of Amun is ten times as large as St. Peter's Basilica, the largest church in the world. So yes, there is size, to impress, but there is skill too."

Everything he says seems charged with another, private meaning. I wish I could order a drink, but it's a Muslim country and there's no alcohol on the menu. I lean back in my chair and bring forkfuls of food to my mouth.

Robert's eyes light up. "Imagine being the architect on *that* job."

"Ah yes," Nabil says. "I would rather build New Kingdom temples than modern hotels, but who will pay me for that? Meanwhile, I poke at the dirt when I can. I find many things of interest."

"Real artifacts, from antiquity?" Robert asks.

"In Egypt, everything you find in the sand is old, but most pieces are too common to be worth much. Sometimes, though, there is something worth finding. I will show you a fine scarab I found near Dendera."

I wait for the pitch. *Unique, special price just for you.* Instead, Nabil invites us to the Winter Palace, the most glamorous hotel in Luxor, where his colleague Samir works. "Samir will leave passes for you to enjoy their private spa, so you can refresh after visiting the archeological sites. Then we will meet for dinner, and I will show you my scarab."

I don't understand what's going on. It's not a ploy to seduce me because I've already been seduced. Plus, Robert is included.

Robert thanks Nabil, then says, "I have a joke for you."

I close my eyes again. *Please, don't.* I already know it's not going to be funny.

"This guy finds an old coin," Robert says, "and he wants to sell it to an antique dealer, so he tells the dealer it's the genuine article because it says so, right on the back. Twenty-five B.C."

Nabil smiles graciously. "Very good. I will remember that." I try not to cringe.

We finish our meal and confirm our dinner tomorrow, at the Winter Palace. Robert and I return to our hotel room. He closes the door, sits on the edge of the bed to take off his shoes.

A wildness rises up in me. I straddle him, grab his fingers and push them against me. I open my legs as wide as I can, bite his mouth, and feel him get hard.

We fuck, at last.

I pretend he's Nabil.

THE SCARAB
1977

I am determined to see everything that Luxor has to offer, every row of ram-headed sphinxes and papyrus-topped columns, every tomb and hieroglyph and statue of Ramses. I especially want to see Hatshepsut's Temple at Deir el-Bahari. If I can't have Artemis—warrior, goddess of chastity and fertility—then I will have Hatshepsut, Egypt's only female pharaoh, and one of its greatest.

Robert and I go to Deir el-Bahari early the next morning, before the sun has fully risen. Hatshepsut's temple is a monument three terraces high, rising from the desert floor and set against the surrounding cliffs. According to the Egyptian patriarchy, a woman couldn't be king, so Hatshepsut is depicted as a male pharaoh, with male attire and a false beard. I study the guidebook and imagine her enjoying the power of her male persona as she sat on her throne, overseeing the construction of the great temple at Karnak and directing her lover—the architect Senmut—to create a monument to her glory.

Despite her achievements, Hatshepsut was erased by those who came after. Her name, visage, place in history—eradicated, even on her own monument. The toothless old dragoman who attaches himself to us points out carving after carving of the same scene. On the left is Anubis, jackal-headed god of the underworld, ready to welcome Hatshepsut to the afterlife. On the right is Hatshepsut, her face scratched out by loyal followers of subsequent pharaohs. "Anubis," the dragoman declares, as he points dramatically to each carving. "Anubis, okay! Hatshepsut, kaput!"

After a while, Robert and I start chanting the refrain along with him, shouting *Okay!* and *Kaput!* The dragoman merely smiles his toothless smile and beckons us to the next wall. When we are ready to leave, he asks for *baksheesh* so softly that I don't mind dropping the coins into his hand.

I picture Hatshepsut with Senmut, her lover, whose task is to carry out her wishes. And I picture Nabil, another architect. His olive skin, his beard. Not a false beard, but a real beard framing a man's greedy mouth between my legs.

When we return from sightseeing, Nabil's friend Samir meets us at the Winter Palace and presents us with passes to the spa, waving away our thanks. "We have a saying in Egypt. When you are a guest in my country, you are a guest in my home." Robert presses his hands together with a bow that looks more Indian than Egyptian.

We relax in the sauna, steam room, and California-style pool, washing away the morning's dust, then go back to our hotel. It's early afternoon, the hottest part of the day, so we close the heavy curtains and sleep until six.

When I get up, I feel gritty and tense, as if I haven't rested at all. The hours seem endless until we can meet Nabil for dinner. We are meeting at the Corniche Restaurant, on the grounds of the Winter Palace, where Samir will join us. Curious, I look up the Winter Palace in the guidebook and learn that Agatha Christie wrote *Death on the Nile* while she was staying there. Another Hercule Poirot mystery, like *Murder on the Orient Express*. It feels like a secret message, an affirmation of what is meant to be.

Finally it's ten o'clock, and we head back to the Winter Palace, where Nabil and Samir have secured a table on the patio. Samir's brother is there, too, along with his wife. Nabil has brought the scarab he told us about. He holds it in his palm—a blue-green oval, intricately carved—and explains that it stands for the human soul emerging from the mummy and flying to heaven to be resurrected.

"In ancient Egypt," he tells us, "the scarab beetle represented rebirth. It was associated with Khepri, God of the rising sun. Just as Khepri reappears each morning, from a place of darkness, to roll the sun across the heavens, this little creature also reappears—from excrement, waste—to begin anew."

Robert winces. "From excrement? Literally?"

The wince annoys me. It feels prissy, feminine. Nabil dips his head. The gesture is polite, with no tinge of irony.

"The scarab beetle rolls its eggs in dung and pushes the ball across the ground, just as Khepri rolls the sun across the sky. Then, when it is time, the little ones crawl out and new life begins—transformed, resurrected, from what may appear ugly and worthless." He studies the scarab. "When the Egyptians saw the young beetles emerge, they concluded that the father was able to self-create, simply by injecting his sperm into the dung ball. Inseminating it with his will."

Nabil is speaking to me, surely, but I have no idea what he is trying to say. Sweat trickles down the back of my neck. The air is thick, heavy with heat.

Then Nabil shrugs. "A myth, obviously, but it indicated the scarab's power over death. Such was its power, in fact, that a replica like this one would be laid on the place of the deceased's heart, which was removed during embalming. This enabled the dead one to bypass the test of having his heart weighed at the final judgment. Under the scarab's protection, the heart could not bear witness against him."

"Hey," Robert quips. "What about the beetle's good and bad deeds?"

"Perhaps the beetle is incapable of both good and bad." Nabil tosses the scarab my way, and I catch it. "What do you think?" he asks me. "To slip into heaven by replacing the human heart with a strange little bug that perpetuates itself and needs no other for its pleasure?"

I meet his eyes. "I don't think it's that easy."

"No. Probably not."

There is a long silence, and then I open my hand. Slowly, Nabil takes the scarab from my palm.

Samir signals to a waiter to bring a pitcher of lemonade and another of ice water for Robert. No citrus. The sister-in-law, a regal-looking brunette who reminds me of Frida Kahlo, gives me a veiled look. *I see what you're up to.* I look the other way.

Lanterns come on across the patio. I hear the splashing of evening swimmers. There is an orange three-quarter moon, a scattering of stars. Nabil drapes his arm across the back of my chair.

When we return to the hotel, Robert is the aggressive one. He pulls me on top of him, digging his thumbs into my hips as he thrusts into me. I do it again. I pretend he's Nabil.

We decide to stay in Luxor one more night.

By now, we've visited all the important sites on both banks of the Nile. I consider heading further south to the colossus of Abu Simbel, the monument that was relocated when the Aswan Dam was built. It hardly seems right to be so close and not see it. Yet it's a six-hour trip each way, twelve hours on a bus with Robert. I can't sit next to Robert that long.

With no plan for the extra day, we sleep late. Neither of us seems in a hurry to leave the room. I settle into an armchair and open the novel I've brought but haven't started. Robert sits at the desk adding up our expenses in the spiral notebook, calculating how we can finish the trip on the budget he prepared.

I refrain from pointing out the cost of the room we are sitting in. It's not part of that budget. It's separate, mine.

At noon, while Robert is in the shower, the phone rings on the nightstand. It's Samir. His brother is inviting us on a felucca ride. His wife, the one who looks like Frida Kahlo, isn't joining us. She has to visit her mother, tend to her children. The reason is unclear, and I'm not interested. I only want to know who else is coming.

Samir assures me that, of course, our mutual friend Nabil will be there. "We would like you to enjoy this special experience before you leave."

I remember what Nabil said about the street vendors. How they want to help the visitor find the very thing, the one special thing, that will satisfy her longing.

My imagination spikes. I tell myself that I'm acting like an adolescent. Then again, I didn't call Samir. He called me. Us, that is. Robert and me.

I don't know what I'm imagining. I'm not imagining anything.

"We will meet you by the little dock in front of Chez Farouk at eight o'clock," Samir tells me. "Then you can have dinner after our sail and prepare for your return to Cairo."

"That's so kind of you," I reply. "We'll be there."

I can hear Robert in the shower, the beating of the water against the glass. Not water from the Nile—or maybe it does come from the Nile. Everything in Luxor comes from the Nile, returns to it.

The felucca will glide down the river and pull up to the dock. It has been set in motion, as if the boat is already moving toward us.

I am not thinking about anything in particular. I'm not weighing different scenarios or considering the heft of my heart. I'm just sitting there, the phone in my hand.

Here are my thoughts, which are not really thoughts.

Robert and I are not a couple, except in a passive way. We aren't married, don't live together, don't tell each other *I love you, I love you.* We met at a concert because a mutual friend was playing percussion. We liked the same movies. We both wanted to go to Europe.

A hard little beetle settles beneath my ribs, and I push the button on the phone marked two, for room service.

Robert is showered and dressed when the porter arrives with the tray. "Thank you," I say, gesturing at the desk. "Just put it here, that's fine."

Robert is clearly surprised. "What's the occasion?"

"All part of the splurge," I tell him. "Back to hard rolls in a paper bag tomorrow."

He lifts the glass dome to admire the plate of warm pancakes. The plate is a delicate porcelain, with a blue-and-gold design. "Looks great."

I don't mention the syrup I requested, made from the juice of fresh oranges. The scent of the citrus is imperceptible because of the mint leaves in a little silver dish, for the tea. The scent of the mint is too strong. Only a person who is already suspicious would wonder what other scent it might be masking. Robert is not that person.

I don't mention Samir's phone call either, or the felucca ride.

I don't mention my longing to be good.

By six-thirty, Robert is a mess. His skin is covered in red welts, his eyes and nose are running, and he's thoroughly miserable. He's not worried, however. His allergic reaction has never been the anaphylactic kind, when your throat constricts and you can't breathe.

I know that; it's why I dared to do what I did. And yet, for a moment, I wonder if I trusted that knowledge too readily. What if we're both wrong?

The possibility fills me with terror. I don't want to hurt Robert. All I want is an hour.

He blows his nose. He looks awful, but not like someone about to die. My racing heartbeat subsides.

"Poor you," I say. "Do you want a cool compress, some Tylenol?"

He shakes his head. "I just need to get through it."

My voice is full of sympathy. "Well, I'm here if there's anything I can do. We can see how you feel in a bit."

In a bit—by seven fifteen—Robert is no better, but he's no worse either. "What do you think?" I ask. "Would it be okay if I go out for a while, maybe take a walk along the river?"

He waves me away, his eyes shutting. "Go. Walk."

I nod. He told me to go. He wouldn't have said that if it wasn't okay.

I put on a thin cotton dress. Underneath it, my flimsiest

underwear—a scrap of bright blue, the color of lapis lazuli. If Robert had opened his eyes, he would have seen, but he doesn't. I run a comb through my hair. "Back in a while," I call. "Feel better!"

My feet remember the way to the restaurant. There are no diners, it's too early, and yet there is Nabil, leaning against the outer railing of the deck, smoking a thin brown cigar, as if he's waiting for me. Surely the universe has arranged this, a convergence of forces that had no choice but to move toward the same irresistible center. I think of the syrup made from oranges—my doing, not a divine plan—but wave it way, just as Robert waved me away.

I am early, but so is Nabil. Samir is not there, nor his brother. A kingfisher swoops from one tall palm to another, brushing the leaves with its tail.

"Nabil," I say.

He turns, sees me. The tip of his cigar glows red. "Ah," he smiles. "You've discovered my secret vice." He squashes the cigar against one of the girders that support the deck. I understand that he's referring to smoking, not to clandestine meetings.

"Where is Robert?" he asks.

I keep my eyes on his. "Sick. He's not coming."

"I'm so sorry."

"I'm not."

"I came early to have a secret smoke." His expression is unreadable.

"Secrets are good."

This is terrible dialogue. Could I be any more blatant? Only if I stepped toward him and put his hand under my skirt.

"Sometimes," he says. The word is neutral, yet I hear it as an affirmation. "Then again," he adds, "it's always better when they are not necessary."

"You mean, hide nothing?"

"I mean, do nothing that needs to be hidden."

His message is clear, but I refuse to hear it. It doesn't fit with everything that has led to this moment.

I refuse to let this turn into an exchange of bodiless quips. To be dismissed.

"Unless it can't be stopped," I say. "Like Fate. Or Allah's will. Only we have to do our part, or it will pass us by."

A bird screeches as it tilts skyward. Behind us, someone turns on the colored lights over the entrance to Chez Farouk.

"Arden." His voice is firm. It is the voice of a parent, not a lover. "You are from a different culture," he says, "and I don't criticize you for your different ways. But you cannot come to a Muslim country and take the idea of Allah's will and turn it to your own purpose. No one knows Allah's will. And no one can alter it."

I stare at him, like a child who's been scolded by an adult, and that is more shattering, more final, than if he had said, "I'm not attracted to you after all."

And then, all at once, I'm flooded with rage, the way the water floods Egypt. "You're the one who started this. No man talks to a woman the way you talked to me, no matter what their damn religion is."

"Yes. You are right."

"Then why did you do it?"

"It was a mistake. I apologize."

"A mistake?" I can't believe he said that. "Like picking up the wrong coat? You would never have said that to an Egyptian woman."

"No. I wouldn't."

"But you said it to me." In my world, that meant: Accept the consequences, do what you described. But Nabil is not part of my world.

"I am in charge of building a new hotel. I cannot be some-one who seduces American tourists."

I want to smack him. I am a person, not a category. "So that's it?"

His face softens. I suppose he is trying to be kind. "Go back to Robert," he says. "Finish your vacation. Then go home. Every-thing will be clearer in your own culture."

"Forget about Robert," I snap. This has nothing to do with Robert. "We're just traveling together."

I am beside myself now. There is no privacy here, behind the restaurant. I can't make a scene. But I can do something.

It only takes a few seconds. I brace my left palm against the girder, and with my right hand I reach below my skirt, rip off my flimsy underpants, and kick them onto the ground by his feet. The overlapping triangles of lapis lazuli lie in the dirt like the petals of a discarded flower. I picture Nabil having to pick up the bright scraps of cloth, hide them in his pocket before the others arrive. "Smell those," I tell him. Then I wheel around and run up the path, back to the hotel.

If this were a movie, I would find Robert having a dire and unforeseen reaction to the citrus—something about the differ-ence between Egyptian oranges and the ones from Florida and California—that has escalated to a throat-grabbing seizure while Nabil and I are fucking in a dark corner behind Chez Farouk.

Because surely, in that movie, we would fuck. There would be voices and maybe even music from the restaurant, a soundtrack for the sounds he and I are making behind the building. Maybe I would still have my shirt on, and Nabil would be sucking my breast through the fabric. Maybe I would be whimpering with pleasure.

Maybe it would be too late by the time I return to the hotel and Robert would die from anaphylaxis, or maybe I would rush him to the hospital and save his life.

But it is not a movie. It is my real life, and none of these things happen.

I don't have sex with Nabil. Robert doesn't die. He just feels like shit for a few hours because of the welts and the itching. By the time we board the train for our return to Cairo, they've subsided.

TUMBLING AFTER
2013

There were no mathematics for grief.

The grief of a wife.

The grief of a mother.

The grief of a daughter.

Grief was not a pie chart. If Arden got two pieces because she was both wife and mother, it didn't mean that Danielle, as daughter, only got one. The pie was not divided into thirds. Each piece was everything.

That was the truth that kept washing over Arden as she held her granddaughter and the reality of the train wreck slammed into her again and again.

Each day brought questions, condolences, paperwork. Lawyers who thought Arden should sue, neighbors with food. People from the railroad, the media. Death certificates, to prove they were really dead. Social services, because of Danielle. Tears and hugs from well-meaning friends.

As far as anyone knew, Leigh had left no will. At thirty-five,

Arden hadn't had a will either; it had never occurred to her that she might die. No will meant no instructions—which meant that Arden had to reach out to Ivan Chernowski, Danielle's father, whom Leigh had finally broken up with two years earlier. Arden had no idea if Leigh and Ivan had a formal custody agreement; probably not, knowing Leigh. She couldn't imagine Ivan wanting custody of Danielle, since he'd scarcely seen her in those two years, but you never knew what someone might suddenly want.

Meanwhile, the people from Child Protective Services agreed to give Arden temporary custody for thirty days, since Ivan's name wasn't on any official document—not even, it seemed, on Danielle's birth certificate. Leigh had been angry at Ivan when Danielle was born and had, Arden discovered, listed Brad Pitt—whom she'd never met—as the father.

It was classic Leigh, getting back at Ivan by picking a more successful actor to play the role. Arden felt a flicker of admiration for the moxie of a daughter who, no surprise, had complicated feelings about the concept of fatherhood.

"We do require," the social worker told her, "that Danielle begin therapy. I can give you a few referrals, if you'd like."

Arden couldn't see dragging the girl to a therapist; it was another thing, like the notion of Ivan as a full-time parent, that she couldn't imagine. Danielle didn't want to talk about her feelings. All she wanted to do was burrow under the covers with toddler cartoons blaring in the background.

"I'd like to wait a bit," she said. "Let her feel what she feels, before trying to make it better."

Ruby, the social worker, gave her a skeptical look. "I'm not sure that's wise. Studies have shown that timely intervention is the key."

Arden folded her arms. "A couple of weeks is still timely."

Ruby's eyes softened. "Every child is different," she said.

55

"Take a little time, if you think it's best. In the meantime, here's a card. Eleanor Cardoza. She's very good." She extracted a card from her purse and laid it on the table. "I can contact the school, if that would be helpful. There's a lot to attend to, in a situation like this." Then her expression grew stern. "You've been in touch with Danielle's father?"

Arden stiffened. "Not yet. I plan to do that today."

"He doesn't know?"

"I have no idea what he knows. I don't think they released the names of the victims yet." Victims. A hideous word. "If he even reads the newspaper. Who knows what he reads, besides scripts."

In addition to acting, Ivan was the director of a theater company with a complicated schedule that took him out-of-town for long periods of time. He was handsome in an exaggerated, flamboyant way, and Arden understood why Leigh had been attracted to him. But that didn't make him a good parent.

"He needs to be told," Ruby said.

"I understand. And he will be."

Ivan Chernowski was the least of Arden's concerns. Number one was Danielle herself, curled into a ball with one of her mother's nightgowns wrapped tightly around her, rose-covered satin with a pattern of silver leaves coiling down her back like ivy.

Number two was the other person who needed to be told. Leigh's actual father. Arden had looked him up on the internet. It seemed that he was still alive.

In Arden's opinion, Ivan had been a bad father from the moment he became one. He hadn't even been in the delivery room when Danielle was born, but she had, and so had Connor. Ivan was touring with *True West*, alternating the parts of the two brothers and full a manic certainty about how this would catapult his career to a whole new level. That elation, Arden was sure, meant he was sleeping with at least one woman in the troupe.

Then Leigh went into labor eleven days early. Everything happened quickly, and there was no time to reach Ivan who, in any case, couldn't—or wouldn't—have left in the middle of a performance.

Arden had squeezed one of her daughter's hands while Connor held the other. They had seen the newborn baby before Leigh did, and Arden had burst into tears. Tears of joy—and of sorrow too, because she knew that Ivan wasn't going to be there to raise this child. Leigh would have to do it alone, the very pattern she'd wanted to save her daughter from repeating.

Yet Danielle was nothing like Leigh. Leigh had been an easy baby, merry and adaptable, while Danielle was solemn, intense, precise about her likes and dislikes. As she moved from infancy into childhood, the traits grew more pronounced. Each food— banana, muffin, sausage—had to be cut into pieces the exact same size and couldn't touch on the plate. Tags on shirts were not permitted, and her stuffed bears had to be lined up from largest to smallest. Once, when Arden babysat, she had let three-year-old Danielle play with a cookie tin of buttons and found her organizing them by color and size.

And then there were Danielle's "pictures." The previous winter, she "saw" her mother slip on the ice, and it turned out that Leigh really had. Another time, she "saw" Leigh become upset at losing her purse, even though they were miles apart.

Arden worried that Danielle was trying to get attention, but Leigh was sure it was the sign of a special sensitivity and Arden didn't want to argue with her. It was something that pleased Leigh about her daughter—rare enough that Arden didn't want to spoil it.

That was another reason she wasn't eager for her granddaughter to be dissected by this Eleanor Cardoza; Danielle's psyche was already tender and quirky, even before the crash. Arden was confident that she could put it off for a while, as long as the Child Protection people could see that Danielle was being well cared for.

She couldn't put off calling Ivan, though. It was the kind of task she would have asked Connor to handle, but there was no more Connor.

Each time Arden remembered that cruel impossible fact, it brought a fresh wave of pain—as if she had to keep learning it, again and again. Even then, there was no time to truly feel it. To stop, be still, and do the one thing she desperately needed to do—to mourn. Instead, she had to fill out forms for Social Security, Citibank, the Administration for Children's Services.

And stay vigilant, to keep from feeling the other devastating truth. The knowledge that had crashed into her like an iceberg when Officer Navarro called.

Arden steeled herself and phoned Ivan Chernowski.

"Arden!" he boomed. Performing, as always. "Great to hear from you. It's been a long time."

Meaning, Arden thought, that he hadn't bothered to check on his only child. She clenched her teeth. She understood that Ivan didn't know about the train, but she was too exhausted to be rational. "I'm calling for a reason," she began.

An inane preamble. Obviously there was a reason. They weren't old friends who called each other just to say hello.

Suddenly, she was furious at Ivan—for being alive, when Leigh wasn't. "I'm calling," she snapped, "to let you know that you're Danielle's only surviving parent."

It was a stupid, oblique way to put it, but she couldn't bring herself to say: *Leigh is dead.*

Ivan's voice grew sharp. "What are you talking about?"

"Danielle. Your daughter."

"I know who Danielle is." The heartiness was gone. "Surviving parent. What the hell does that mean?"

"Exactly what you think it means." Arden made herself say it, because she didn't trust him to understand. "Leigh is dead."

"For fuck's sake, Arden. What happened?"

She explained about the sleep apnea and the dangerous curve, but Ivan didn't seem to understand. He kept asking about automatic sensors and emergency brake systems, as if he were arguing with her so he could prove it couldn't have happened. Arden wanted to throw the phone at him. Did he think she was playing some kind of sick joke? "Go look it up on Google if you don't believe me. The Hudson Line. The first accident in Metro-North history to result in passenger fatalities."

That seemed to shut him up. "Jesus," he said. "I'll get there as soon as I can. The understudy can manage for a day or two."

"You don't need to come. You just need to know."

"Of course I have to come. To get Danielle."

Arden cut him off. "No, you do *not* have to get Danielle. I have custody." Only for thirty days, but there was no reason to mention that.

"A girl needs her father."

I'll call Brad Pitt, she thought, wanting to be mean and make him suffer the way he deserved. "Not necessarily."

"I'm coming to get my daughter," Ivan repeated, and slammed down the phone.

Arden stared at the black rectangle in her hand. It was jiggling like crazy—no, it was her hand that was trembling. Telling Ivan about the accident had brought it to life again. A train car tumbling into an abyss. Exploding metal. Bones shattering as they hit the rock.

There were times when your life changed because of something you did. And there were times when you did nothing, but it still changed.

An engineer you would never meet, dozing off for a few seconds. That was all it took.

Arden heard a small sound and whirled around. It was Danielle, framed in the doorway, her eyes wide. Her mother's nightgown was wrapped around her.

"Danielle. Sweetheart. What is it?" She hoped Danielle hadn't overheard the phone call. She couldn't have known who her grandmother was talking to, but the tone had been unpleasant.

Arden swore, again, to shield Danielle from unhappiness. The funeral, two days from now, would be awful. But after that, no more pain for Danielle. Ever.

Danielle pulled the nightgown tight. "I saw her."

"Who?" Arden asked, though she knew.

"Mommy." Danielle looked five years old, not ten. "She said she was sorry. She didn't mean it."

"Darling, darling." Arden swooped her up, taking care not to disturb Danielle's hold on the nightgown, and murmured every word of comfort she knew to assure Danielle that she wasn't alone, abandoned in her grief.

They were just words. Arden already knew they wouldn't help. They were a placeholder, not a path. She didn't know where the path could possibly be. Not this time.

A SIDE TRIP TO ROME

1977

From Cairo, there is no easy way to get back to America. People assure us that you can fly from Egypt to Israel, though not in the other direction, and from Tel Aviv to New York. "Easy, many flights. American Jews want to visit Israel, and the planes have to make a round-trip." But Robert and I don't trust it. What if the border agent at Ben Gurion Airport sees our Egyptian entrance stamps and won't let us in?

We decide to take a no-frills EgyptAir flight from Cairo to Rome, and go standby from Rome to New York. We're warned that we might have to wait hours or even days at Fiumicino Airport, especially if we want two seats on the same plane, but it's the only affordable option.

We retrieve our suitcases from the carousel at Fiumicino and make our way to the counter of the airline with the next flight to JFK. As we wait in line, Robert counts our remaining lire. Most of the bills, left from our time in Venice, are faded or held together with Scotch tape; much of the Italian currency is like that. Still, we're glad to have the cash, since we need something to eat. Robert guards our spot in line while I look for a place to buy bread and cheese. I hand the vendor a bill, and he drops a dozen pieces of candy and gum into my palm as change.

I am so, so done with this vacation. I picture my apartment in Brooklyn, the plants on the fire escape that my neighbor promised to water. I'm sure they're dead, but I'll get new ones. A new jacket. A new boyfriend.

When I return with the food, Robert grabs my arm. Amazingly, there's a seat on a flight to Kennedy that is now boarding. The ticketholder didn't show up, and we are next in the queue. Robert assumes that I will take it.

I stare at him. His pale skin, the way his mouth is opening and closing. I can't imagine the two of us being together, once we're back in the States. I compare him to Nabil, and I can't stand him. Then I remember what a horrible person I am, and I can't stand myself.

"You take it," I tell him. "Go ahead. I don't care."

I'm certain that he will argue, insist that I go. Instead, he nods. Maybe he's anxious to be done with me too. Then he presses a wad of paper into my hands. My airline voucher and receipt, the rest of the tattered lire. Stupidly, I give him the candy and gum. Robert takes them, as if in exchange. "Safe travels," I call, but he's already being ushered down the jetway as a baggage handler grabs his suitcase.

I tighten my grip on my own suitcase, the bag of bread and cheese. He's gone.

The airline agent is getting ready to close her station. "Excuse me," I say. "I'm on standby. When is the next flight to JFK, please?"

She purses her lips, then taps on a keyboard. "It appears that the flight scheduled to leave at eighteen twenty-five has been cancelled. There are no other flights until tomorrow."

"That can't be right."

"I'm afraid it is. You're welcome to check with other carriers."

I shake my head. I can't buy a whole new ticket on another airline. "When is the first flight tomorrow?"

She taps some more. "The first flight is scheduled to depart at eight thirty-two. However, since you're on standby, I would advise you to be here by six o'clock."

That's seventeen hours from now. I'm starting to regret giving the seat to Robert. "Right," I say. "Thank you." Then I add, "*Grazie.*"

"*Prego.*"

I cram the bread and cheese into my daypack and try to project an aura of confidence for the benefit of anyone who happens to be looking. *I can do this.* It's not impossible. I'll find a quiet corner to wait, sleep, until the morning flight.

If I can get on it. I might not.

Suddenly, I'm angry at Robert. He shouldn't have let me give him the spot; he should have been gallant, no matter what I said.

But Robert has become used to me getting my way. I am the one who decides, and he is the one who accedes. I insisted on Egypt, on Luxor. Now on this. He did what I told him to.

Still, I can do something more interesting than sit at the airport for seventeen hours. My Eurail pass is good until the end of the month. I can catch a train to Roma Termini and explore the city. Turn the delay into an extra day of sightseeing.

I feel a surge of elation. Robert and I never made it to Rome— we were going to, but went to Istanbul instead—so I will do this, the thing we missed, on my own. I remember Nabil's remark about St. Peter's Basilica, and how it would be dwarfed by the Temple at Karnak. *My house of worship is bigger than yours.* I give a defiant sniff. We'll see about that.

I turn back to the airline agent. "*Scusi,* please. Is there a locker where I can leave my suitcase overnight?"

She nods politely, though I've detained her again. "Of course. At the end of the terminal, near the exit. There is a blue sign."

"Great. Thank you."

I spend a dollar's worth of lire on a locker, stow the suitcase, and make my way to the shuttle that will take me to Roma Termini. I have no idea how far it is from there to St. Peter's, which I am now determined to see, along with whatever else I can. Fountains, piazzas, frescoes. I remember reading that Rome has over four hundred churches.

I hurry to the platform, into the last car, and slip into an empty seat on the aisle. The window seat is occupied by a young man who looks like he's trying to channel John Lennon. Long hair, granny glasses, a red bandana around his head. Peach fuzz covers his baby cheeks. "Hey," he says. "American?"

I give him a perfunctory smile. "What else?"

"Berkeley," he says proudly.

"New York."

"Crazy customs line. How long did it take you?"

"I'm actually on my way back," I explain, "but I can't get on a flight until tomorrow, so I figured I'd head into Rome for a while."

"Cool."

I don't know what's *cool* about not being able to get on a flight until tomorrow, but I let it go. It's only a thirty-minute train ride, and there are no empty seats.

"I'm meeting up with some friends later," he tells me, "but we could hang out till then if you want. You know. See what there is to do."

His whole manner is painfully callow, with the John Lennon glasses and artfully faded denim shirt. Berkeley High School, I think, not the university. On the other hand, I have almost no money—cash, that is, the credit card is not to be used—so it might be smart to tag along with someone. Plus, I notice a map in the pocket of the denim shirt. A guide to the city, something else I don't have.

He sees me eyeing the map, pulls it out, and opens it so we can both see. "I'm figuring the Colosseum, for sure, and the Roman Forum. Maybe the Trevi Fountain?"

The Trevi Fountain is one of the places I meant to visit, when I handed out worksheets to my students in Brooklyn and dreamed about a summer trip. It all comes back to me, like a memory from childhood. The girls with their school uniforms and Charlie's Angels hairstyles. The sweet aromatic smell of the mimeographed pages, damp and purple from the copier.

"I need to go to St. Peters," I say. I want to prove that it's bigger than Nabil made it sound. I know it's stubborn and childish, but that's what I want. After that, I want to go home.

"Sure. Whatever." He turns the map, trying to find St. Peter's.

"I'm Arden."

"Paolo." He gives an awkward laugh. "No, not really. It's Paul. But I figured I'd go by Paolo while I'm here."

I fight the urge to roll my eyes. "Go for it. Maybe you can blend in."

To me, the sarcasm is obvious, but he doesn't seem to hear it. He probably thinks I'm praising his idea.

This is not going to work, I decide. I feel another flare of anger at Robert.

"I can't find St. Peter's," Paolo/Paul says, turning the map again. "I think it might be the same thing as the Vatican."

"St. Peter's is a giant church," I tell him. "The Vatican is where the Pope lives, and I'm pretty sure you need a ticket or a tour guide. The church is free, but I heard the lines are insane."

The kid gives me an arch look. "I can get us in. I'm an expert at line-cutting." He must have seen my dubious reaction because he adds, "Trust me, you wouldn't believe how easy it is.

Nobody's paying attention. They're just taking pictures or looking at the guidebook. So hey, if you want to see the Pope's house, I'll make it look like we're part of one of those tour groups. I do it all the time."

I'm sure he's making this up. Maybe he slipped into a movie theater once or twice, but this kid from Berkeley High isn't sharp enough to get past the Italian ticket-takers. I remember them from Santa Maria Delle Grazie in Milan, when Robert and I went to see *The Last Supper*. They stamped our tickets at four separate checkpoints, each time with a more extravagant flourish. Really, the kid has no clue. Trying to sneak into the Vatican with this Paolo/Paul infant is not how I want to spend my final hours in Europe.

He's not done, though. "I have the kind of face people trust," he tells me. "I look like everyone's kid brother. Clean and trustworthy, but not too handsome? Like someone who might have been behind you in line, but you're not sure because you only looked long enough to think, 'Right, he's fine.' It's a kind of a kick, fooling everyone."

I give him a cold look. "You mean, you're kind of a shit."

"Hey. I'm just getting by, like everyone else."

I push the map away. "How do you know what everyone else is doing?" I get up and walk to the end of the car where I stand for the rest of the trip.

I expect the kid to get the message, but he sidles up to me and hovers at my elbow when we exit the train in Rome. "Come on," he pleads. "Don't be so uptight. We can hang out, like I said. See some ruins."

He really needs to go away. "I don't want to see any ruins."

"Or whatever. A piazza."

It's clear now, how young he is. Seventeen, eighteen at most. I'm not interested in being the Older Woman Who Teaches Him

About Life. I'm not even interested in killing time with him. I have a plane ticket, a bag of bread and cheese, and thirty-five hundred lire, the equivalent of four American dollars, and I just want to get through the next few hours.

But he won't give up. "You're alone, I'm alone, why not?"

"I thought you were meeting some friends."

Tears fill his eyes. "I lied. They bailed on me." He swallows, his throat quivering. "She bailed on me. It wasn't a *them*. I just didn't want you to worry that you'd get stuck with me forever."

He looks both brave and pathetic. I can't stand it. "What happened?" I ask.

He falls into step beside me as we make our way through the station. "Her parents have this place outside of Rome, like some kind of villa? They invited me to visit, after my summer job was over. She went over there first, Bianca, and I was going to join them. I had my ticket. I was all pumped for it."

I know the rest of the story, he doesn't have to tell me, but of course he does. "Then Bianca sends me a postcard—a fucking *postcard*—to say she's met this guy and I shouldn't come. At first, I think maybe it's a joke. Maybe I should do a handwriting analysis or something. But the last sentence is something only she would know, I'm not going to say it, it's too embarrassing, but then I know it's really her who wrote it. A fucking postcard."

I look at him and see him struggling not to cry. "You already had your ticket."

He sniffs. "Yeah."

"And you thought you'd show up, and maybe she'd change her mind."

Then he surprises me. "I'm not that stupid. I just figured, why waste a ticket to Italy?" He gives me a sheepish look. "And hey, I might meet someone else."

I try not to cringe. I am not that someone else. He can't

possibly be thinking that I am. I desperately hope this isn't how I seemed to Nabil.

"It's tough to be on your own," I say, trying to find words that are kind but not false. "I know it's not the trip you imagined, but I'm sure you'll end up having a great time. Different, but great."

He nods, his eyes still wet. "So you want to hang out? I have some weed. I hid it in a pair of hiking socks."

I stop walking. Around us, people are rushing in all directions, heading for the gelato stand, the information board, a complicated network of tracks and exits.

"You need to be careful what you say, Paolo." I keep my voice low. "And especially who you offer weed to. I'm okay, don't freak out, but you never know."

"I knew you were okay. I can tell about people."

Shit. I don't know what to do with this Paolo/Paul. I don't want to *hang out* with him, and I definitely don't want to smoke an illegal substance that he's smuggled into Italy. Yet I can't let him wander around Rome by himself.

I look at my watch. It's quarter to four. I need to be on the ten o'clock shuttle to the airport—twenty-two hundred hours, Italian time. After that, the line shuts down until five-thirty in the morning. No way am I going to get stuck in Rome all night or miss that flight.

It means six hours with this kid, max. To get him settled, and see a bit of Rome.

The thought occurs to me: I could just dump him. But I can't. The kid isn't Robert. He's a thousand times more helpless. Even the girls I teach in Brooklyn are savvier.

"So what's your plan?" I ask. "Where are you going to stay, while you're here?"

Paolo/Paul gives me a goofy look. "I kind of thought I'd see who I met."

"Well, you met me, and I don't own a hotel. What's your next idea?"

I'm thinking of a youth hostel, one of those places with dormitory-style beds. That would be good for Paolo/Paul. He could meet other people his age. Hang out.

It's clear from his hangdog expression that he has no "next idea." I tell him, "Let's find a youth hostel. Let me see your map."

He hands me the map. "You're a good person, Arden. You never would have done what Bianca did."

I lift an eyebrow. "You don't know that."

"You wouldn't."

"Maybe I tried to," I say, "but the guy didn't want me to break up with my nice boyfriend to be with him."

"Is that true?"

I shrug. Then I open the map. "I bet there's a hostel right near the train station. It makes sense, people arriving in the city, needing a place." I toss him a smug look when I see that I was right. "Look." I point at a spot on the map with the words GARIBALDI HOSTEL. "It's right across the street."

Paolo/Paul looks uncomfortable. "Maybe we should wait and see what happens."

"A hotel room isn't going to just happen. Let's go. We'll check you in, and then we can see few ruins before I have to get back to the airport." I've abandoned my idea that I need to see St. Peter's. It's smaller than Karnak. Fine.

Paolo/Paul follows me, but I can see that something is wrong. Was he hoping I'd offer to sleep with him, and now he's pouting? Maybe, but I don't care. I'm going to get this done, do this one good deed, before I go home.

I pull open the door of the hostel and stride to the front desk. "*Parli inglese?*"

An image flashes across my memory. Myself, turning to a

strange man with hooded eyes and asking, *"Parli italiano?"* This is the inverse, or else it is the same. I don't know. I do what I have to do, that's all.

"Of course," the receptionist says.

I don't even look at the kid. I'm on a mission now, and my attention is focused on the woman at the desk. "My friend needs a bed for the night. Three nights, actually." Enough time for him to see a few fountains and piazzas, and figure out what to do—which, obviously, means calling his parents in Berkeley. *Please send money.*

"We are quite full," she says. "It is one day at a time, as space permits, in the common quarters. By this hour, the beds are taken."

Damn. Plus, it sounds like a homeless shelter. Paolo/Paul needs a place where he won't get picked on. "I can't believe that's the only option," I tell her. The kid still hasn't said a word. To be fair, I've hardly let him.

"The only alternative I can offer," the woman says, "is a private room on the top level. We rent it for a three-day minimum, usually for chaperones or guides. However, it is more expensive."

"That's perfect," I say. She quotes a price, payable in advance. I turn to the kid. "This is your lucky day after all. Pay up, Paolo."

"And the passport, please," she adds.

"And the passport," I echo, as if he needs a translator.

Paolo/Paul stares at me. Fresh tears fill his eyes. "I don't have any money."

"Excuse me?" I feel my skin turn cold. Was this whole thing a scam? No, I can't believe it's a scam. He's too pathetic. It's the bandana, the John Lennon glasses. "What were you thinking?" I hiss.

His words are like bubbles of misery, escaping between sobs. "I was going to stay with Bianca's family. They were going to take care of everything. I spent all my money on the ticket." He can hardly get the words out. "That's why I can't stay here." His chest heaves as tears pour down his cheeks. "I didn't know how to tell you. I'm really sorry."

Oh, for fuck's sake. I'm absolutely certain that he isn't playing me. It can't be worth all this humiliation for a lousy room in an attic.

I dig in my backpack and pull out my parents' credit card. "Put it on this. Three nights."

"What are you doing?" he says.

"Shut up," I tell him. My parents said it was for an emergency, and this is more of an emergency than the hotel in Luxor. Anyway, I'll pay them back. This is on me, not them.

The woman takes the credit card, runs it through a machine, and repeats, "Passport, please." Paolo gives it to her, and she hands him a brass key. "All the way to the top. It's the door on the right."

I can't leave him to settle in alone; we've come this far, and I have to finish. I follow him up three flights of stairs to a tiny attic room. There is a cot, a bureau, a crucifix. "Well," I announce. "It's a start."

I walk to the octagonal window and crank the handle to let in some air. Paolo sits on the bed, his face in his hands. "Hey," I tell him. "You're going to be fine. Your adventure is just beginning."

He turns to me, his expression desolate. And then I understand the mistake I've made.

I decided that he needed a parent to take charge and save him—because I wanted to save someone. I risked Robert's life with the orange sauce. Now I have to save Paolo's.

But Paolo didn't lose a mother. He lost a girlfriend. That's what he needs. To be a man, not a son.

I cross the room and drop to my knees by the bed, where he

is sitting. "It really is," I say. "You are one good-looking dude, Paolo. Definitely *not* someone's kid brother." I slide my palm up the inside of his jeans. "You know how hot you are, right?"

It is so easy that it makes me sad. I don't have sex with him, though. What he really wants is a blow job, and I give that to him. He is so young. It takes less than two minutes.

Afterward, I kiss him on each cheek, Italian style. "I need to get back to the airport," I tell him. "But you are going to have a wonderful time in Italy, dear Paolo. You are going to have a wonderful life." I give him my bread and cheese, along with the thirty-five hundred lire.

I'm back at Fiumicino Airport by seven-thirty, nineteen-thirty on the Italian clock. I spend the next twelve hours waiting for the flight to New York, which I get on. Other than getting to JFK, I have no plan. And no money. I don't care. I am certain of only one thing: if I didn't give Paolo everything, it would be like giving him nothing.

It isn't quite as brave as it sounds, because I still have the credit card. The knowledge of that credit card in my pocket makes me feel as if I can slip through, no matter what I get myself into. Get home intact, unscarred.

It is an illusion. But I am young too.

PART TWO

HUSBANDS
AND FATHERS

GREEN BURIAL
2013

Arden delayed the funeral until Connor's relatives could arrive from the West Coast: a sister and her family, a widowed mother. His brother Finn, who had taken over the McRae Farm, found a cemetery near Rhinebeck that did green burials, where you wrapped the body in a shroud and put it straight into the earth, covered with flowers and dirt. That seemed right to Arden; their poor bodies were too shattered to be dressed up in fancy clothes and arranged in satin-lined coffins. Melanie Langmuir, a friend of the McRae family who had become a non-denominational minister, was coming to do the service.

Arden was worried about Connor's mother, who was old and frail: the cross-country trip, the shock of her son's death. Mercifully, her own parents had died the year before. They had loved Connor too. And Leigh, the child who was named after them. Lena and Aleksander.

At first, Arden hadn't wanted anyone at the funeral except the closest family. Then she relented because she couldn't tell Danielle's classmates to stay away—or her own friends, who were Connor's friends too. The Yoshimuras, Nikki and Ennis, who'd shared all those movie nights and beach trips. Leigh's college roommate. And Ivan, who insisted on coming.

There would still be some missing faces. Finn's son, who was teaching in New Zealand. Her brother Hugh, in the hospital for a procedure that couldn't be rescheduled. If there were gaps in the circle of mourners, Arden would just have to hold tightly to Danielle's hand to let her know that the ring surrounding her was unbroken and would keep her safe.

Bridget and Finn, Connor's siblings, had wanted two separate funerals, but Arden insisted on a single service. Partly because she didn't think she could handle two funerals, and partly because it was Leigh who had brought the three of them together with her school project, and it seemed right for everything to end together too.

Melanie Langmuir had asked for a few details she could incorporate into the eulogies, small stories and quintessential moments that evoked the person everyone was there to mourn, yet revealed something they might not have known.

"Of course," Arden had told her. The task felt both hideous and profound, yet it seemed like something she could do. For Connor's mother, who shared the same terrible role, a mother burying her child. And for Danielle.

Leigh seemed easier; Arden had known her daughter from the day she was born and had the whole of her life to choose from. Leigh, at two years old, already displaying her signature willfulness by refusing to leave the playground, even when Arden began to stroll to the exit and pretend that she was leaving without her. Leigh had tightened her arms around the metal pole and stood her ground, singing to the air to show how little she cared.

Autonomy, not authority—that was Leigh, with a bravado that was both maddening and funny.

At four, insisting on wearing a pink-and-purple tutu over her auburn curls, calling it her "ballerina hair." At ten, in her jodhpurs and riding jacket, determined to have her lesson, even though it was bitterly cold and the owner of the stable wanted to close. At fifteen, organizing a rally at her high school in solidarity with the march in Washington for gay and lesbian civil rights. When a boy in her math class asked if she was some kind of lesbian or why did she care, she threw Martin Niemoller's proclamation right back at him. *"First, they came for the socialists."*

The tutu and the rally, then. Two aspects of Leigh's independent spirit.

Finding the perfect anecdotes for Connor was harder. He'd been thirty-three when they met, with thirty-three years of history that Arden would never know—experiences that had made him think he needed to be celibate in order to find his way back to himself. Then polyamorous, so he could unlearn possession and preference. Finally, he had chosen her, only her, and Arden was certain that she had made him happy, in and out of bed, as he had made her happy. But she wasn't going to let Melanie Langmuir talk about that; it was nobody's business, and it hurt too much to remember.

She decided to focus on the farm, which would please his family. There was an endearing story about Connor's inedible jalapeno-apple chutney and how he'd delivered all those peaches and berries to the local churches. Arden had her own memory of that time—sitting next to him in the pickup truck as they made their way down the back roads, helping him carry the crates into the church kitchens, aware the whole time of the man's body that she wasn't permitted to touch. She had wondered, briefly, if it was a clever, or not-so-clever, ploy. But it couldn't be, since she'd already thrown herself at him. No, it just happened to be the idea he was trying on when she met him. Connor had been trained in the scientific method, so he had to experiment and see for himself.

She'd let Melanie talk about the churches, not the celibacy. Not the things that were hers alone.

Connor's father had been Irish but his mother was a Scot, so Arden made sure that the funeral began with the Church of Scotland blessing:

May the sun shine warm upon your face.
May the rains fall softly upon your fields.
Until we meet again,
may God hold you in the hollow of His hand.

For herself, she chose readings from Rumi, Mary Oliver; Psalm 121, Connor's favorite; and Louis Armstrong, singing *What a Wonderful World*.

Once they started to walk toward the graves, the restrained simplicity she had aimed for began to come apart. First it was Connor's mother, who began wailing and insisting that it was her husband, not her son, who was being buried, and where was the coffin they had paid for, with the brass handles, and where was the three-piece suit she had chosen? Finn tried to quiet her, but Arden mouthed: *It's okay*. It was her child in that green grave. She had the right to do whatever she wanted.

Then one of Leigh's college friends broke down, and Arden couldn't help feeling that this particular outburst, in contrast, was a bit theatrical. And then, the way things came in threes, there was Ivan. Late, slinking in, slipping into place right next to Danielle. "Hey, Nellie," he said, putting his arm around her. He bent close, their faces matching, the same sleek black hair and arched brows. Arden glared at him. She longed to tell him to go away, but Danielle seemed glad to see him and she could hardly begrudge the girl her remaining parent.

Melanie Langmuir finished her remarks and recited a closing poem by Rabindranath Tagore.

Bid me farewell, my brothers.
I bow to you all and take my departure.

Everyone filed past the graves where the wrapped figures had been placed, waiting for a turn to toss handfuls of dirt and the flowers they'd been asked to bring. Ivan, still claiming his place next to Danielle, scooped up an excessive amount of dirt and tossed it dramatically onto Leigh's shrouded form.

Arden could feel her anger spike. Go home, she wanted to yell. Leave us alone.

Ivan stepped away from the grave, and Arden could see Leigh again. She looked so small, like a mummy. *Hatshepsut, kaput*, Arden thought, the fragment of memory returning after so many years. Deir-al-Bahiri in Luxor, the city where she was conceived.

She turned to Danielle. "Do want to give your mom a flower?" Danielle shook her head. "It's fine, you don't have to. Can I give her one for you, though?"

Danielle nodded, though barely. Arden took a white rose and dropped it onto her daughter's body. For a moment, it was the only flower. Soon, others would follow and the rose would be buried under lilies, jonquils, irises.

Then she crossed to the other grave, Danielle's hand in hers.

Connor. Her only real husband. She took another rose and held it over the linen-wrapped form.

Suddenly, it was too much. She had given all she had to Leigh, her child. She couldn't do it again, give everything again.

She turned, sought out Connor's mother, who was standing between Bridget and Finn. She held out the rose, signaling with her eyes. *Come. You first.*

Connor's mother seemed to understand. She let go of her two remaining children and inched forward. Arden reached out her hand, mother to mother. A wife was temporary, compared to a mother. Yes, she had loved Connor madly, with her whole heart. But his mother had loved him first, and longer.

She gave the rose to the old woman, who kissed it and let it fall onto the body of her son. Arden bent and scooped up a handful of dirt. "Goodbye," she whispered.

"Grandma?"

She turned. Danielle's voice was tiny. "I want to give Grandpa a flower."

"Of course, sweetheart. Would you like to give him this lily?"

She handed her granddaughter the pink-and-white flower. Danielle's fingers tightened around the stem as she looked at the wrapped figure.

"Thank you for not telling about the lunar eclipse thing," she whispered. Arden had no idea what she was talking about. Then Danielle tossed the lily onto what remained of Connor's body. Her friends, waiting on the side, broke away from their parents and gathered her into a group hug.

A moment later, Ivan materialized next to Arden again. "I know this is kind of a lousy time," he said, "but you need to understand. I'm going to get custody of my daughter."

Arden turned to him. Was he actually challenging her, in the middle of Leigh's funeral?

"I'm just saying," he added, "in case you weren't planning on taking me seriously. It's the least I can do."

Her voice was tight. "That's noble of you. But not necessary. I've got this."

"She's my child. Not yours."

"Oh, really?"

"We all know I'm her father," Ivan said. "Just look at her."

"Father. As in: sperm donor."

"As in: yeah. That's all the court cares about."

"There's more to being a father. Like actually being there."

"Don't blame me for that. Leigh kicked me out. Not the other way around."

"Smart lady."

"Don't be a bitch, Arden."

Had he really called her a bitch? A woman who had just lost both husband and daughter? Well, let him call her that if he wanted. A bitch was a mother dog that snarled at anyone who came too close to her pups.

Her gaze moved to Danielle, encircled by her friends. She thought of her granddaughter's quirks, how she had to cut the labels off her shirts because they felt wrong against her neck and eat each item on her plate before proceeding to the next.

Arden narrowed her eyes as she turned back to Ivan. He might pretend that he'd been lit by the Flame of Fatherhood but it was pure bullshit. He needed to drop the act and go back to being his regular selfish self.

Leave us alone, she wanted to snap. Danielle stays with me.

"She's my daughter," Ivan repeated. "Whether you like it or not."

"Your sperm."

"Why are you so angry?"

That stopped her. Because she knew why.

FACTS AND LIES
1977

While I am in Europe with Robert, New York City has a twenty-five-hour blackout, and the city is engulfed in darkness. Elvis Presley performs in his last concert and dies of a heart attack three weeks later. David Berkowitz, known as the Son of Sam, is captured after a year of New York City murders. A man named Roy Sullivan is struck by lightning for the seventh time.

I am aware of none of this. I am twenty-four years old, and I think my own story is the only one that matters.

I'm glad to be back in my home country, though it isn't until I retrieve my suitcase that it strikes me how odd it is to be returning alone, as if my traveling companion has died along the way. I assume that Robert made it back and that one of us will call the other. Meanwhile, I take the subway to Brooklyn. To my apartment, and the dead plants.

I knew they would be dead. I gave a key to my neighbor so she could water them once a week and rescue my grandmother's wedding-ring quilt if there were a fire, but we aren't really friends so I knew she would forget. I dump the plants in the trash can. Then I take a long hot shower and walk to the post office to get the mail that's been held for my return. I stop at the bank, pick up some New York food. Potato salad and deli meat, a freshly-made bagel.

When I return to my apartment, the phone is ringing. I know it's Robert, and I let it ring. The thought of seeing him, sleeping next to him, makes me ill.

Then I tell myself: Don't be rude. He wants to know if you got home safely. I pick up the phone with my fingertips.

"I can't believe I left you in Rome," he blurts, before I've finished saying hello. "I should have waited till there were two seats on the same plane."

"It's fine," I tell him, though he is right. He shouldn't have listened when I told him to go. He should have thought for himself, insisted that I take the first ticket. Only someone incredibly selfish or passive would do what he did. Robert isn't selfish, but sometimes being passive and being selfish are just two ways to step on the same road.

"Besides," I add, "we could have been there for days, waiting for two seats. Singletons made more sense."

It's true, but has nothing to do with who took the first of those singletons. Robert doesn't seem to notice. I told him it was fine, so it must have been fine.

I hear him give a small sigh. Then he says, "Well, I'm glad you're back."

I can't think of anything more to say. Not: *Let's get together soon.* Not even: *Hey, great summer.* I only want one thing: to end this call.

I clear my throat. "I just got in, actually, and I'm beyond jet-lagged. I really need to crash."

"I know how you feel," he says.

Does he? I don't care. I hang up without saying goodbye.

— ♦ —

It's not easy to stop seeing someone, especially if you've just spent ten weeks together. Robert has no reason to think I don't want to see him, here in America. He has an idea about who I am: a nice person, trustworthy, loyal. If not exactly a girlfriend, close enough.

Until Egypt, that's mostly who I was. Robert doesn't know about the orange sauce I ordered from room service. Nothing happened, but that was Nabil's choice, not mine. It still counts as betrayal.

Robert calls twice a day. Each time, I put him off. Finally, he asks, "Arden, what's going on?" I consider lying, but for once he's too quick. "Forget the phone," he says. "We need to talk in person."

We agree to meet at a bar on Charles Street. I have five hours to think up a credible lie or brace myself to tell the truth.

And what is the truth? *I'm tired of you.* I was never excited about you in the first place, but we had the right things in common. I picture a Venn diagram, our circles overlapping in a shaded area called "Summer Trip to Europe."

The bar is nearly empty, so we settle at a table in the corner. Robert orders a beer and I ask for a dirty martini with Grey Goose, no gin. He raises an eyebrow. It's a serious drink for five o'clock. I tilt my head in acknowledgment. It's going to be a serious conversation.

He waits until we have our drinks, then says, "So, Arden. Is this about me leaving you at the airport? I can't tell you how sorry I am. I wish I could turn back the clock, do it differently."

I stare at the olives, lined up on their silver spear. "No," I answer. So far, I'm telling the truth. It happened long before the airport.

"Then what? I thought we were having a great trip."

I really don't want to be having this conversation. I would have been glad to let everything fade away, no scenes, no recriminations, just some nice memories of museums and cathedrals and cobblestone streets.

I can feel Robert pushing me to answer. I see his pursed lips and carrot-colored hair, the way he's leaning forward, edging into my half of the table. My reluctance shifts into meanness. "How great?" I ask. "Great scenery, or a great time together?"

"Both." There is a defensive edge to his voice now. "We had some great times."

"Like when?"

He gives me a shrewd look, as if he's figuring out what I'm up to, though he doesn't understand why.

"Luxor," he says, daring me not to remember how I straddled him in the hotel room and he dug his fingers into my hips as he thrust into me. Of course I remember. It was the hottest sex we ever had, because I was pretending he was someone else.

Maybe he thinks this is what I want—to recharge our tepid American relationship by channeling that Egyptian heat. Maybe he thinks this is a new kind of foreplay. *Let's pretend we're at a hotel in Luxor.*

A hotel that I was paying for, with my parents' credit card. Because I hoped it would make me different. Make us different.

"Luxor," I repeat.

"I'd say that counts as a great time."

"Really?"

His smile is sly. "Yes, really."

"No, it doesn't." I don't want to do this, but he's making me do it, with his insistence on claiming something as his, ours, that had nothing to do with him. "It wasn't what you thought." I look right at him. "I was pretending you were Nabil."

It's true but secret, not something I meant him to know. I say it now, though. To end this.

To my surprise, he tells me, "I was pretending that too."

My eyes widen. I'm astonished that he would admit such a thing. Yet what man wouldn't want to be the elegant, irresistible Nabil?

I remember everything now. Nabil's arm, draped carelessly across the back of my chair, and his shockingly casual statement. *When I taste a woman, I stroke her with my beard, and the smell remains.* I can't imagine any man, Egyptian or American, thinking he had the right to say something like that. He would be slapped.

I didn't slap him. Because I wanted him to do that to me, and he knew it. I fucked Robert instead.

Suddenly, I see everything differently, as if Robert's words have been turned inside out. Because Robert is not someone who speaks in images or innuendos. He is literal, exact.

I hear the words we've just exchanged, as if someone has played them back for me. I told Robert, "I was pretending you were Nabil." And he answered, "I was pretending that too."

Literally. Pretending that the other person—me, Arden— was Nabil.

That it was Nabil he was fucking.

I pull the martini across the table, as if I'm afraid Robert will take it. He is waiting for me to speak, but I can't. He has ruined my fantasy, the memory of my fantasy. It was all I had.

Nabil is no longer my private, phantom lover. By claiming him, too, as his own lover, Robert is stealing him from me.

"I can be like that," Robert tells me, leaning closer. "More spontaneous. That's what I realized. In Luxor."

He means: a better lover. I cringe.

He is still talking. "That's why I hope I didn't screw things up by the stupid thing I did at the airport. Let me make it up to you."

I don't give a shit about the airport. Or I do, but it doesn't matter, because the person at the airport is exactly who Robert is. Someone I can boss around, even if I'm wrong.

Maybe he really does want to have sex with men. Go ahead, I want to tell him. Then I think, He would probably do it, if I told him to.

Robert shakes his head. "I don't know why I walked away like that. I was going to turn around, but they were closing the door to the jetway."

"It's fine," I say. "Everything is fine."

I can see him preparing for another round of explanations, but there are no words that will change what has already happened. I think of Paolo/Paul, the boy in Rome, following a girl to Italy who has told him not to come.

I can't believe Robert really wants me this much. He's inventing a girlfriend with my face. "It's fine," I repeat. "We both wanted to go to Europe, and we went to Europe. We didn't have a big fight; it's just time to go our separate ways."

"But why, before we even give it a try?"

I grip the martini glass. "There's nothing to try. Summer's over."

"You're mad about the airport," he insists. "I understand, but I'll make it up to you. Just tell me what you need me to do, and I'll do it."

I can't stand any more of this. I shove the martini glass at him and stand up. "I'm leaving. Don't follow me."

I push past the tables, and then I'm out the door. Robert is not behind me. I dare to exhale. I did it.

Only I didn't because he calls that evening. Leaves cards, flowers, outside my apartment. A stuffed bear with a red bow. Day after day. I am going out of my mind.

Robert asked what I needed him to do. I need him to go away.

But he won't. He's like a terrified child, grabbing me around the neck, pulling me underwater. If I try to save him, I will drown. I can't shake him off and swim away. I have to kick him to make him let go.

That's what I tell myself, when I come up with my plan.

My plan is simple and unoriginal: to start dating someone else, as quickly and ostentatiously as I can. It has to be someone completely unlike Robert so it's obvious what I want. And it has to be someone in Robert's circle so he will hear about it.

I have coffee with Theo, the mutual friend whose concert brought us together last spring. Theo isn't a candidate—he and Lynette have been together for years—but he knows a lot of people and likes having parties. I tell him that I'm dying for one last bash before the school year begins. Is he planning anything, maybe a serotinal celebration? I explain that serotinal means late summer.

Theo loves my serotinal idea; it's a perfect reason to throw a party. I mention that it would be better if Robert isn't there.

Theo gives me a knowing look. He doesn't ask for details, but assures me, "No Robert." I'm confident that he'll keep his word.

Theo is fun-loving, generous, and a talented drummer. He is also a talker, so I'm equally confident that he will tell Robert when he sees me with a new man at the party.

I spot Jonah right away. He's a musician, too, a bass player, a big man with an animal energy. Not feline, like Nabil. More like a bull or a bear. I picture him with a hairy stomach, vigorous in bed.

I choose him, and it's clear that he's chosen me too. What will happen next is easy to foresee. What I don't foresee is Robert's devastation.

I am so sure that once he understands that I've moved on, he will move on too. I am easily replaceable. *Well-educated woman in her mid-twenties. Must like literature. No citrus.* That's why, when Lynette calls to tell me about his misery, I am stunned.

"He thinks the world of you," Lynette confides. She is whispering, as if divulging a secret that I've begged her to share. "Like a prize he never dreamed he could win. And then he lost you. If you don't want him anymore, it means he wasn't good enough."

I hear Nabil's words, strangely similar to hers. *"It means he has failed you; he hasn't shown you anything good enough to satisfy your longing."*

"How do you know all this?" I ask.

"Theo. Robert cried on his shoulder."

"Honestly," I say. "That is such melodrama. It was a summer trip, not some great big love affair. We got along, but a relationship has to catch fire. If it doesn't, it doesn't."

"Maybe it caught fire for him."

I think of the notebook where Robert kept track of our expenses. How he liked to convert francs into dollars, centigrade into Fahrenheit.

Our best sex was when I pretended, in Egypt. Used him.

He never really burned for me, unless that's what he thought burning was. Never reached under the table to run his hand along my thigh. Never pushed me against a wall and pressed his mouth to mine.

"No," I say. "It didn't. He's making this up so he can feel sorry for himself."

"I can tell him you aren't all that great, if it would help."

"Ha. Not a bad idea."

"Like, the girl's no treasure. If you only knew."

I laugh, though it's not a happy laugh, as another idea forms in my mind. It's not an idea that someone who wants to be generous and good would have. I've forgotten about that. Or maybe I remember, but I don't care.

I consider the traits that Robert has ascribed to me. Sensitivity. Decency. Trustworthiness. If I prove I'm the opposite, he will be repulsed. Relieved to be rid of me.

The insensitive, untrustworthy thing I do has to be believable, of course. Based on something real that only Robert would recognize, like whatever Paolo/Paul's girlfriend wrote on the postcard that made him know she was serious. Something private that I've twisted, proving that I'm not a good person after all.

Thoughts tumble across my brain, like a deck of cards. They fan onto each other so quickly that there's no time to register each individual card. All I see is the top card. The final one.

This wasn't part of my plan. It's worse. But I do it. I toss my kindness in the trash can, next to the dead plants, and hear myself say the words.

"It's hard to believe he's so hung up on me," I tell Lynette, "since he's really into boys. That's what he likes."

"Boys?" Her voice drops. "How do you know?"

"He told me."

I can't accuse Robert of something he hasn't actually done, but I can repeat what he said. "He likes to pretend it's a guy, not me, when we have sex."

Nabil. Not any guy.

"Holy shit."

I can already see Lynette running to Theo, who will tell Robert what I said and ask if it's true. *"What the hell, bro?"* Maybe Theo will decide that it is true, even if Robert says no. Either way, I've betrayed Robert in an uglier way than if I'd slept with another man. He will understand that I am not the person he imagined. He will be disgusted, and he will let me go.

What I don't know until Lynette tells me, weeks later, is that there was a scandal at Robert's school over the summer—a teacher made inappropriate remarks to a student, and the headmaster had to fire him because the parents threatened to sue. I don't know that those parents, who are wealthy and well-connected, are avid supporters of the Save Our Children campaign started by the born-again pop singer and Florida orange juice spokesperson Anita Bryant. Keep perverts away from our children. I don't know that the school, worried about enrollment, has embraced their cause.

I meant to be cute, not literal, when I said "boys." It was supposed to refer to men. I don't see that no one thinks it's cute.

I don't see my own impatience. If I had waited a few more weeks, Robert would have given up.

I am aware of none of this. I am twenty-four years old, and the only story that interests me is my own.

BLOOD
1977

I don't go to bed with Jonah Orenstein, the man at Theo's party, for three more weeks. Our mutual interest is understood, but he tells me that he's leaving on a tour with the band, and I need to know if he's really going to call when he gets back.

He does. We go out for pad thai, then walk across the Brooklyn Bridge, through lower Manhattan, all the way to his flat in Tribeca. His body is the way I imagined, thick and strong. Different, which is what I want. Sex is lusty and straightforward. We take a shower afterward, and he washes my hair.

I don't think about Robert while I wait for Jonah to return or after the pad thai and the shower. A new school year has begun, and I am occupied with my students during the week and with Jonah on the weekends. Whatever reflection I do is directed at the yellow parakeet I've acquired, replacement for the dead plants. Technically, no pets are allowed in my apartment, but I interpret that to mean mammals who scratch walls, shed, bark, or pee on the carpet. I name the parakeet Big Bird and talk to him while I sit at the kitchen table grading papers and writing scraps of poetry.

Reeds loose in the water,
a big unhurried moon.

A scene so still
you could start at Polaris, and peel back
the whole black calyx of sky.

Robert hasn't called since Theo told him about Jonah. I take
his silence as a graceful exit from my life. I am wrong.

Jonah and I are not in love, but we enjoy each other and I am
oddly content. I feel relaxed, voluptuous, like a woman in a
painting, as I lie naked against the pillows. We watch old black-
and-white movies on TV, eat when we feel like it, cartons of
spicy take-out or stews that Jonah cooks in a cast-iron wok.
There is music in the background, always. Jazz, blues. Eric
Clapton, Freddy Mercury. There are no train schedules to worry
about, no expenses entered into a special notebook.

Jonah is easy to be with. He likes to sing, make love, take
showers together in the tiny rectangular bathroom. The shower
is a white metal box with streaks of rust and a plastic curtain,
bolted into the corner of a tiled floor made of black-and-white
hexagons. Cracked linoleum shows through the places where the
tiles are missing. A taped-together window leads to a fire escape.

I could have gone on like this for a long time, and maybe I
would have, if I hadn't gotten up from the toilet one afternoon in
the teachers' bathroom at school and found big clumps of something red and slimy dropping from my body.

At first I'm relieved, since I haven't had a period since Istanbul. I'm sure it was Istanbul because I remember being desperate
to find a restroom in Gülhane Park and dragging Robert up and

down the paths through the world's saddest zoo. They had a donkey, a horse. I remember making a snippy comment about the horse, and Robert saying, "That must be all they can afford. Exotic animals cost money." I knew he was right, but I was irritated by the way he made everything about money. I wanted him to be sad about the sadness. Finally I had to go back to the Topkapi Museum and use the restroom there.

That was my last period, though my periods have been screwed up since the beginning of the summer, when I had two in a row as we train-hopped through northern France. I assume it's the traveling and the jetlag, and that things will eventually return to normal.

I look at the slime in the toilet and am sure this is a giant delayed period—menstrual waste, accumulating during weeks of messed-up biorhythms and erratic time zones, releasing at last. Still, it's dark and gloppy. Scary.

I wonder if I should show it to a doctor—but how? Scoop the whole wet mess into my purse? I stare at the bowl, trying to memorize the clots of blackish-red. Then I push the handle. There is a swirl of red as blood spirals down the drain.

I take a tampon from my purse. I've been carrying it around so long that the paper is dirty and torn. I rip off the remaining wrapper and shove the tampon inside. More blood comes out. Not a lot, but enough to scare me. It freaks me out more than the clumps. Maybe I do need to see a doctor.

I make my way down the staircase, gripping the banister, and tell the school secretary that I'm unwell and ask if someone can please cover my last two classes. I take a taxi to the Women's Health Clinic.

As I wait to be called, I alternate between the conviction that I have uterine cancer and the certainty that it's just a funky period, an all-at-once ejection of the summer's unused glop. Or an embryo. I shudder. Jonah and I are too new to deal with an embryo. On the other hand, if that's what it was, then it's already over. I remember reading that one of every six known pregnancies ends in a spontaneous rejection, mostly because of abnormal chromosomes. Nature's way of eliminating fetuses that aren't viable.

Nature, then. As long as it's not cancer, the other options will let me slip through. Funky period or spontaneous abortion. Either works.

My name is called, and I'm ushered into an examining room. Blood pressure, temperature. Paper gown. After a few minutes there's a polite knock on the door, and the doctor comes in. Her nametag says K. Smithies. She's tall and thin, with high cheekbones and silver hair in a French twist. She asks about symptoms, last menstrual period. Any fever, vomiting, dizziness?

She asks me to lie back, feet in the stirrups, while she examines me. She is gentle as she removes the tampon, which I've forgotten about. The examination seems to take a long time. Finally she smooths the paper gown over my exposed knees. "Why don't you sit up now, so we can talk?"

She is much nicer than my regular gynecologist, yet her niceness is scaring me. It must be cancer after all.

I swing my legs over the side of the examining table so we're face-to-face. "You lost a fair amount of blood," she tells me. "It appears to have stopped, though we'll need to get you on a saline drip and monitor you for a while. The good news is that your baby is just fine."

I blink. "What baby?"

The gentle smile returns, but it's laced with something sterner, as if I'm pretending to be surprised. "Surely you are aware, Ms. Rice, given everything you've reported. You're nine or ten weeks pregnant. I can be more precise later."

I shake my head. She must be confused. I've only been with Jonah for a month, and I'm meticulous about birth control. Unless it happened right away, some kind of fluke?

No. She said nine or ten weeks.

I turn pale. No. Yes. My perplexity turns to horror. Robert, not Jonah.

I have a sick, unfunny thought. Nabil. The third person in the bed. The holy spirit, inseminating the dung ball with his will.

A bubble of hysteria rises in my throat. I try to stifle it, and what comes out is a snort. I want to apologize to this nice Dr. K. Smithies. I'm not laughing at her or what she's told me.

"You truly didn't know?"

I explain about the time zones and the jetlag. She makes a few notes on a clipboard. "I understand. And yes, travel can disrupt the body's rhythms."

I fix on the word *disrupt*. Clearly, that's the explanation.

"I'm on the pill," I tell her. "And I'm super-conscientious. Maybe this is some kind of hormonal mix-up?"

"No birth control method is one hundred percent foolproof." She reaches for a pen. "I haven't checked your hormone levels—we'll need to do a full workup—but your uterus is telling us what we need to know. You are definitely pregnant."

I wait for the speech about my options, but she's busy making notes in my chart.

"Then what happened today?" My eyes narrow. "I didn't do anything, if that's what you're thinking. Like, tried to get rid of it and pretended I didn't know."

She looks up, her gaze level. "I'm not thinking anything like that. My concern is for your health and wellbeing."

"Then *why*?" I repeat.

"It could be any number of things," she replies, "and we may never know. The most important thing is to keep it from happening again. For the baby's sake, and for yours."

The baby's sake. My relief when she didn't say *cancer* shifts into anger. "It's not a baby. A pregnancy, okay. But not a baby, with a diaper and a bottle and great big eyes. You're not supposed to say that."

She doesn't even flinch. "Fair enough, Ms. Rice. Let's just focus on the situation at hand. I need to draw some blood and get you on an IV drip to replenish the nutrients you've lost."

My rebellious energy dissipates as fatigue overcomes me. I fall asleep on the gurney while the saline solution drips into my body. When I wake up, a nurse gives me a list of instructions, a packet of vitamins and iron pills, three sanitary pads, and a number to call if the bleeding resumes.

By the time I return to my apartment, it's evening. Big Bird is squawking at me. Like him, I'm hungry, but I'm too keyed-up to think about food. Mostly, I'm worried about how to avoid Jonah while I take care of this and get un-pregnant.

And Robert. Shit. Do I owe him anything? Maybe, but I'm not opening that door. Let him get over me, move on. That was the point. If I reel him back now—*I just thought you should know* —after making sure he's drifted free, then the whole cruel thing I did, through Lynette, was simply that. Cruel.

Still, the fact of Robert is tugging at me. I need to make sure he really has moved on.

I phone Lynette. I'm not thinking clearly—it's probably the blood loss, and the shock—because it's as if I've forgotten our other conversation, when I took something Robert trusted me with and twisted it into an ugly half-truth.

I ask her how Robert has been, if they've seen him lately, or Theo has. There is an odd silence. Finally, she says, "Do you honestly not know?"

It's almost the same question that Dr. K. Smithies asked. "Not know what?"

Another silence. Then Lynette gives a deep sigh. She explains that her best friend Abby is dating the head of admissions at the boys' school where Robert is—or was—librarian. The boyfriend made Abby promise not to tell a soul, but Abby told Lynette because telling your best friend isn't like telling the whole world, right?

And now Lynette tells me. Her voice is grave, prim. She tells me how Robert was ousted from his job for "perversion" and blacklisted by the National Association of Private Elementary and Secondary Schools. How he left town and no one knows where he is. "His life is totally destroyed," she declares.

I can hear the drama, and it pisses me off. As if she hadn't been part of that destruction.

I told her something ugly and mean so Theo would tell Robert, and Robert would know I was a horrible person and let me go. If my ugly words traveled beyond that, it was Lynette's doing, not mine.

I want to point that out to her, smack away the primness. We did this together. I ignited the blaze; Lynette made sure it spread.

Then, all at once, my wooziness disappears. In its place there is the starkness, and the horror, of what I did. We are not equal in this, Lynette and I. Nothing would have happened if I hadn't lit the match.

I clench the phone as sweat gathers on my forehead, slithers down my back.

Robert must know the source of the words that ruined his life; there is no one else it could have been. And he must know that they were intentional, meant to hurt. He must despise me. Well, that was what I wanted.

Not that way. Not by harming him like that. Even though it was true.

And then, as if from nowhere—the words forming themselves, rising up, filling my brain—the thought I didn't want to have. What if I got it wrong?

What if Robert meant exactly what he said: that he too was pretending to be Nabil, instead of his regular self? Agreeing with me, the way he always did.

It was the simplest answer, but I'd never considered it. Because I didn't want to.

I needed a way to get rid of him. So I made something up.

The phone is burning my fingers; I can't hold it a second longer. "I need to go," I tell Lynette. I drop the phone. Blindly, I careen from wall to wall, knocking into Big Bird's cage. He lets out a screech of protest.

My self-loathing has no borders; it spills past my skin, onto the floorboards. My parents would be horrified. This is not the person they strove and sacrificed for me to become. The person they were speaking to, and for, when they raised their glasses at our Thanksgiving table.

Then, in a flash of memory, I realize where I learned the words that came to me in Deir el-Medina. *Let it be for the good of all.*

It was their toast, my parents' toast. Lena and Aleksander, sharing the bounty that the new country, America, had given to them.

I let out a sob. I long for a way out of this evil thing I have done. For penance, atonement.

Big Bird is still screeching. Outside the window, I hear the wail of a siren, two men arguing in Spanish. The sanitary pad fits snugly between my legs, in case there is further seepage. Hopefully, there won't be.

And then I see it. The path.

I cannot possibly terminate this pregnancy. It proves that Robert is not what I said he was. It is realer than my words.

I understand that having a baby is not simple, but women do it all the time.

The baby will remind me. Of what I did, and who I am. I will place this baby like a scarab on my heart.

Jonah will believe the baby is his. There is no reason for him not to; we are lusty, monogamous. And it will come early, in just seven months. Many babies come early. Of all my deceptions, this one will be the easiest.

I worry that Jonah will be upset about the pregnancy, but he is delighted. Four months later, he decides that we should get married. He thinks it will be great fun to dress up and have a party; he will set our wedding vows to music. I tell him we don't have to, though I'm relieved when the ceremony is over and we have signed the papers.

When Leigh Alexandra Orenstein is born, Jonah is the legal father. She is small, barely six pounds, so she passes for a seven-month baby instead of one who is full-term. Dr. K. Smithies knows the real due date, but she honors my request to keep it between the two of us.

What it means, though, is that Jonah thinks there are still seven weeks until the baby is due. He is on tour with the band when I go into labor, and I am alone when I look into Leigh's eyes for the very first time.

COME BACK

2013

Leigh, Danielle, and their two cats, Tinkerbell and Tiger Lily, had been living in a winterized cottage in a small town near the Hudson. It was a rental property, separated from the main house by a vegetable garden with a chicken wire fence and parallel beds of pachysandra that rimmed a narrow path. The owners of the cottage had been told about the train wreck—Finn did that, thankfully—and Arden had emailed to ask if they could please look after the cats for a few weeks while she sorted things out.

The owners had sent a gracious reply, assuring her that they would stop by the cottage to feed the cats and scoop out the litter box, but hadn't offered to take the cats on a permanent basis. Arden's building didn't allow pets, so that wasn't an option. She had expected Danielle to plead for the cats, yet Danielle seemed to have forgotten about them. She wondered if Danielle thought, somehow, that her entire house had been destroyed in the crash. Tables, chairs, cats. In a way, it had.

It was time, Arden knew, to call Eleanor Cardoza, the child therapist. The social worker—Ruby, that was her name—was probably right: Danielle needed to talk to someone who wasn't in the midst of her own grief. Plus, Arden needed the therapist's help in getting home-schooling approved for longer than the miserly four weeks the district had authorized. It would be heartless to send a girl like Danielle back to school before she was ready—and to what school? The one she'd gone to, in the town on the Hudson? And how was she supposed to get there from Arden's apartment? Later, once the custody business was settled, they'd find a school in Manhattan that Danielle liked. For now, though, home-schooling was the only option.

Plan for the cats. Therapist appointment. Tutor.

Arden was well aware of what was not on her list. Crying. Raging. Facing the brutal justice of her pain.

There was no room for any of those things, not while she was struggling to hold Danielle's life together.

"I don't *want* to talk to someone," Danielle said.

"You just have to show up," Arden told her. "If you want to talk, fine. And if you don't feel like it, the first time, that's fine too."

"First time?" Danielle glowered at her grandmother "First, out of how many?" She shook her head. "It's no. I'm not going."

"You have to, sweetheart."

The needy child was gone, replaced by an obstinate adolescent. "Oh really? And what are they going to do, if I don't? Arrest me?" Danielle extended her arms dramatically. "Cuff me now."

"Danielle," Arden said. It was funny and not-funny. "You have to see someone because you're a minor with an open file at the Child Welfare Department. Therapy is one the things they require in order for you to stay here with me."

"Fine," Danielle countered. "I'll just stay with Olivia." Olivia was her best friend in what Arden was already thinking of as Danielle's old life.

Arden gave her a stern look. "This isn't like a sleepover, Nellie. It's about where the Child Welfare people think you should live. Your mom didn't leave any instructions, so they get to decide."

"What about my dad? I could live with him and be in his plays. Like those child stars, when a teacher comes on the set to help them with their homework."

Arden struggled to keep her voice neutral. "Your dad hasn't really been in the picture lately." It seemed like the kindest way to put it. The last thing she wanted was to make her granddaughter feel worse by underscoring Ivan's absence.

"That's not because of him," Danielle said. "It's because of her."

Leigh wouldn't let Ivan see his daughter? Arden could hardly fault her, yet she couldn't imagine Ivan trying very hard. It didn't seem fair to blame Leigh for that.

She studied Danielle, whose fists were now clenched under her arms. She understood that adolescent girls rejected their mothers and idolized their fathers, especially the ones who weren't around, but the flowers on Leigh's green grave were still fresh. Couldn't they let Leigh be perfect for a few days before making everything her fault?

"These things are complicated," she managed to say.

Danielle shook her head again. "You think you know everything, Grandma, but you don't."

"I'm sure he thought of you every day. Your dad." Arden sent a silent plea to the unknown Eleanor Cardoza. *Help me out here.*

"That's not who I'm talking about. I'm talking about *her*." Danielle narrowed her eyes. "You think she was oh-so noble and pure, with her Save the Whales and People for the Ethical Treatment of Animals. But she wasn't. She had boyfriends and girlfriends. That's why Dad couldn't stand it, and he left."

"You mean she had friends?" Arden tensed. "And your dad didn't like that? He didn't want her to have friends?" It was classic: an abuser who wanted his partner all to himself. Ivan was worse than she'd realized.

"I didn't say friends," Danielle corrected her. "I said boyfriends and girlfriends. She said you could love lots of people. You didn't have to prefer one person over another, as long as they all agreed and respected each other."

Arden turned ashen. That was polyamory talk. She remembered Connor in a Japanese restaurant, long ago. Did *Connor* have something to do with this?

No, he couldn't possibly have advocated polyamory to her daughter. This was just Danielle's way of being angry at her mother for dying.

If you had loved me more, only me, you wouldn't have left me.

She remembered Danielle standing in the doorway, wrapped in Leigh's nightgown, staring at her with big haunted eyes. *She didn't really mean it.*

Mean to die, clearly. Leave her.

"Dad thought it was gross, and I did too," Danielle said. "He told her she had to give them up or he was finished. But she wouldn't."

"Danielle." It took everything Arden had to stay calm. "You really need to be sure of what you're saying." Arden made herself hold absolutely still, not even a twitch of her jaw to reveal the turmoil that was taking place inside—because there were two things that couldn't be true at the same time. On the one hand, the only person she'd ever met who was more literal than Danielle was her biological grandfather, the long-banished Robert Altschuler. If Danielle said that Leigh had multiple partners, then Leigh had multiple partners.

On the other hand, there were Danielle's "pictures"—which

might be exactly what Arden had suspected. Exaggerations, a ploy for her mother's attention. Another reason Danielle needed to see a therapist.

Arden put her hands on Danielle's shoulders and looked her granddaughter in the eyes. "How do you know all this, Danielle?"

"I saw it."

"You really saw? Real, actual people? Or was it one of your pictures, the pictures you see in your mind?"

"My pictures are real. Remember when I saw Mom fall on the ice?"

Arden took a deep breath. This was not a conversation to push Danielle through, to make it turn out the way she wanted.

"Sometimes when people are very close," she said, "they can sense when the other person is hurting."

"And the train," Danielle reminded her. "I saw the train."

Arden remembered the girl's nightmare, how she had writhed on top of the blanket and cried, "I saw." Arden had almost seen it herself too, but later, when she already knew. Terror had raced through her body, as if joining her to those she loved by letting her feel what they had felt.

Maybe that was what Danielle meant about boyfriends and girlfriends. Leigh must have said something, and Danielle made a picture in her mind, afterward. Arden knew that Leigh had been cold to her daughter, though it pained her to admit it. Could she really fault Danielle for wanting to believe that she "saw" what was happening in her mother's life? It seemed real to her, because it was all she had.

Arden shivered. Let the therapist figure it out. Eleanor. Someone she could pay, who would find answers.

Her hands were still gripping Danielle's shoulders. She exhaled slowly and willed her fingers to relax. "You have to be careful, sweetheart. If you say something that's sort of true, but not exactly true, you can end up hurting another person very badly."

"I can't hurt her by telling you," Danielle said. "She's in heaven. I thought maybe God wouldn't let her in, but He did."

Arden shut her eyes for a moment. "There's a lot to sort out," she said, finally. "That's why it's helpful to hear what someone else has to say. A fresh perspective."

"You mean, a therapist."

"You're a smart cookie, Nellie." She met Danielle's gaze. "Will you do it, meet her, see what you think?"

"What if I hate her?"

Arden weighed her options. If she convinced Danielle to meet Eleanor Cardoza, she would have done what the social worker asked. If Danielle refused a second meeting, that would be Eleanor Cardoza's failure, not hers.

"Then you don't have to go back."

It was the best she could do.

Arden had thought that Eleanor Cardoza would want to talk to her first, for background, but the therapist declined. "I have what I need from her file. You and I can talk later, after Danielle and I have gotten to know each other."

"I understand," Arden said. "At the same time, there are things you should know."

Eleanor's voice was soft. "I know she lost her mother in a dreadful, traumatic way."

There's more, Arden wanted to say. Her visions. And the polyamory. Will you find out if it was true? Who Danielle's mother—my daughter—really was?

That was the question she kept circling back to, and the possibility that Leigh—her free-thinking sprite, the charmer who put a tutu on her head and sang to the horses—hadn't been a particularly nice person, not when it came to her daughter or to the father of her child. And if she hadn't been, then whose responsibility was that, if not the mother who had carted her from husband to husband?

Arden was having trouble breathing. The last of those husbands was Connor McRae, a man she had trusted entirely. Surely this had nothing to do with him. If it did, the earth was crumbling beneath her.

Before Connor, there was Jonah Orenstein, a man who had walked away when she told him the truth, just as she was about to walk away first. Then Michael Tate, whom she never should have married. And before all of them, Robert Altschuler, whom she had ruined.

She was spiraling down a crazy-hole. Maybe she was the one who needed therapy.

Loss was hard enough, if you were certain you knew whom you'd lost.

The appointment with Eleanor Cardoza was set for Thursday morning. Wednesday was Danielle's first session with Nora, the tutor assigned by the school.

With Danielle in Nora's care for a few hours, Arden decided to make a quick trip to the river town where Danielle had lived with her mother. She needed to get a sense of the task that awaited her. How many clothes and possessions Leigh actually had. Whether she could bear to go through them, or should just call the Got-Junk people to come and take everything.

She arranged to get a key from the owners, the Fremantles. Shelly, the wife, gave an effusive speech about what a tragedy it was. Arden waited for her to ask what she could do to help, so she could tell her, "Take the cats." But Shelly merely said, "Why don't you hold onto the key, for now? That way, you can come and go as you like."

"Yes, good idea." Arden took the key, thanked her, and eased out of the Fremantles' kitchen. She crossed the yard to the cottage, picking her way around the overgrown pachysandra.

The cottage smelled of cat pee. Arden found a can of air freshener under the kitchen sink and sprayed the baseboards. Then she collected the overripe bananas lying on the counter, an open box of Raisin Bran, and a yellow onion that had started to sprout, and threw them in a garbage bag. She'd told herself that she would simply look, assess the situation, but it was impossible to smell cat pee or see black bananas and do nothing.

They called it "the cottage," which made it sound cute and small, but there were five good-sized rooms. A living room, kitchen, bedroom for each of them, and an enclosed porch that Leigh had turned into a studio for her framing business. She had liked finding photos of everyday objects and making them beautiful by the way they were presented. Strips of ribbon and wallpaper, frames within frames. That was Leigh, Arden thought. Creative ways to wrap the ordinary and make you notice.

Arden swallowed, vowing not to fall apart, and strode down the hall to Leigh's bedroom. She stopped at the closed door—feeling, already, how much harder this would be than the kitchen. The dishes and towels were going to Goodwill; maybe Leigh's clothes should go to Goodwill too. Stuffed into cartons. Taken away.

And yet, before that, she had to see her daughter's clothes, her earrings, her makeup. Mourn her in the details. Privately, specifically. Arden turned the knob and went inside.

The three pillows she always slept with were still bunched from sleep; a few strands of Leigh's auburn hair lay across the sky-blue silk. Arden bit her lip, then lifted the tendrils with her fingertips and put them in her pocket. She ran her hand over the textured bedspread, the bedpost with its acorn-shaped finial, the pleated lampshade. Each thing said *Leigh*. The flair she'd had, even as a child, an extravagant carelessness that always ended up looking intentional and perfect.

There was a book face-down on Leigh's nightstand. Arden picked it up, eager to know if it held the answer to the question she hadn't yet put into words. Then she frowned, disappointed. It was nothing special, just a collection of anagrams and acrostics. She put it back on the nightstand.

Idly, she opened the night-table drawer. For a crazy moment, she thought there would be a Gideon Bible. Or a notepad, with the name of the hotel.

Instead, there was a collection of items, carefully laid out. Something made of feathers, and something else that was clearly a dildo. Arden drew back. Not items she was meant to see, but okay. Her gaze moved to the other items. A vibrator. Leather ties, a blindfold.

She stiffened. What if Danielle had wandered in, searching for a pencil or a hair clip, and opened the drawer? What was Leigh thinking—or was she thinking at all, the way someone needed to, when she had a child?

She slammed the drawer shut. Leigh, she wanted to cry. Don't be this person. I saved you, when you might have been a bloody clot in a toilet, when I didn't even want you—and then I did, I wanted you so much. Everything I did was for you.

I want you now. I don't care about the dildo. Come back.

The traffic was outrageous, and Arden was late getting home. She phoned from the car, twice, and the tutor, Nora, was nice about waiting, though it was clear that she thought a ten-year-old could stay in a doorman apartment for thirty minutes without being in serious peril.

Arden tried to pay her for the extra time, but Nora refused. "The school pays me, not the parent. But I can't stay late next time, just so you know. I have a whole schedule."

Arden apologized, assured her that this was a one-time occurrence. Then, when Nora left, she asked Danielle, "So how did it go?"

"Grandma. It's fine. It's just math and stuff. You don't have to stress."

Yes, I do. Arden pictured the cottage, the nightstand. She'd fled without getting rid of its contents, and the trash bag with the bananas and the raisin bran was still in the middle of the kitchen floor. Well, she'd retrieve it on her next visit.

She exhaled again, then eyed her granddaughter. Suddenly, the need to do something was urgent. "Let's go the pet store," she said. "We can get a bird."

Danielle looked confused. "A bird?"

"I don't think Tinkerbell and Tiger Lily are going to work out," Arden admitted. "Not here. They don't allow pets. At least, not pets with fur and claws. But I had a bird once, a parakeet. They're pretty to look at, and no trouble at all."

"A bird." A smile spread across Danielle's features.

Arden allowed herself a moment's relief. This one thing, she could do. Get right, in the tapestry of *wrongs* that wove through her life.

A PARROT STORY
1978

I am twenty-five years old, yet somehow I think that a marriage based on a lie is going to work.

At first, it seems to. Jonah delights in my nursing body, just as he delighted in my pregnant body, and adores Leigh, who is easy to adore. She is a sweet baby, a snuggler. He makes up songs for her on the harmonica, and she watches his hands and face, entranced by the sounds they make. I prop her against my body, skin to skin, as he invents goofy riffs, and give thanks for my good fortune.

I could easily have slipped up and ruined this. For seven months, I had to synchronize the math and the calendar. Joke about my early weight gain, keep the baby's flutter-kicks to myself. Luckily, Jonah was on the road with the band for long stretches of time in the spring and didn't keep track of the *What to Expect* chapters the way I did.

The final weeks were the hardest, knowing that the baby would come while he was on tour. There was no way to ask him to stay home, as long as I claimed that I wasn't due until the end of June. I had to insist that I could finish out the year at the girls' school in Brooklyn and move into his Tribeca apartment with time to spare.

Leigh arrived in mid-May, as I knew she would. I was alone in my third-floor walkup when I called a taxi to take me to the hospital. Big Bird, the parakeet, saw the baby before Jonah did. But I didn't slip. I pulled it off.

That summer, with Leigh in a sling across my chest, I'm as happy as I can remember being. Everyone is happy for me too. My parents, who are living in Arizona, come to visit, eager to see the grandchild who bears their names. Even my brother Hugh, who has never been especially interested in me, calls weekly and asks for pictures.

In the middle of this happiness, I develop an odd, almost perverse ritual. I check the calendar every day and try to remember exactly where I was and what I was doing a year ago. This same day, last summer. Which country and city. Which museum, plaza, cathedral. With Robert.

I don't know why I am doing this, but I don't miss a day.

One morning at the end of July, I take the cloth off Big Bird's cage and see that he is dead. He is lying on his back, wings folded, beak up. I let out an anguished cry.

I call the vet, though I understand there is nothing the vet can do, except to agree: *Yes, he's dead.* Stupidly, I'm remembering Monty Python and the dead parrot sketch. *It is an ex-parrot. It has ceased to be.*

A vet tech kindly explains that this can happen for any number of reasons. He lists the possible causes: heat, disease, dehydration, exposure to a toxin that doesn't affect humans but can be fatal to birds. When he mentions that the coating on a Teflon pan, especially at a high temperature, can produce fumes that are deadly for birds, I hang up.

I made tortillas last night and moved Big Bird's cage into the kitchen for company. Jonah was at a rehearsal; the baby was asleep. I wanted to talk to Big Bird, the way I used to, in Brooklyn. Recite my fragments of poetry while I cooked to see how he liked them, their cadence and flow.

I understand that I killed my bird, but I can't tell Jonah, who is asleep in the bedroom. It's another thing I can't tell him. He will think that I'm not the person I claim to be, and he will be right.

I pull a box out of the closet, the box for the Marc Fischer pumps I'm still hoping to fit back into, and dump the shoes on the floor. They fall on their backs, heels up, like Big Bird. The shoebox will be the bird's coffin, the tissue paper his shroud.

I put the shoebox in a canvas shopping bag, with Big Bird wrapped inside, then lift Leigh out of her makeshift crib and place her in the Snugli I've strapped across my chest. She stirs, but doesn't wake. I cover her with a shawl so she will stay asleep. Quietly, I leave the apartment.

I walk west along Spring Street, toward the river. I can't put Big Bird in the trash, and there's no backyard where I can bury him. I have the idea that I'll toss him into the Hudson, let him be carried downstream toward the Statue of Liberty. It seems like a proper send-off for a loyal bird. But the wind picks up and Leigh awakens, hungry. She starts to cry. I am still blocks from the water.

No one is paying attention, so I let her nurse under the shawl while I walk. I move slowly, gently, my hand on her back. The canvas bag bumps against my leg.

Finally I come to West Street, and realize that my plan makes no sense. I can see the Hudson, but I can't get near it; the ruins of the collapsed Miller Highway are still there, blocking access, while the city figures out what to do. Maybe I can walk north, to one of the Chelsea Piers, but I have no idea if I'm allowed to walk to a spot where I can toss my parakeet into the water. Maybe a sign will say No Littering, or the gulls will swoop down on Big Bird and eat him like garbage.

Leigh is fretting now, and I can tell that she has a soiled diaper. I want to cry too. There is nothing I can do except turn and retrace my steps back to the apartment. I pass a man selling fruit and newspapers, a bike chained to a streetlamp. I pass a wire trash basket. Tears begin to pour down my face. I drop the canvas bag into the basket.

When I get home, Jonah is awake. "Where the hell were you?" he shouts. He is worried in a way I've never seen. "You're gone, the baby's gone. I'm thinking it's some kind of emergency. Why didn't you wake me?" Then he registers my tear-streaked face. "What happened?"

"It was my fault," I tell him, and I start to cry again. "I didn't realize what would happen. I didn't take care of him."

"Who?" He is obviously confused. Leigh is unhappy, but alive. And not a *him*.

"Big Bird," I manage, still sobbing. "I threw him in the trash."

"The parrot?"

"Parakeet."

"You threw him in the dumpster, out back?"

I shake my head. What does it matter which trash can I tossed him into?

"He's dead." My sobs are making it hard to speak. "It was the frying pan. The Teflon."

It's clear that Jonah isn't following, though I understand that he wants to be kind. He runs a hand through his hair, still messy from sleep. "Shit, Arden. I'm really sorry."

"Me too."

Leigh squirms, whimpers.

"I have to change her," I tell him. I push past Jonah, who looks lost. Then I stop and put my hand on his arm. "I need to change her diaper, that's all."

His flesh is warm, solid. I remind myself: Don't mess this up.

Jonah is not my image of a husband, but he is open and exuberant, with a good heart. He sings, cooks, kisses my stomach and face and nursing breasts. He has accepted Leigh—come to love her—when he had no plan to be a father.

Unfortunately, he is not her father.

Sometimes I think: Does it matter? Why is it different from using a sperm donor?

Even at my most optimistic, I know that's a stupid analogy. A sperm donor is a solution. Not a lie.

Still, I have no intention of telling Jonah, ever. My child's name is Leigh Alexandra Orenstein. It's the only name she will ever have.

I don't return to my teaching job in Brooklyn. There is no simple way to commute, and I have a baby. I find editing work I can do from home, for a textbook company. I carry a sack of pages home on the subway, with instructions about how to coordinate the material in the chapters with the exercises in the workbook. Topic sentences, gerunds, metaphors and similes.

Jonah has a chance to cut a record, a solo. If it catches the attention of the stations and their listeners, it could be a game-changer. "Go for it," I urge. Jonah doesn't care about money or fame, though he likes the idea of recording a song that he wrote. I want him to succeed. I want him to be happy.

He goes to the West Coast for three weeks, and I'm glad to

have the apartment to myself. Leigh and myself, that is. Jonah is a big man and takes up a lot of space. With him away, I can exhale. Say whatever I want, without worrying that I'll make a mistake.

Leigh gets her first teeth. Two front ones, and then tiny fangs.

I remain irrationally upset about Big Bird.

While Jonah is away making his record, I go to the publisher's office to turn in my pages and pick up some new ones. The money is good, and we need it. Jonah won't get paid until the record is out—and, even then, nothing unless it sells.

I take Leigh with me on the subway. She's no longer a tiny infant, but she likes being strapped to my chest and I like feeling her there. I have a bag slung across my left shoulder with the chapter galleys, another bag on my right shoulder with diapers, bottle, wipes. I put a hand on Leigh's back. My other hand cups her little feet in their pink-and-white socks.

When I get to the publisher's office, I notice a woman in the waiting area with a lopsided haircut and a frazzled expression. Her child is older than Leigh and is sitting in a foldup stroller, but otherwise we are the same. The woman catches my eye and laughs. "Do you do your cross-referencing while she's napping? My little monster never sleeps. Thank God for Sesame Street."

The mention of Sesame Street reminds me of Big Bird, and I flinch. "I do try to work when she naps," I answer, "but mostly I end up working late at night."

"Same here." She extends a hand. "Juliet Montgomery."

"Arden," I say. "Arden Rice."

The woman Juliet points to the stroller. "Zack. He also answers to Zachary, Zacko, and Wacko." The boy looks up and offers a pleased-with-himself grin. Leigh turns to meet his gaze, as if she knows the grin is for her.

Juliet sees Leigh's face and exclaims, "Oh, she's precious. That hair! And just look at those eyelashes. Did she get them from her daddy?"

I think of Jonah's dark hair and dark brown eyes, heavy lidded when he's turned on, bright when he's singing. "Not really."

Juliet doesn't seem interested in my answer. She's already moved on to the next thing. "Aren't you bored out of your mind with the difference between *its* and *it's*, *accept* and *except*?"

"My stuff is more about topic sentences. Compare and contrast."

"Huh. What grade do you have?"

"Seventh," I tell her.

"That's why. I have fourth. Seventh sounds better. Want to trade?"

I have no idea if she is being serious or just having fun. Either way, the conversation is tiring me. I'm used to Jonah and Leigh, neither of whom requires so many words.

Juliet and I are summoned to confer with different editors, but the meetings are short and we end up leaving at the same time. She follows me into the elevator, pivoting the stroller with a brisk, confident twist. "Are you taking the subway?" she asks. "Which one? Uptown or downtown?"

Her questions are starting to irritate me, but I try to be polite. "The IRT," I say. "Downtown." Then I add, "Or I might walk to the park."

The idea has just occurred to me, and it does seem like the perfect thing to do. It's a gorgeous fall day, and there is an entrance to Central Park nearby.

"What a great idea!" Juliet says. "Let's do it."

I didn't think I was inviting her. On the other hand, Jonah is away, and there's nowhere I have to be. Juliet and I fall into step as we cross the lobby and push through the revolving glass door, onto the sidewalk. It really is a spectacular day—amber and scarlet leaves, air so clean and crisp that you want to bite it and swallow it whole.

Juliet eyes the bags dangling from my shoulders. "If you want, we can stop by my apartment and you can leave your stuff there. It's only a couple of blocks. Instead of lugging it around, I mean. I have an extra stroller you can borrow."

I wonder, briefly, if she's a crazy person who wants to lure me to her apartment so she can kill me and steal Leigh, then decide that she's overwhelming and maybe a little bit lonely, but not crazy. "Sure," I say. "That would be great."

Juliet chatters as we walk. "Stephen, my husband, is on one of those corporate legal teams. You know, mergers and acquisitions?" I have no idea what she's talking about, but I nod. "So we have this huge place because we have to entertain clients. It's kind of over-the-top, so don't freak out."

When we approach the Beaux-Arts building where Juliet lives, I understand what she means by *over-the-top*. A uniformed doorman rushes to open the door, and we step into a lobby with a two-story ceiling, marble floor, and medieval-looking tapestries on the walls. A potted ficus stands like a sentinel by the reception desk.

I am not used to so much space. In the apartment I share with Jonah, everything is under or on top of something else. A wire basket with bags of rice and coffee beans fills the space under the sink. Cereal boxes are lined up on top of the refrigerator, spines out, like books.

I can't help wondering why someone with money, which Juliet clearly has, would want to do the kind of tedious work we are both doing. If I ask her, I am sure she will tell me. And then she will ask me a question, and I will have to answer, and she will decide that we are friends. I don't want any friends. I just want to take care of my baby, cross-reference textbook pages, and not have to lie.

We take the elevator to the tenth floor. Juliet does another tilt-and-pivot with the stroller, where Zack has now fallen asleep, and unlocks the door to her apartment. It's even grander than I imagined. There are pale thick rugs on the wide-plank floor. Modern, expensive-looking lighting. An L-shaped couch.

I can't believe I've met someone who lives here. I know there are people who live like this, but they are not the kind of people I know.

A sentence forms in my brain, hard as a diamond. *Someday I will live in a place like this.*

I remember another sentence that also filled me. *Let me be good.*

They're such different longings, yet one doesn't preclude the other. I don't see why a person should have to choose.

"Home sweet home," Juliet declares. "Don't say I didn't warn you. Do you want some iced tea? Perrier?"

"This is incredible," I tell her. Then the question slips out. "Why in the world are you toiling over *its* and *it's* when you live in a place this?"

I worry that I've offended her, but she waves a hand. "I have to do something with my brain, and that was my degree, English. So I figured: Why not? It's part-time, and I can quit if I hate it. Which I might."

Her explanation isn't so different from mine, except mine starts with the main reason: we need the money. Before Leigh was born, when Jonah and I did nothing but listen to music and make love, I didn't think about money. Now it's all I think about. The thoughts loop endlessly in my mind.

Leigh needs things. Those things cost money.

I can't rely on Jonah for that money.

Because Jonah's record might tank. Because Jonah doesn't care about money, and he'll never earn enough to get us out of that tiny apartment with its two-burner hot plate and cracked linoleum.

Because Jonah shouldn't be responsible for providing Leigh with the things she's going to need.

Because it's not right for me to lie around and play with my baby, when I ruined a man's life.

I don't know which is the real reason. None of them are. They all are.

"What about you?" Juliet asks. "You get to do topic sentences, but still."

I shrug. "A lot of reasons."

"Like what?"

"English degree." I hold up a hand and tap on each finger. "Check. Part-time. Check. Has nothing to do with diapers. Check."

"And?"

I tighten. Juliet is pushy or perceptive or both. When I don't answer right away, she waves her hand again. "Hey, everyone has a story. Or sometimes we just do things, right? I don't know, I might try macrame." Then she says, "You can toss your stuff on the chair. I'll get the other stroller. If Zack wakes up, which he won't, tell him I eloped with the doorman."

I wait while she goes down a hall, into another section of the apartment. I put my hand on Leigh's rump and whisper in her ear, "What do you think of all this, my little pumpkin? A hall *inside* your apartment. Not a hall you go down to *get* to your apartment."

Leigh makes one of her cooing noises. I think she recognizes

the word *pumpkin*. It's one of Jonah's words for her. Round vegetable words. Pumpkin, cabbage, tomato.

Juliet returns with a second collapsible stroller and a blue
insulated bag. "We can put our drinks in here." She lifts a multi-
colored object from the handle of the stroller. "And look, isn't
this a darling mobile? It attaches right to the bar."

I am overwhelmed by the number of possessions she has.
Extra strollers with darling mobiles, special bags for going to the
park. I want these things too. I want them more than I want an
L-shaped couch and expensive lighting because I want them for
Leigh.

"Actually," I say, "I should probably change her, maybe feed
her, before we head out? It's been hours since we left the house."
The house, I think, annoyed at myself. It's not a house. It's a crappy
little railroad flat.

"Sure," Juliet says. "Why don't you go to the guest room, for
some privacy? It's through there, second door on the right."

Guest room. In my own *not-a-house*, Leigh sleeps in a padded
box I made for her. Until now, it seemed sweet and creative.

I say, "Great, thanks," and carry my little girl to a room, like
the stroller, that is simply extra, if someone happens to need it.

Unlike the understated décor of the rest of the apartment,
the guest room has a bizarre, Amazon-jungle theme. There are
palms and ferns and spider-plants, jade-green throw pillows. In
the corner, there is a fake parrot on a wooden stand. The parrot
is so realistic that I'm not sure, at first. He has technicolor feathers
and bright glass eyes. He doesn't blink when Leigh and I enter
the room. The eyes are not real.

He's not even an ex-parrot, who has ceased to be. He never
was.

I look at the fake parrot and mourn Big Bird yet again. He
was the only one who knew my true story.

WOLF MOON
1979

Jonah returns from California. The record is in production, but he doesn't know what will happen after that. It's about what else is out there and which ones gets picked up by the stations. The industry is unpredictable.

To me, this is his big chance, our big chance, and it's important to care. But Jonah doesn't see it that way. He wanted to cut a record, and he got to do it, this cool thing that most people never get to do. His song, *Wolf Moon*, is on its own now. If it's not a hit, so be it. He can still play his music in clubs and festivals, go on tour with the band. Life is still good.

On the one hand, I admire that about him. On the other hand, I want my baby to have a darling mobile. A music box with a ballerina on top. Her own room.

Jonah's energy fills the apartment again. He tosses Leigh in the air. "How is my pumpkin girl? My round little tomato." She laughs with delight, and he dances her around the room. When she falls asleep, Jonah encircles me with his big body.

We doze for a while, and then he wants to take a shower together. He runs his fingers through my hair, presses me against the white metal box. We are wet, slick with soap. I start to slip. Instinctively, I grab at the flimsy shower curtain, but our weight is too much. The curtain tears away from the plastic rings. Water spills over the curb of the shower, onto the broken tiles. I want to cry, but I can't do that to him. I can't let him see what is on my face. *I don't want this anymore.*

I care about Jonah, but this is not the life I want: a railroad flat with a rusted sink and windows that have to be propped open with a stick. Maybe it's because of Juliet Montgomery, or maybe it's something else, set in motion long ago.

There is nothing I can do right now. I need to wait for *Wolf Moon* to become a success. But I am not someone who likes waiting.

I have a blank composition book, relic of my teaching days, with stitched binding and a pebbled cover. I press my finger along the crease to flatten the page. Then I pick up the pen I have placed on the table. It's a pen from a bank, with the bank's name along the side. Not our bank; we have no extra money to put in a bank. Just a pen someone gave Jonah to write down the address of a club.

Jonah is at a friend's loft, playing music. My baby is asleep. I feel the silence of the apartment. An image forms in the center of that silence.

> The river is threaded with light.
> Reddish strands of an absent sun
> float to the shore.

I read what I've written. Reddish strands, like hair, floating on the water. An absent source of light.

It's Leigh, obviously. All I write about is Leigh. My words return to her, the way the water in Egypt returns to the Nile.

The river is moving too slowly.

Wolf Moon is taking too long. I need my own plan.

I fix on Juliet Montgomery, who came into my life for a reason, surely—offering a hand, a chance. It's time for me to do my part. To hail the boat that can ferry me across the water, onto dry land.

Juliet and I exchanged phone numbers that day at the park, though I feel certain that she has to call me and not the other way around. Otherwise, it would seem as if I'm looking for another free something. But the days pass, and she doesn't call. I decide that it's better to run into her naturally. In fact, I need to stop at the publisher's office, so maybe we will meet there, as we did before. I wait after I've gotten my new pages, but Julia doesn't appear. For all I know, she has quit the textbook job and taken up macrame.

I'm confident, however, that she's still in the same apartment. The address is not on the slip of paper with her phone number, but I know where it is. I can see the striped awning, the stone lintels. I can easily find it again, stroll past it on my way to the park.

I walk to the subway, contemplating my idea—and grow less certain. What do I really I want from the encounter I am picturing? A dinner invitation for the two couples and their babies? Juliet's husband, Stephen, is a rich corporate something. I can't imagine a conversation that would interest the four of us. Besides, dinner at their apartment is not going to make Jonah long for a different kind of life. He likes the life he has. If we are lucky and *Wolf Moon* generates serious money, Jonah would never use that money to move to a building with an awning and a marble lobby. He doesn't care about things like that. He is charmed by the box-bed I made for Leigh, nestled in a corner of our bedroom.

I didn't do it to be charming. I did it because Leigh needed a place to sleep.

Juliet is not the solution. I tell myself, again, that I have to be patient.

Wolf Moon is not a hit. The timing is wrong. Musically, it belongs with Van Morrison and early Springsteen. But people want disco now, and funk. *Grease*, and the Bee Gees. Jonah's lyrical reflections, with their haunting chords and dissonant bass, are not what they want to hear.

I am more upset than he is. "It's not fair," I say.

"The music business is never fair." He gives a philosophical shrug. "I knew that going in. You can't hang your happiness on making it onto the charts. You just have to make your music, play for yourself."

"You mean, accept your lot as a struggling artiste."

He opens his hands. "I'm not struggling. I'm a happy man."

Now I feel like a shitty person because I want to cry: *What about me?* If I do, he will tell me what a great life we have, we have everything we need.

I want to fling the most overused counter-argument back at him. *You have a family to consider.*

Not really. The same reply I gave Juliet when she gushed about Leigh's eyelashes.

I say something that is close to what I feel, but not the whole thing. "What about the future?"

Jonah wraps his arms around me. "Hey, we'll deal with that when we get there. A hundred things can change. It's crazy to overthink it."

I don't know what to say. We are talking two different languages.

I imagine myself calling Juliet and asking if Leigh and I can stay in her extra room for a day or two, the one with the jade-green pillows and the fake parrot. Use her extra stroller. We will make ourselves small. They won't even know we are there.

It's not that I want to leave Jonah. It's just that I need a plan, and I can't seem to think when there are broken tiles and rusted metal cabinets and no bed for my child.

"What happens now?" I ask him. "With the record?"

"You mean the actual records, the ones they produced?" He gives another shrug. "I think they'll let me have me the unsold ones if I pay for the shipping. I can sell them myself at my gigs."

I picture a stack of boxes in a corner of the apartment. Where? Next to Leigh's little homemade crib that she's already outgrowing?

I don't want to be a guest in Juliet Montgomery's apartment. That is not a plan. It's a reprieve, the space before a plan. Like the room in a youth hostel that I got for the boy in Rome. A blow job instead of a true love.

Jonah wants to go out for Thai food. "Let's get some Penang curry and tom yum. Give our little tomato a taste of something more exciting than mashed-up bananas."

We go to the Thai restaurant, even though we can't afford it. I tell myself that it's a special treat because of Jonah's disappointment about *Wolf Moon*, though he is an expansive mood and doesn't seem disappointed at all.

After a week of waffling, I call Juliet Montgomery. She seems pleased to hear from me and suggests meeting at the entrance to the Children's Zoo. It's a difficult trip, three flights of stairs and two different subways, but I agree. Juliet will obviously take a cab. I can't ask her to bring an extra stroller. I need my own stroller, so I find the credit card that I hid, months ago, in the back of my underwear drawer.

I hid it from myself, not from Jonah, who has no idea that I have it. I remember my trip to Europe and the power I felt, knowing that the credit card was there if I needed it. That credit card belonged to my parents; this one is mine. I got it when I returned from Rome, though I never used it. I use it now. I buy a lightweight stroller that is safe for toddlers up to thirty pounds or three years. Leigh is six months old and weighs sixteen pounds. I do this for her now, and for her future. It doesn't feel like overthinking.

I meet Juliet at the Delacorte Clock, just as its bronze menagerie of bear, goat, hippo, kangaroo begin to play "The Farmer in the Dell." I discover that my hunch was correct. Juliet has quit the job with the textbook publisher, but instead of macrame, she's learning Ikebana, the art of Japanese flower arranging. Her husband is working on a big corporate something with a Japanese firm, and Ikebana is her way of connecting with the culture. Maybe they'll go to Japan at some point, after the deal closes. Who knows?

I agree. Who knows? I pretend that my own life is full of this kind of *maybe*, instead of *maybe* we'll fix the bathroom window.

Once we get to the Children's Zoo, though, we are more alike than different as we push our strollers over the hexagonal paving stones, pointing out the penguins and sea lions, the baby goats and sheep. Zack and Leigh are equally entranced. Juliet wants to go to the gift shop. She buys Zack a stuffed penguin and insists on getting one for Leigh as well. She talks incessantly, leap-frogging from topic to topic.

After a while we leave the zoo and push the strollers along

the leaf-strewn paths. It is sunny and crisp; red and brown leaves lie in piles beneath the bare branches. The street vendors are still out, selling slushies and pretzels and cold drinks from their little carts.

It's a peaceful day, and I am filled with hope. Things will work out. Jonah is short-sighted but not stupid. And he loves Leigh. He might even love me, though we don't use that word. It's more as if we eased into being together and just kept going. And yet, oddly, he is my husband. He has been inside my body more times than all the men before him combined. The only person who has spent more time inside me is Leigh.

The weather turns cold. The trees are glazed with frost, and the leaves are gone. I make a stuffed chicken for Thanksgiving. The oven is too small for a turkey.

Thanksgiving was always my favorite holiday. My father would tell the story of how his family arrived at Ellis Island on Thanksgiving, a day they had never heard of in their native Poland. We would hold hands and go around the table saying what we were grateful for. My brother Hugh would say, "I'm grateful for football and for not being a girl, like Arden." Then I would say, "I'm grateful for not being a boy and having to smell bad, like Hugh." And then my mother would shush us and declare, "Let's just be grateful for our good lives, and wish the same for all."

With the cold weather, there are no festivals or tours for Jonah. The upscale restaurants don't want his kind of music, nor do the companies that hire singers and pianists for their holiday parties. I suggest looking for temp work in a Broadway production or giving private lessons, but he is not interested. "It'll pick up after the winter," he tells me.

The cartons of *Wolf Moon* arrive, a Christmas non-present.

We shove them under the bed. I sense them there, every time we make love.

After the winter is still months away. "What do other musicians do?" I ask.

Jonah's reply is vague. "Sometimes it's busy, sometimes it's slow. You just have to roll with it."

I hate that expression. I need a better plan than *roll with it*. Something I have more control over.

Leigh is nine months old. We see Juliet and Zack once or twice a week: an indoor play area in a glass atrium, the park for the snow. We mention our husbands only in passing.

I allow myself three items a month on the credit card, using the money I earn from the textbook company to make the payments. I can never pay the whole bill, so the interest mounts.

Jonah pays the rent; it's a rent-stabilized apartment, absurdly cheap. Between the two of us, we manage to cover food, phone, heat. Then Leigh gets a bad cold, and I realize that we have no health insurance. I can't believe it never occurred to me. The last medical expenses I had were for her birth, covered by my insurance from the private school.

Leigh gets better, but we still have no insurance.

Money and the future are all I can think about, but I can't talk to Jonah about either. It's like what he said about the music industry: *I knew that going in.* I knew who he was and how he lived. Any deception was mine, not his.

Meanwhile, Jonah makes up silly songs for Leigh. The Pomegranate Song. The Tomato Song. I wonder if he could make money doing children's parties, but he looks so hurt when I suggest it that I say I was only joking.

Leigh has outgrown her clothes. She can't wear songs.

My thoughts jump from one idea to another, like Juliet's conversation. Jonah is a good man, and I am lucky to be with him. He is also my husband.

Jonah is not the right father for my child. He is not the father at all.

I need to wait, be patient.

I need to act. Patience won't pay for winter clothes.

I am slow and confused in a way I don't understand because I have always, always been decisive and quick. Finally, because I need to talk to someone, I call Hugh. We weren't close, growing up, but he is my brother. He says I have to tell Jonah how I feel and make him promise to find some kind of job. That Jonah has a responsibility, as Leigh's father.

I don't say, "He's not her father." I say, "Yes, okay," because Hugh is right. I tell Jonah how worried I am, and he agrees to take the next thing that comes around. It's not as good as actually going to look for a job, but it's something.

Empowered by Jonah's promise, I call the principal at my old school in Brooklyn. Could they use a music teacher, even part-time? Someone to do the after-hours things that the real music teacher doesn't want to do, or the union won't let her do? Work with the band to prepare for the all-country competition. Create music for the spring play. Maybe an after-school songwriting class.

The principal loves my idea, and I am elated. I found a solution. I didn't need Juliet Montgomery after all.

But Jonah is disgusted by my proposal. "I don't do junior high school bands. That's not my kind of music."

"You said you would take anything."

"We must have different definitions of anything."

His words are so harsh, so unlike him, that I recoil. He sees, softens. "We're not homeless, Arden. We just have to ride this out. I've been here before, trust me."

Do I? I'm not sure. I think back to the party where I met him. Jonah was supposed to be a way to get rid of Robert, nothing more. Yet he was so natural to be with. He sang while he tossed rice and vegetables in the wok. He washed my hair.

Even so: Is this the life I intended? The life that Leigh and I need?

Juliet signs up for a Mommy-and-Me gymnastics class. I should sign up, too, she tells me. It's only two hundred and fifty dollars for twelve sessions. The little ones will love it.

Jonah and I burrow under the covers. He lifts my hair, kisses my neck. In the morning, when I start to change the sheets, I find unopened bills from Con Edison and the phone company under the bed. I want to throw them at him. What was his plan, to sing a Broccoli Song to New York Telephone?

I can't do this anymore. When Jonah goes out to jam with a friend, I call Juliet. I try not to sound as if I'm begging, though I am.

"Can Leigh and I stay in your guest room for a couple of days? The one with the parrot." I don't know why I said that, about the parrot. In case she had two guest rooms, I suppose. Anything was possible, for someone like her.

Jonah is not there, but I'm whispering anyway. "I promise it won't be long, just until I can arrange some financial help from my brother." I swallow, on the verge of tears. "I wouldn't be asking if I weren't desperate."

"Oh my god," she whispers back. "Did he hit you?"

Jonah? Of course not. I won't let her think he did something awful, even if it's an easy explanation that will make me seem blameless.

"It's nothing like that. I'll explain when I see you. If we can come?"

I assume she will say, "Of course, come this very instant."

But she hesitates. "It's a tad awkward, this particular evening. Stephen has the Japanese people here. Do you think it could wait till tomorrow?"

No, it can't. I finally have the nerve, and Jonah is out, and I can't do this tomorrow when he might be on the couch singing the Tomato Song to my daughter.

I swallow. "Not really." The phrase that keeps circling back, reminding me.

"Right." I can almost hear her working it out, how she can whisk us straight to the jungle room, without the Japanese businessmen knowing. "Okay," she says, finally. "Ask the doorman to buzz me when you're here. You might have to wait in the lobby for a few minutes, but we'll make it work."

I pledge my undying gratitude and tell her I'll be there as soon as I can. Then I buckle Leigh into the stroller and give her a set of plastic rings. "You need to play quietly, okay? Mommy has to pack a few things."

I don't know what to take, what I need, now that I'm really doing this. I survey the apartment, trying to understand that I will never see it again. Never have this family again.

It doesn't matter. I've made up my mind.

Suddenly, I'm moving at lightning speed. I grab Leigh's blankie and pacifier, the folder with my passport. My wallet, my phone. Everything important goes into a backpack; diapers and clothes are jammed into a black garbage bag that I shove into the stroller behind Leigh.

I am almost ready to leave when I hear the sound of a key in the door. My pulse jumps. Jonah is the only other person who has a key.

No. He is jamming with Eduardo.

But it is Jonah. He sees me stuffing a sleepsuit into the backpack and says, "What the hell are you doing?"

"I thought you were with Eduardo."

"He's sick." Jonah stares at me and says, again, "What the hell is going on?"

I close my eyes. It's too late to back down, and I don't want to.

"I can't live like this." There is a long silence. Then I open my eyes, meet his. "*We* can't live like this, Leigh and me. I need to know that she'll have clothes and a real bed, health care, whatever she needs. Not just the Tomato Song."

I wait for him to argue or explode. Instead, his voice is eerily calm. "I see. And what makes you think you get to define *whatever she needs*?"

"I'm her mother."

"And I'm her father."

And here it is, the moment that was waiting for me. Arms open like a lover, waiting for me to step into its embrace.

I can see it as clearly as the pink sleepsuit in my hand. There are two roads, and both of them are full of pain.

I can tell Jonah that I'm leaving anyway, and *I will see you in court*, and we will see who the law thinks is a better parent. Because we are married, there will be legal battles, which cost money. There will be no winners. Leigh will be the one who suffers most.

On this road, I will break Jonah's heart by wrenching his daughter away from him and pitting her loyalty to me against her loyalty to him. We will cut her into pieces like a ham and fight over the pieces for the rest of her life.

On the other road, I will break his heart by telling him that Leigh isn't his daughter after all. Not his pumpkin, his little tomato.

Why must I be the one to choose? But who else?

He is waiting for me to speak. The man who washed my hair.

I am pinned to the moment, sick with despair. Despair makes me reckless.

Go ahead, I think. Hate me. It will be simpler, in the end.

"No, you're not," I say.

He isn't expecting this. "What?"

"You're not her father. Take a paternity test. You'll see."

He still doesn't understand. "Why do you think I'm not?"

"I know you're not." I put the pink sleepsuit into the backpack and zip it shut. It is a cruel gesture. Leigh watches from the stroller.

"You know I'm not? Then who?"

I lift a shoulder. "The guy I went to Europe with, that summer."

Jonah is still confused. "How do you know?"

I can see him trying to work it out, trying to decide if I was still screwing someone else when we got together.

This is going to destroy him, but there is no other way.

"I knew from the beginning," I tell him. "She wasn't premature. She came right when she was supposed to. Nine months after her conception." I have to make sure he understands. "Seven months after you and I slept together."

His face turns ashen as my words penetrate. "You're telling me that you pretended all along that she was mine. That you lied from the beginning."

I can't move. I am doing something terrible, unforgivable. I am not the good person I vowed to be at the tomb of the craftsmen.

"You let me believe she was my child." His voice breaks. "You let me love her."

I cannot permit myself to cry. I don't deserve to cry, because I am the one who did this. Tears are for victims.

Even so, I begin to weep. "I'm so sorry."

He looks right into me. "You let me love both of you."

"Jonah—"

His words slice through me like a scythe. "You played me." Then he turns away, flings open the door, and slams it behind him as he leaves.

I am free to go to Juliet's spare room. No one will stop me.

In the end, I didn't slip up, and no one revealed my secret. I did it myself.

THE TOMATO SONG
2013

When Danielle emerged from the therapist's office, Eleanor Cardoza nodded at Arden. "Shall we stay with Thursdays at two o'clock?"

Arden searched Eleanor's face for a message, a clue, but there wasn't one. She stole a glance at Danielle, but there was no message there either.

Still, Danielle wasn't protesting. She wasn't even pouting, just waiting silently. Good enough, Arden decided.

"That works," she said. "We'll see you next week. Same time." She gave Eleanor a faint, hopeful smile and followed her granddaughter into the elevator. "So," she declared, as the doors slid shut, "want to swing by the pet store, like we talked about? I'll bet they have some amazing birds."

Danielle's face brightened. "Can we call my dad? Maybe he can come with us. He likes birds."

Absolutely not, Arden thought. But she told Danielle, "What a nice idea. On the other hand, the pet store is right around the corner. Let's just pop in and see what they have, since we're so close."

The brightness faded. "I guess he can see the bird later. At the apartment."

Arden liked that idea even less but said nothing. She doubted that Ivan Chernowski would travel all the way to the Upper West Side to meet a parakeet.

The pet store had an enormous birdcage in the center, filled with parakeets and cockatiels. Arden watched as they darted from perch to perch, like a flurry of green and yellow leaves. Danielle crossed her arms and studied them too. Then she shook her head. "I don't think so. None of them are what I saw."

Arden's pulse jumped. "What do you mean, *saw?*"

"When I saw my mom," Danielle said. "I saw her with a great big bird, more like a parrot? But he wasn't flying around. He was just sitting in the corner, like a statue."

Arden felt the blood drain from her face. The only bird that fit her granddaughter's description was the big stuffed parrot in the apartment where she'd fled with Leigh, when Leigh was a baby. There was no way Danielle could know about that. Being sensitive to her mother's fall on the ice was one thing. A vision of a stuffed bird from decades before she was born was another.

Even Leigh wouldn't have remembered the stuffed parrot. Nor would Arden herself have remembered, if it weren't for the idea of getting a replacement pet and the memory of the bird she'd had long ago, in that shabby little railroad apartment, and how she'd run away to the place with the stuffed parrot so she could give her child a better life.

Danielle couldn't know any of that—not unless Leigh had told her daughter the story that Arden had told to her, when she was small, about how they had to live in a room that looked like a jungle when her daddy died. It was like the story her father used to tell, about the Ryżu family traveling across the ocean to Ellis Island. *Here is what we went through, to become us.*

Leigh had been a baby, too young to have her own memories, but Arden had tried to make it real for her. Her preferred version of real, of course.

One version: Your daddy died.

Another version: A man who wasn't actually your daddy walked away from us when I broke his heart.

Arden let out her breath. This was not the best moment to decide if her granddaughter had psychic powers or a vivid imagination. "Okay," she said, "not a bird. Is there another animal you'd like?"

Danielle thought for a moment. "Maybe a goldfish."

"Great idea." Anything would be a great idea, as long as it was something she could actually give her. "In fact, let's get two, they're small. And one of those striped ones. I think they're called angelfish."

"They're not angels," Danielle said. "Angels are see-through."

"Angelfish. It's just a name." Arden's enthusiasm shifted into the anxiety that was becoming her new normal. Angels and visions. Then again, maybe it was just Danielle being her literal self. A fish was not an angel.

She couldn't help wondering if she was really prepared to take on a child at her age, and—no point soft-pedaling the obvious—a child who was higher-maintenance than most.

It was a foolish question. You were never prepared for what life threw at you. Even if you were the one who tossed the baseball through your own window.

A salesperson came up to them, a young man with blue hair and a Harley Davidson tee shirt. Arden showed him the fish they wanted, and he went to get a plastic carrier with ferns and a plant called hornwort that was supposed to make the fish feel like they were in the ocean. She told Danielle to pick out a tank that would fit in her room. It used to be called the guest room, and before that it had been Leigh's room, but Arden made sure to say "your room."

They bought a tank, a heater, fish food. The young man with the blue hair told Danielle how to clean the tank, and she wrote everything down in her careful script. Then she turned to Arden. "I really want to show Dad my fish. Can we invite him over?"

Arden kept her eyes fixed on the orange fin of the largest goldfish. The girl had lost her mother. How could she possibly oppose her desire to see the only parent she had left? "Of course," she said. "Let's get these fellows settled into their new home and then you can call him."

Excited by the plan, Danielle chatted happily in the taxi as she held the water-filled carrier on her lap. When they got home and had set up the tank, Arden gave her the phone to call Ivan. Danielle tried three times, but he didn't answer. "Why don't you leave a message?" Arden suggested.

Danielle hit redial, and Arden listened as she left an earnest message that nearly brought tears to her eyes.

"I'm sure he'll call back the second he checks his voicemail," she told her. "Now, how about we fix ourselves some dinner? Have you ever made stuffed manicotti? I could use some help."

Danielle wanted to see the recipe. "It says for eight."

"We'll cut it in half. Divide by two. We can have leftovers tomorrow."

Danielle frowned. "You can't divide an egg by two."

"We'll just use the yolk. I'll show you how to separate it."

"That's a yolk. Not half an egg."

"It absolutely works," Arden said. "It's what chefs do."

She understood her granddaughter's need for an orderly world, especially now. Yet she remembered cooking with Leigh at the same age, and how Leigh had liked to toss whatever appealed to her into the pot, and it always ended up tasting delicious.

Everything hurt. Even the happy memories.

She gave Danielle a paper and pencil so she could work out the fractions, then sent a silent message to Connor, Leigh, the social worker whose name she couldn't seem to remember.

I'm doing my best. I hope it's good enough.

When Danielle was asleep, placated by Arden's assurance that her father was probably in the middle of a play and would call later, Arden took out the list she had made days ago. She put check marks next to *therapist*, *new pet*, and *tutor*. Those were the Danielle items. There were still the Leigh items: the contents of her cottage, including the night-table drawer, and one more search for some kind of will or provision for her daughter.

Arden already knew she wouldn't find anything. Leigh wasn't like that. The methodical orderliness of her biological father had skipped a generation, finding a home in Danielle, who liked to organize buttons. Leigh was passionate about the things she cared about, but that didn't include planning for a distant future. Whatever plan they arrived at would be determined by the lawyers and social workers.

And then there were the Connor items. His clothes. His books. All the things he had touched that she couldn't bear to look at.

Arden squeezed back the tears that she wouldn't be able to stop if she let them come. When she was thirty-eight years old, she had finally let herself love someone besides Leigh, and that person was Connor. There were others she had almost loved, but never with a whole and open heart. Only him.

She knew when she had started to love him. It was the

moment when he gave a tomato to a little girl with braids and told her that he was a tomato elf. Arden could remember the feeling that had washed over her. Two overlapping feelings, like a double exposure. Another little girl, and another man who tossed the girl in the air and sang the Tomato Song. The memory hurt, so she'd always pushed it away. But now there was a new image, superimposed on the first: Connor, opening that wound and healing it at the same time. A perfect red tomato, because everything was brand-new, like the day you were born.

Knowing it was probably a bad idea, she retrieved their wedding album from the bottom drawer of the credenza and set it on the table. Opened it. There they were, looking so happy. Connor's arm was around her waist, pulling her toward him.

And there was Leigh, radiant as her maid of honor. Leigh had taken credit for the marriage because of her school project on sustainable agriculture and her insistence on seeing the horses, and Arden had let her.

It was impossible not to weep now, big wrenching sobs that shook her whole body. She'd been holding herself together, but not tonight. She needed to let herself feel it, all of it. Not just grief, but fury.

Why hadn't the engineer paid better attention? Why didn't the railroad screen for sleep apnea? Why did they have a track with such a stupid sharp curve?

And why were the two people she loved most on that particular train, together?

Her skin turned cold. Because of her. For her special birthday. The perfect day to deliver the punishment she had eluded for so long.

She felt ill, sickened by her own thoughts.

They were the ones who bore the punishment, Connor and

Leigh. Not her. Their bodies, falling, breaking on the rocks. Her pain, her loss, was nothing compared to theirs. How dare she claim it?

If this was really a punishment, then she had slipped free once again, tossed the sack of suffering onto someone else.

The cold seeped into her bones, her cells. She didn't know how she could go on—except for Danielle, who needed her and had no one else.

Quirky, solemn Danielle, child of her child. She would ferry Danielle to adulthood. Raise her, as she had raised Leigh—by herself, after everyone else had left.

Well, not exactly. There was a missing part of the story.

Leigh's actual father hadn't left them. She had made him go away.

Whenever she'd thought that Leigh really ought to know, she hadn't been able to bring it up. It had felt too awful to tell Leigh that she'd been lying to her all these years, keeping her from the father who was, in fact, alive somewhere.

Later, it was because of Connor too. If she told Leigh, she'd have to tell Connor—and she couldn't. She'd finally turned into a good person. If he knew she'd done something so awful, he would think badly of her, and she wouldn't be that good person anymore.

But now there was Danielle. No siblings, no mother, a jerk for a father. Connor, the man she'd thought of as her grandfather, was gone too. Yet there was a real grandfather, alive, connected to her. Someone Danielle needed—because she needed, and deserved, every bit of family she had left.

Arden wiped her eyes and closed the wedding album. She knew how to find Robert. She had done it before, right after the train crash, just to see if she could. She hadn't looked at anything on his page, only wanted to see if he was still alive.

She booted up her laptop, logged onto Facebook, and typed his name into the search bar. There were five people named Robert Altschuler, but she knew which one was him. It was the square face with the furrowed eyebrows, the distinctive hair—partly gray now, but she could still see the original color, the same glorious auburn as Leigh's. That was why Jonah Orenstein had called her his little tomato. Round and red. Arden had never liked red hair on a man, but on Leigh it was stunning.

She clicked on Robert's profile to see what he had posted. Who he had become. Whether he had survived her cruelty.

She scrolled quickly through the posts. There were photos of leaves, water, waving grass. Patterns, the sort of thing Danielle would like. Close-ups of the natural world, but no people, so there was no way to tell what kind of life he had.

It didn't matter. Whoever he had turned into, Robert needed to know about Danielle—which meant he needed to know about Leigh. Arden clicked on the rectangle for *message* and began to type.

She was reading in bed when the phone rang. Ivan, returning Danielle's call—with his usual disregard for other people's lives, since it was long past Danielle's bedtime.

"Hey," he said. "I wanted to wait till Nellie was asleep. I hope it's not too late for you?"

Arden set her book face-down on the blanket. "No. It's fine."

"So," he began, "here's the thing. And yeah, it's kind of awkward."

Arden waited. He wasn't calling about the fish; that was obvious. Well, let him say what he had to say. She wasn't going to offer the prompt he was clearly waiting for.

She knew, already, that he was going to back out of his

grand gesture about wanting custody. He traveled for weeks at a time and worked long hours at the theater; there was no way he could raise a child. He was just being dramatic, trying to claim a starring role in a play he had no intention of bringing to the stage.

Ivan cleared his throat. "I got the message about the goldfish. And I know I said I was going to fight you for custody."

Arden could write the speech. *Love to, but. Best for her, really. Her mother would have wanted.*

"I meant what I said at the funeral," he told her, "but it's just not realistic. We're getting ready to do *Streetcar* and then *Diary of Anne Frank*. Princeton, Cambridge, New Haven. Eight cities, all over the damn country. I'm directing, and I have to give two hundred percent. I can't be worrying about homework and flossing and being there after school."

"Because you assumed Leigh would do that," Arden snapped. She couldn't listen to this ridiculous lament; was she supposed to feel sorry for him? "And then she had the nerve to get herself killed."

"It's not my fault, Arden. Her death, or any of it. She's the one who told me to leave."

"The way I heard it, you gave her an ultimatum. That means you were the one who chose to walk away when she didn't do what you wanted."

"What I *wanted*," he said, "was a partner who wasn't some kind of free-love whore."

"Oh really? Because you never got it on with a cast member in one of your plays?"

He didn't answer. There you have it, Arden thought.

She was livid now, as if all the accumulated frustration was pouring out of her, into this conversation. She'd been shocked—and yes, repelled—by what she discovered about Leigh. But Ivan had no right to tell Leigh who to be if he wasn't going to be faithful himself. Put her first.

Give up something for her, like I did.

Arden closed her eyes. Calm down. Focus.

When she opened them again, her voice was steady. "So you're telling me that you don't want custody of Danielle."

"I can't assume custody of Danielle. That's more accurate."

"I need it in writing. Notarized."

"Whatever you want."

"That's what I want." Her voice hardened. "But you'll have to be the one to respond to your daughter's invitation. About the fish, and whether you'll come to see them before you leave."

"The problem is," he said, "I've already left. I'm calling from upstate."

"I'm not going to carry a message for you."

"Understood. I'll call her tomorrow."

Arden wanted to say *you damn well better*, but held it in. You couldn't bully a man into being a father. All you could do was give him a chance. Or not.

She ended the call. Then she checked Messenger app, in case there was a reply from Robert Altschuler, which there wasn't. Well, it had only been a few hours. Even an impatient person, as she certainly was, could appreciate that he might need a little more time.

LOVELY YOUNG WIDOW

1979

As Jonah slams the door behind him, I am filled with despair. When I decided to leave, I never pictured myself talking to him while I did it. It was just me and my baby, gone.

But I can't stop, even to register my anguish. I have to keep moving, do everything right now, finish this, before Jonah returns.

I stuff another trash bag with clothes, baby food, bunny, and lift Leigh into the Snugli to make room in the stroller for a second bag. It's all the collapsible stroller can hold. I carry everything else on my body, like a packhorse. My baby in front; my backpack behind. I leave the rest for Jonah. Frying pans, towels, linens, Cuisinart, everything I brought with me from Brooklyn. It can't repay what I've taken from him, but it's all I have to give.

When I arrive at Juliet's apartment with my trash bags full of clothes, her husband Stephen is guarded. I can't blame him. I look like a homeless person—which, technically, I am.

"We're glad to help out for a few days," he says. "I under-stand that you have a brother in Denver who will be arranging a long-term solution?"

Stephen doesn't want me here, that's evident; he's humoring his wife, at least for the moment. "Yes, exactly," I say. "I really appreciate it."

He gives me a pointed look. "There aren't going to be any dramatic scenes, I presume. A husband banging on my door in the middle of the night."

I shake my head. I didn't tell Jonah where I was going. And even if he guessed, he only knows Juliet's name, not her address. Plus, I feel certain that he's not going to search for me. I've robbed him of the reasons he might want to.

The assurance I gave Juliet about Hugh, my brother, is a bit less certain. I do think Hugh will help me, but I don't know how much or how soon.

And I can't, can't call my parents. They were so delighted to see me settled and happy, with a baby named after them. Lena, Aleksander. I can't ruin that. Not yet.

"No worries," I tell Stephen.

Juliet rolls her eyes. "He's just showing off. No one bangs on doors around here. We have a doorman."

Stephen surprises me by laughing. I can see the affection between them and I feel better, even though I understand that he still doesn't want me here.

"No drama," I repeat. "And yes, just for a few days."

"Come," Juliet says, and ushers me to the guest room. The parrot has been moved into a corner to make space for the por-table crib Juliet has set up. "I had this in the closet," she tells me. "From when Stephen's sister visited? It's not an actual crib, but I think Leigh can make do for now, don't you?"

I stare at the portable crib. It has a baby-sized mattress, surrounded by white netting. There is even a stuffed lamb, with perky little ears lined with blue satin. It is not a padded box.

I burst into tears. Juliet puts her arms around me. "Just ignore Mr. Show-Off. Stay here as long as you want."

I don't know how to thank her, but she says there's no need. Besides, who can resist that darling Leigh?

"There's a bathroom down the hall, on the right. And just raid the refrigerator whenever you want."

She makes it seem so simple—and, strangely, it is. Stephen is at his office all day and leaves us alone. Leigh sleeps deeply in her new bed.

Then Stephen has to go to Japan for a week. No big deal, Juliet says. This happens every few months.

Supposedly, I will be gone when Stephen returns, though I'm not. I haven't even called Hugh. I sleep when Leigh sleeps, eat when she eats. I'm like a baby myself, retreating into a time before there were words. If there are no words, there can be no lies.

I have now hurt two men who did nothing wrong. And there is no punishment, just this pretty guest room with jade-green pillows and a stuffed lamb.

I don't know how long this might have continued before Stephen put his foot down. What happens instead is that he returns from Tokyo and tells Juliet that he will have to go back for six weeks to oversee the transition, merger, whatever it is. I can almost see the gears turning in Juliet's mind. A week is one thing, but six weeks is too long for her husband to be far away. She tells Stephen that she and Zack will go too. Zack needs his Daddy. It will be an incredible experience for all of them.

The apartment? Arden can look after things. *Things* means collecting the newspaper and mail, watering the plants, and being there every Wednesday when the cleaning people come. Free rent, in exchange for taking care of these *things* while the Montgomery family are in Japan. The refrigerator and pantry are stocked; I should use everything up, or it will go bad.

It's a lifesaver that I'm sure I don't deserve, but my little girl does. We can stay in this haven on Central Park West while I figure out how to reboot our lives.

I try not to think about Jonah and whether he is okay, although I'm sure he is not.

I try not to feel my sorrow and guilt. Guilt is not the same as regret.

I did what I had to do.

Obviously, I snoop. I'm alone in Juliet Montgomery's apartment, Juliet Montgomery's life, so I can't help looking for clues about how she got to have a life like this.

I don't take anything, not even a dime from the pile of change on Stephen Montgomery's dresser. What I want to steal is the invisible something that got Juliet this life, not one of their expensive knickknacks. I go through one room at a time, but there is nothing to find. Stephen and Juliet are not very interesting people. They have a lot of clothes and shoes, shelves full of books and records. There is no copy of *Wolf Moon*.

By the third week of their trip, I decide that I'd better start figuring out a plan. I need a job and a place to live. But what kind of job will let me bring Leigh? I have no one to leave her with, and child care costs money. Anyway, I can't. Won't. We've made it this far together.

She's an easy baby; there must be employers who wouldn't mind if I brought her with me. But then, right there in Juliet's living room, Leigh takes her first steps, and I realize that she's not a baby anymore. Her days of snuggling quietly are coming to an end. Already, she is grabbing at everything and getting angry if I won't let her have it.

I give in and call Hugh. He is concerned for me and furious at Jonah. "Jesus," he says. "I can't believe he turned down that band idea at your old school. It could have led to something. The people at those private schools all know each other. Something would have opened up."

I feel myself grow defensive, protective of Jonah. "That's not the career path Jonah wanted to open up."

"You sound like you're taking his side."

"There aren't any sides. There's just what happened."

Hugh gives a contemptuous snort. "Sorry, Arden, but I don't understand how a person could refuse work that he thought was, quote-unquote, below him, rather than support his own child. How he could stand there and let you walk away with his kid."

My fingers tighten around the phone. I had to have known, when I dialed High's number, that this moment would come. Like the moment with Jonah, when I gripped a pink sleepsuit and understood what I had to say and do.

I can tell the truth, or I can lie. If I tell my brother the truth, he will think I'm a bad person and he won't help me.

If I lie, he will think Jonah is a bad person. And then he will help me.

There is no real choice. I need his help, so I lie. I dirty Jonah Orenstein's good name. I sacrifice him—for Leigh, the small helpless person who is counting on me.

And Hugh saves me. Juliet gives me a place to rest, but Hugh gives me a way to go on. He's like the credit card my parents tucked in my pocket when I went to Europe, to be used if I truly needed it. A twenty dollar bill sewn into my hem.

I'm aware that I am very lucky. I have been gifted with both luck and shrewdness. Together, they get me through.

Hugh is right about people at the private schools knowing each other. The same network that blacklisted Robert Altschuler rallies to my support. The principal at my old school in Brooklyn gets me bumped to the top of the substitute list, bringing steady work, followed by a summer school job, and then a real job at a sister school nearby. A teacher has left unexpectedly, her husband got transferred across the country, might I be able to step in?

Leigh and I have already moved into the little garden apartment in Brooklyn that Hugh is paying for until I can "get my feet on the ground," as he put it. It's an Italian working-class neighborhood where everyone looks out for each other. The couple next door has a deli that has been in the family for three generations. Carmela, the wife, whispers to me that she needs to get her mother-in-law away from the cash register and the customers. The mother-in-law, who used to run the deli with her husband, has a good heart, but she's a talker. People are in a hurry now and don't like waiting while she chatters. If this keeps up, they'll lose business.

The mother-in-law needs a new occupation, and I need a babysitter. Carmela and I make a deal. I can pay for childcare, but not much. "It's not about the money," Carmela assures me. "You'll be helping me too. And Nico, who's too chicken to tell his mother she can't work the register anymore."

The mother-in-law, Mrs. De Luca, is delighted to watch Leigh, whom she calls Lia, and help the lovely young widow.

I've invented a vague and touching story about the death of my beloved husband. I'm sure Carmela De Luca thinks the widow story is a fabrication and the real story is that I got knocked up and my parents kicked me out. It doesn't matter to me; everyone thinks what they want to think. Mrs. De Luca has convinced herself that I'm Italian, and that Rice is pronounced Ricci.

I don't worry about getting divorced because I have no intention of ever marrying again. I wonder if Jonah will pursue a divorce, if only to be rid of me. But I hear nothing, so I assume he doesn't care. He never cared about formalities. The wedding was just for the party. And the music.

I like my new job at the Brenner School. The girls are older than the ones I used to teach and not as innocent, but I enjoy their probing minds. My favorite class is a senior English course called "Seminal Works of Contemporary Literature." We're reading *The Bluest Eye*, *One Hundred Years of Solitude*, *The Cider-House Rules*, *Ragtime*.

One of the students in the class is a tall blonde named Savannah Tate. It's clear that she comes from serious money. The Brenner School has a robust scholarship program and works hard not to create a two-tiered structure, with uniforms and standard-issue backpacks, but it's obvious where each girl stands in the hierarchy. Savannah is right at the top, not only because of her privilege but because she's athletic and unafraid.

I get a taste of Savannah's power in the third week of school. It's barely October, but Brenner has already started preparations for its homecoming weekend. Each homecoming has a theme that's meant to be uplifting and family-friendly. This year, it's the Muppets, homage to the release of *The Muppet Movie* in June.

Everything has been approved—logo, graphics, color scheme—when Savannah Tate decides that the Muppets are too sappy. She wants *Alien* instead. Something gritty and future-oriented that shows how kick-ass women can be. She wants Ellen Ripley, not Miss Piggy.

It's a ridiculous idea. There's no way that chest-bursting aliens can replace Kermit and Fozzie and *The Rainbow Connection*.

But Savannah has made it her cause. Female empowerment—isn't that the message the school wants to instill in the next generation?

She gives an impassioned speech in the school lunchroom, where I am on duty. Then, when the entire student body is clearly on her side, Savannah freezes. Her expression grows pensive, solemn. "No," she says.

She waits. The crowd waits with her, as if they can't breathe until she does. "I was wrong." Another pause, impeccably timed. "Maybe Ellen Ripley is the future, but Miss Piggy is *us.*" There's a rustling, and she holds up a hand. "Think about it. Miss Piggy *knows* she's a superstar, and nothing will stand in her way. She can flutter her eyelashes or come in with a karate chop. It's up to her. Either one. Or both. *She* decides! What could be a better role model for us? Isn't that what the Brenner School is all about?"

Everyone cheers. Now they want Miss Piggy and the Muppets. Savannah bows her head.

Good Lord, I think. The girl is something else. I'm certain it makes no difference to her what the homecoming decorations look like. She just wanted to see if she could change their minds. Twice.

I've never met anyone with Savannah Tate's absolute confidence. I admire her, though I wouldn't want to be her.

A wisp of memory darts across my mind. A younger Mary Arden Rice, charged with a new and intoxicating sexual power, telling a man: "I admire the Pyramids, but I wouldn't want to buy them."

The man's slow, seductive smile. The things he said.

Nothing happened, yet that evening led to Leigh, my daughter, as surely as if the man had opened my legs and penetrated me with his seed.

I feel my face grow hot. I can't believe I'm thinking about this, in the middle of a school cafeteria. I wipe the back of my neck with a napkin.

It's a fleeting spark from a coal that has burned itself clean. In four months I will be twenty-seven years old, and I can't imagine desiring a man ever again.

LACROSSE SEASON
1980

Hugh wants me to come to Denver for Christmas, but I can't afford the airfare and I won't let him pay for one more thing, so I thank him and say no. His wife, Georgia, sends a box of clothes and toys for Leigh. My throat catches as I go through the carton. I hate remembering how I never had any use for them, Georgia and Hugh, as if they were too boring for me. Their kindness fills me with shame.

The De Lucas invite Leigh and me to spend Christmas with them, and I accept. Leigh is nineteen months old and absorbs everything. The lights on the tree and around the doorframes. The red candles, the smells of cinnamon and pine. After dinner, I call my parents in Tucson and put Leigh on the phone; she babbles happily, enchanting them. I tell them that Jonah has an important holiday gig and is sad to miss the call. They believe me. It is the same made-up reason I gave for not coming to Tucson.

I understand that I can't sustain this deception forever, but today is not the day to tell them about my failed marriage. It's Christmas, my mother's favorite holiday. I picture my parents sharing the *opłatek* wafer with their Polish friends, the special unleavened bread with a picture of the nativity pressed into the dough. Eating carp, pierogi, herring. The bits of hay my mother has spread under the tablecloth, a reminder that Jesus was born in a manger.

I wish my parents a merry Christmas and promise to send pictures of Leigh in the outfit they sent. Then it's a new year, a new decade. Mrs. De Luca shows me how to make stuffed manicotti, the way her mother made it, back in Italy. I teach my daughter to sing "The Wheels on the Bus." Leigh forms her first three-word sentence.

I began to repay Hugh, a little at a time.

It's spring term at the Brenner School. Lacrosse season begins.

Lacrosse is Brenner's premier sport, and Savannah Tate's record as goalie when she was only a junior has made her its undisputed star.

I know nothing about lacrosse. When I was in high school, I was occupied with John and Yoko, Woodstock, People's Park. I need to know about lacrosse now, though, if I want to be part of the Brenner community, which I do. I desperately need to be rehired as a permanent member of the faculty, so I do my homework.

I learn that women's lacrosse goes back to 1890, when a woman named Louisa Lumsden introduced it to a Scottish girls' school after seeing a men's game between the Caughnawaga Indians and the Montreal Lacrosse Club. One of Lumsden's students, Rosa Sinclair, started the first American team in 1926. The girls at Brenner love to quote Sinclair's well-known statement: "It's true that the object in both the men's and women's lacrosse is to send a ball through a goal by means of the racket. But whereas men resort to brute strength, the women depend solely on skill."

Those in the know call it *lax*, an abbreviation for *la crosse*, referring to the X made by the crossed sticks. It's an ironic term, because girls who play lacrosse are the opposite of lax. They're intense, fearless, the goalie most of all. She may not be the one who scores the points, but she's the one who determines which team will win. Exactly the spot, I think, where Savannah Tate would want to be.

Brenner's obsession with lacrosse means that the members of the team are in a special category, although no one says this aloud. If a girl on the lacrosse team needs an extension on an assignment or an absence from her last period class, it's understood that she will have it. After all, the glory the team achieves on the field benefits everyone. I don't like it, but as the non-tenured newbie, I know to keep quiet. For a while, anyway.

What happens next is so predictable that it's hard to believe I don't see it coming. I'm too busy creating elaborate lesson plans full of multi-modal learning to prove how valuable I am, making the best ever nutrition-packed meals for my toddler. My tolerance for people who aren't trying equally hard is minimal.

I understand that Savannah Tate works hard on the lacrosse field. Maybe it's too much to expect the same level of commitment in the classroom. And yet, it doesn't seem too much to expect a sincere, respectful attempt to fulfill the requirements of an assignment, instead of trying to bullshit the teacher as if she's too stupid to notice.

In my contemporary literature class, spring term, we are reading *Slouching Toward Bethlehem*, *Sophie's Choice*, *Interview with the Vampire*, and *I Know Why the Caged Bird Sings*—a selection heavily weighted toward female voices, which seems right for these sharp, ambitious young women. The midterm assignment is to analyze one of the novels through a lens of the student's choice.

When I read Savannah's midterm paper on feminist aspects of good and evil in *Sophie's Choice*, I am puzzled, uneasy, and then livid. Savannah has submitted a beautifully formatted paper in a special folder with a plastic cover. When I begin to read, however, it's evident that she hasn't actually read the book. She's read the opening and the closing chapters, that's all. The analysis is shallow and flat-out wrong. She makes a big deal out of the Brooklyn setting, as if that gives her access to Sophie's psyche.

I can almost see Savannah's smug little smile at how well she's pulled this off—as if her cleverness as an athlete means that she's clever in other ways too. More clever, certainly, than an earnest young teacher who will be impressed by a plastic folder and neatly-blocked paragraphs.

And even if I can tell that she hasn't read the novel, why would I make trouble? I'm a one-year temp, and she's the star goalie.

Anger gathers in my fists. I feel the two things I need, colliding in my brain. To keep this job, for my daughter's sake. And to be upright, virtuous, after so many lies.

Surely, I can have both. This can't be a world where they are incompatible.

My frustration morphs into fury. I didn't get myself out of a broken-down railroad flat so I could be passive and stupid.

Oh, I know this feeling, this place where righteousness tips into rashness, but it's too fast. Something unstoppable pushes into my fingers and toes.

I am not powerless. I have the power to say no.

I give Savannah a D. Not an F, since she did turn in a paper. It will be her midterm grade in my class. I am aware that varsity athletes are not allowed to play if they receive lower than a C in any of their academic courses.

No one can fault me. I'm just upholding the standards in the Brenner School Code of Ethics.

It doesn't take long for the pushback to begin. Savannah doesn't come to me herself, however; she has the coach do it.

"I appreciate that you have high expectations of your students," the coach says, his expression as polite as mine. "I wouldn't dream of interfering in your classroom, no more than you would dream of telling me how to manage my team. But a D does seem a bit excessive. There was no plagiarism, correct? She did write a paper of the required length?"

I'm not going to debate this. I cross my arms. "Since you wouldn't dream of interfering, I'm not sure what you're asking."

The politeness drops away. "Savannah needs a C on her midterm report card."

"Savannah has earned a D."

"I need my goalie."

I shrug. "Maybe another girl would benefit from a chance to show what she's capable of. Isn't that how Savannah got her start last year?"

The coach gives me a long, unflinching look. Then he says, "You seem like a decent person, Miss Rice, but you're out of your depth here. Savannah is a legacy student, three generations. Her family's continued loyalty means a lot to the school."

Ka-ching, I think, though I know this is how things work.

Then the coach adds, "Savannah's a credit to the school in her own right, you know. A solid academic record, solid leadership. She'll be graduating in a couple of months. Vassar, I believe."

"Well, then," I say. "Let's hope this experience will inspire her to even greater heights at Vassar."

The coach understands that he's not going to win this one,

and we part cordially. I wait to see who will be sent next. I expect it will be the dean of students or even the principal. Instead, it's an elegant, well-groomed woman who introduces herself as Kira St. Cyr. Savannah's mother.

"I'm absolutely delighted to meet you," she tells me. "I've always believed that literature is the foundation of our civilization. She who does not read good literature remains emotionally undeveloped."

I have no idea what this is supposed to mean, but I'm sure she will soon connect it with her daughter's grade. "What can I do for you?" I ask.

Her expression is full of the world's sorrow. "Not for me. For a child."

"Any particular child?" If Kira St. Cyr is a Shakespearean actress, then I'm her straight man.

"We need to adjust Savannah's grade in your course."

"We?"

"You, Miss Rice. The situation is not acceptable. I'm quite certain there is another solution." Before I have a chance to reply with a counter certainty, she amps up the pathos. "It's my daughter's emotional stability that concerns me the most. Her self-confidence, at this vulnerable juncture between girlhood and womanhood."

Clearly, Savannah Tate learned her flair for the dramatic from a pro. But this classroom is my theater, not hers. "As I'm sure you know, Mrs. St. Cyr—"

"Ms. Her father and I are divorced."

"Ms. St. Cyr." I give her a deadpan look. "True self-confidence comes from the knowledge of having earned what one has received."

"Savannah has earned a higher grade than a D."

"And you know this because—?"

"I'm just trying to help my child, Miss Rice. It's what a mother does."

I want to ram my fingers into her throat. How dare she tell me what a mother does for her child?

I manage to contain my fury, though barely. "I understand your point of view, Ms. St. Cyr, but the subject is closed. I don't change grades because someone's mama complains. If you want to help your daughter, tell her to read the *good literature* on the syllabus, instead of trying to fake her way through an assignment. Overestimating oneself isn't the same as self-confidence. As I'm sure you know."

I'm aware that I've probably gone too far. A bitch-slapping contest with the lacrosse coach was one thing. But my snippy, self-righteous speech to the reigning matriarch of a legacy family may have cost me my job.

The next day there is a message in my box, letting me know that Michael Tate would like to see me. I prepare myself for a rich, entitled asshole who intends to bully me into letting his precious daughter have what she wants. Instead, Savannah's father is delighted that I told Kira St. Cyr where to shove it.

"Very little would please me more," he says. "Not that we talk often, thank goodness, but she couldn't wait to phone and tell me how rude you were—and, of course, how I had to fix it. It goes without saying that I liked you immediately."

I have no idea what to make of this speech. It has too many layers, most of which are none of my business. The only relevant part is the bit of flattery at the end, which I need to squelch quickly.

"Whether you like me is beside the point," I tell him. "Your daughter tried to scam me. I caught it. End of story."

"I couldn't agree more."

I give him a curious look. "Then why are you here?"

"I have my own perspective," he replies. "Hear me out."

Michael Tate wants me to go easy on Savannah, but for a different reason than everyone else. He doesn't give a crap about lacrosse. Savannah has already been accepted by Vassar, and it would take a failing grade or two to put that in jeopardy. According to Michael Tate, his ex-wife doesn't care about lacrosse either. She just wants her daughter to have a spotless record.

Michael's aim is equally simple: to get Kira off his back. It was an unpleasant divorce, he explains. He was the one who wanted it, leaving Kira, as the discarded spouse, hell-bent on retaining—or accruing—as much power as she can. The best way to do that is through their children. Until they turn eighteen, anyway, when custodial negotiations will come to an end.

They are nearly there, Michael tells me. Their son Charlie is twenty-one and doing well. All Michael has to do is make it until Savannah's eighteenth birthday, in August. After that, he can deal with his children as he wishes, without having to deal with Kira too.

This English paper business has gotten to her, though. And, of course, the English teacher's refusal to cooperate. Kira has offered her version of an early retirement package: if Michael will take care of this one annoying problem before Savannah graduates, she will leave him in peace. Now. He won't have to wait until August.

"What does any of this have to do with me?" I ask.

"Whatever you'd like it to." His smile is broad, benevolent. "A good word with the president of the school board, if that would be helpful. I'm sure you would be a valuable addition to the faculty."

I stand up. "Get out."

He looks startled. "Excuse me?"

"Get out of my classroom."

"You misunderstand me."

"I doubt it." I narrow my eyes. "I don't give a shit about your marital power struggles. I'll pay for my own lousy choices. Don't try to bribe me into getting involved with yours."

He stands too. "Your reaction seems excessive."

"Not to me."

"You're a difficult woman."

"Thank you."

"Truly, Miss Rice, I didn't mean to offend."

"Yes, you did. But I'll get over it."

"What do you want?"

"Nothing you can possibly give."

"Try me."

Oh, this is the stupidest sort of hostile non-flirting. I have no patience for it. "Go away," I tell him. "Tell your daughter to read a book before she thinks she has the right to analyze it."

"Was her paper really that bad?"

"It was a three-thousand-word smirk."

He laughs, clearly delighted.

"Feminist aspects of good and evil in *Sophie's Choice*," I add.

"Good Lord," he says. "Poor Sophie was hardly a feminist. Her life was shaped by one man after another."

"You've read the book?"

"Of course. I read a lot."

"More than your daughter."

"She's too busy being a jock."

It's my turn to laugh. "Oh, fine. I won't tell the principal about your attempt to bribe me."

"I'm sure she would approve. She's a huge lacrosse fan."

I shake my head. He *is* a rich asshole, but he's fun to banter with.

"I've changed my mind," he says. "It'll probably be good for

Savannah to get a reality reset before she goes off to college. She's gotten pretty full of herself."

"You think this will humble her?"

"On second thought, not a chance. She'll just hate you."

I try not to smile, unsuccessfully. He sees and smiles back.

"Just to be sure I understand," I tell him. "You came here to make me change your daughter's grade, but now you're okay with leaving it as it is."

"You were right," he says. "It won't help the school to let students think they can manipulate the faculty. I'll tell Polly that I support you one hundred percent."

Polly—Paula Thomas, to me—is president of the Brenner Board of Trustees. I don't want any favors from Savannah Tate's father, but I let it go. This isn't the hill to die on. I have a daughter of my own who needs my paycheck. "She'll have to sit out the next game or two."

"She will," he agrees.

Though I didn't intend to, I offer a small concession. "I'll give her a chance to redo the paper. If she can turn in something that would merit an A, I'll upgrade her to a C. But I won't accept a new paper for a couple of weeks. It will take her that long to read the book and write something credible."

"A couple of weeks means a couple of games."

"Exactly."

"I'm sure Savannah will enjoy being welcomed back by her grateful teammates." Then he gives me an amused look. "Would you like to attend that game with me? We can sit in the bleachers and do the Wave."

The invitation is inappropriate, not meant to be taken seriously. "Not really, but thanks anyway."

"What if it were followed by dinner?"

I can't have heard correctly. "Are you asking me out?"

"It seems so."

"You must really want to get me fired."

He gives another laugh. "No worries. Polly's an old friend. You won't get fired for having dinner with me. Especially since you're going to make Savannah redo that terrible essay."

I think about Leigh, who would need a babysitter—not Mrs. De Luca, who goes to bed at eight o'clock. Any other sitter would be a stranger, and expensive.

Then I think about the whispers that would most certainly spread through the school, faculty and students, if I were spotted in the bleachers with Savannah Tate's father, and the very real chance that this would ruin my future there, no matter what he thinks.

I decline a second time and tell Michael Tate that my free period is nearly over. I have a sophomore creative writing class to teach, so he'll have to forgive me for asking him to leave. It's not until the next day that I realize I've given Savannah Tate the same chance for a do-over that my brother Hugh gave to me. I'm fairly certain that neither of us deserves it.

ANGEL FISH

2013

After Danielle's third session, the therapist wanted to meet with Arden privately. Arden was relieved, because she would finally know what Eleanor Cardoza knew. And worried, because of what that might be.

She timed the appointment for when Danielle was with Nora, the tutor. Better if there had been a friend to leave her with, but there were no friends in Manhattan. Not yet, anyway. Another item to add to the list.

Eleanor Cardoza's office was in a modern high-rise building on the Upper East Side, not far from the college where Arden had taught for the past decade. Modern American Poetry, Twentieth Century Female Voices. They had offered her a tenure-track position if she completed the PhD she began years ago, but she'd thanked them and declined. Part-time teaching was fine with her. All of the pleasure and none of the politics.

After the train wreck, the dean had sent a note urging her to take bereavement leave for as long as she needed. Arden had no idea how a person could tell when they no longer needed to feel bereaved, but told him that she appreciated the flexibility and would let him know. For now, she needed to focus on Danielle.

She got off the crosstown bus at the familiar stop—ignoring the urge to turn left, toward the college—and made her way to Eleanor's building. Eleanor buzzed her into the fourth-floor reception area, then ushered her into the office.

Arden settled into a blue wingback chair and looked around. She hadn't been inside Eleanor's office before, only the waiting area. Eleanor gave her a reassuring smile. "Thank you for coming in, Mrs. McRae."

Arden winced. She wasn't Mrs. McRae. She'd been Mary Arden Rice during and between her various marriages. But she merely said, "Of course. My granddaughter is my priority."

Eleanor folded her hands. "Tell me about Danielle. What she was like, before the accident."

What Danielle was like. Arden thought of the orderly buttons, the way foods couldn't touch on her plate, how she couldn't bear tags and seams on her clothing. "Sensitive," she said. "Careful. She always had very specific likes and dislikes."

"Was her mother like that too?"

Hardly. Leigh was the opposite. Daring, impulsive, eager for the new and unknown. "Not at all," Arden said. "Leigh was someone who could grab a scarf and a belt and a skirt, and put them together in a way you thought was going to be just awful, but turned out to be amazing."

"She liked to do things her own way?"

"Always."

"So Danielle *is* like her."

Arden frowned. "I suppose. When you put it like that."

"Two people who liked to do things their own way. It's understandable that they'd clash."

Arden shook her head. No, that part wasn't right. *Clash* made it sound like rivals battling for dominance. Leigh and

Danielle were more like two species of fish living in the same tank, swimming around each other.

"They didn't clash," she said. "They had different styles, but they were still a unit. Close in their own way." She wasn't sure if that was true, though she hoped it was. "It was just the two of them," she added, though Eleanor already knew that. "Danielle's father wasn't really around."

"People can clash and still be close," Eleanor said. "Sometimes they clash because they're close. Extreme intimacy between mother and daughter—especially, as you say, with no siblings or father in the picture—can be quite stressful."

Arden really had to object now. "That's not necessarily true. It wasn't like that for Leigh and me. We were in a similar situation, in fact, at various points in her life."

When I was between husbands, she thought. But that was none of Eleanor's business.

"Each dyad has its own dynamic," Eleanor said. "For Danielle and her mother, it seems to have been far more fraught, with more hostility."

"I have no idea what you're talking about. What hostility?"

The therapist rested her chin on her clasped hands. "Mrs. McRae, your granddaughter was, and is, furious at her mother."

"You mean, for how she died?"

"No. For how she lived."

Arden thought of the night table drawer, the things Danielle had said.

Eleanor gave her a long, pensive look. "It's hard when someone dies before you have a chance to stop being angry at them. The guilt and anger get frozen in place, and you have to work extra hard to soften them, without the other person there to work on it together."

Arden nodded. As a theory, it made sense. Still, what exactly had Leigh done that was so dreadful? Being a bit promiscuous wasn't the worst thing a mother could do.

That meant it wasn't the worst thing Leigh had done. There was more.

Her features tightened. She didn't know what the *more* was, and she didn't think Eleanor Cardoza did either. That was why Eleanor wanted to meet with her. To see if Arden knew something—something Danielle hadn't told her therapist, but might have told her grandmother. Or her grandmother might have learned another way.

Her concern for Danielle moved to the side, replaced by alarm about Leigh. Arden loved her granddaughter, but Leigh was there first. A baby strapped to her chest, for whom she had done whatever she had to do. She remembered what she had felt about Connor's mother, at the funeral. *You loved him first, before I came along. You loved him longest.*

"What *about* the way her mother lived?" she asked. "What made Danielle so angry?"

"That's what we need to find out." Eleanor unclasped her hands and let them drop to her lap. "Danielle is experiencing what we call complicated grief—grief that triggers issues that were already there, under the surface or out in the open, like jealousy or anger or shame. When that happens, the anger or shame gets all wound up in the grief, so it's hard to just feel the grief, for what it is."

Arden gave another nod.

"With children," Eleanor continued, "it can include a kind of magical thinking. Feeling irrationally responsible and then overwhelmed with guilt because of what they think they've done."

Arden's frown returned. "I'm not sure I follow."

"As in: 'I was mad at my parent, wished her dead, and now she is.'"

"Is that what Danielle said?"

"Children rarely say that sort of thing directly. But they may feel it, especially if the parent did something hurtful that didn't get repaired."

Arden flinched. "Did Danielle tell you about her visions?"

"The things she sees and, as she puts it, 'just knows'?"

"The things she *thinks* she sees." Arden fixed her eyes on Eleanor's. "We have to consider the possibility that much of what Danielle reports is simply not true."

"It's an interesting conundrum, isn't it?" Eleanor said. "On the one hand, there are countless well-documented instances of someone sensing what's happening to a person they're close to, even if that person is far away. We might not understand how it works, but it does."

"Meaning that Danielle's visions might be true?"

"Perhaps. I can't say."

"And on the other hand?"

Eleanor shrugged. "Certainly, she could be inventing things. For any number of reasons. To give form to her anger. To be in control. It's hard to say."

Arden leaned forward. "So we can't assume, if she said her mother did such-and-such, that Leigh really did it?"

Eleanor gave her an odd look. "Is that your main concern? To keep Leigh blameless?"

"I'm just trying to make sure I understand you."

"Yes, you understand me. We assume nothing."

Arden sat back, releasing her breath. "You'll keep working with her? Danielle?"

"Of course. We've hardly begun."

"And you'll recommend that she continue to stay with me? Permanently, that is."

"Is there another option? You've said that her father won't contest your petition for custody."

"That's right." Ivan had sent the notarized letter, as promised. For once, he had come through.

"Danielle is lucky to have you," Eleanor said, her voice softening. "You're lucky to have each other. It's a dreadful loss for you as well."

Tears welled up in Arden's eyes. It felt as if she had lost Leigh twice. First, the real person. And now, the Leigh of her memory, the Leigh she thought she knew.

The baby in the Snugli had grown into a toddler, a schoolchild, an adolescent. Arden remembered how upset her own mother had been when she wanted to do something that Lena was sure would result in injury, financial ruin, dishonor to the Ryżu family back in Poland, or all three. To try anything for herself, Arden had to slip past them, where they couldn't see. Lie. Rebel. Leave.

She hadn't wanted that to happen with her own daughter. Leigh was allowed to try things. Snowboarding, bungee-jumping. Sex with men and women, if that was what she wanted.

Maybe Leigh had been a little wild, and maybe Danielle had irritated her, but that didn't mean she'd been *hurtful*—Eleanor's word, harsh and unfair. Surely someone who'd had a good mother, as Leigh had, couldn't have turned out to be a bad mother herself.

Arden squeezed back her tears. Stop it, she told herself. This conversation was about Danielle. It wasn't a referendum on her own parenting.

"I wanted to wait a bit before meeting with you," Eleanor was saying. "But at this point, now that things are starting to surface, I think it's important for us to keep in touch. Perhaps we can speak again in a couple of weeks?"

"Yes, of course." Arden rose, following Eleanor's cue. She was glad the meeting was over. She'd wanted answers but there hadn't been any, just new questions.

They said goodbye, and Arden hurried down the stairs instead of waiting for the elevator. Sixty-four steps. It felt good. On impulse, she went into a shoe store on Lexington and bought a pair of high-end walking shoes. Then she stopped at the college to tell them that she was ready to return. She needed to get busy again.

Danielle needed to get busy too. She needed a school, friends, not just a tutor. Arden had fought for home-schooling and won, but it was time to find her granddaughter a real school. Figuring out the past was important, but Danielle needed a life right now.

When Arden got back to the apartment, the tutor Nora was in tears. "The fish," she sobbed, gesturing down the hall.

Arden hurried after her to Danielle's room, where they'd set up the tank. Danielle was crouched in front of the glass, staring at the angelfish as it floated upside-down.

"I don't know what happened," Nora said, her voice full of distress. "We were doing her math in the other room. Then we came in here."

Arden gazed at the dead fish. Her fingers tightened around the bag she was holding. A shoebox, tugging at her memory.

Carefully, she set the bag on the floor and knelt beside Danielle. She thought of all the reasons an angelfish might die. The wrong kind of water: too cold, too warm, a chemical imbalance. Over-feeding, starvation. A hundred different reasons, and you might never know. "I'm so sorry, sweetheart."

"I think it was meant to happen," Danielle said. "Because it's an angel fish. So it's a real angel now. In heaven."

Arden tensed, dreading what she was sure Danielle's next words would be. *With my mom.* But Danielle's words were matter-of-fact. "We should probably get it out of the tank, so it doesn't freak out the other fish."

"Yes," Arden said. "Good idea."

She wondered if she should offer to replace the dead fish. It seemed like the obvious thing to do. New pet, new school.

"I feel just awful," Nora said. "The thing is, I have to go to my next house. I mean, now that you're back, is it okay if I leave?"

Arden pushed herself to her feet. "Of course. I'll walk you to the door."

She followed the tutor down the hall. Keeping her voice low, she asked, "How does Danielle seem to you, in general? I'm thinking I should start looking for a school so she can be with kids her age, but I don't know if she's ready."

Nora lifted a shoulder. "I wouldn't know. I just go where they send me. Sometimes it's a kid with an operation, where they can't go to school for a few weeks? I just do the lessons so they can keep up."

"Right," Arden said. Well, what had she expected the tutor to say? The girl hardly knew Danielle. Plus, she was twenty-something years old.

When she was Nora's age, she'd been preparing for a summer trip to Europe. When she was Leigh's age—Leigh's final age, the last age she'd ever be—she had decided, for the second time in her life, that she was done with men. No more husbands or lovers. *Just me and my girl.*

Of course, Connor McRae was waiting in her future, but you never knew what was waiting in your future. A man with a basket of apples. A train engineer with undiagnosed sleep apnea. You just had to go on, without knowing.

DINNER
1980

I never expected to see Michael Tate again, so I'm astonished when he sends a photo in early September, care of the Brenner School, of Savannah in a Vassar sweatshirt. On the back, he's written, "The coast is clear. Dinner?" Below, his phone number, followed by: "As ever, Michael."

It feels incredibly arrogant, and I can't imagine why he would be interested in having dinner with me, months after our sole conversation, other than a need to prove that I will eventually say yes.

There are, however, multiple reasons to say no. Although his daughter is no longer my student, the power imbalance is still there. When a single mother with a low-paying job has dinner with a wealthy older man, motives are suspect all around.

And there is me, specifically. I am not someone who goes out for dinner. I have retreated from everything non-essential; no lunches, movies, not even a drink after work. The best way to avoid hurting a third man is to have nothing to do with any man. I have planted my flag on the moon of motherhood, and that's that. My dinner companion is Leigh, who is now big enough to eat at the table. On the first Sunday of every month, we go up-stairs and have dinner with the De Lucas.

I have, at last, told my parents the truth. I kept my failed marriage from them for an absurdly long time, although I wonder if they suspected. I said it was a lifestyle conflict and our differing attitudes about money and security couldn't be re-solved. It is, in fact, the truth, though not the whole truth. The desperation that drove me to leave Jonah was fueled by my fear about money, but it was also fueled by the lies I carried. They were like burning coals, shoved into the Snugli next to Leigh.

Michael Tate knows nothing about any of this. I am just a woman he met once who stood up to him, something I'm sure is a rare occurrence. He wants a final round that he can win, or maybe he simply enjoys a good joust.

And, because he is clearly a man used to getting what he wants, there is a more than reasonable chance that dinner will be followed by an invitation, or expectation, that we will proceed to his apartment. His bedroom.

I can't imagine kissing or touching or being intimate with anyone ever again. That alone is sufficient reason to say no.

On the other hand, Michael Tate is a mature man, and I feel certain he could handle a polite refusal with his ego intact. I remember our conversation, which I enjoyed. I surprise myself by saying yes. I tell Michael that I will meet him at whatever restaurant he selects; there's no need for him to know where I live. He gives me the address of a restaurant in midtown Manhattan, and I arrange for Mrs. De Luca's granddaughter to watch Leigh. She is elated. She adores Leigh and is eager for babysitting ex-perience.

I take the subway from Brooklyn and bring cab fare for the trip home.

And my credit card.

Michael is an attractive man, in the way that a certain kind of successful man is attractive. He has an air of confidence, penetrating blue eyes, a compact body in expensive well-fitting clothes. His hair is unfashionably short, grey at the temples, but it suits him. The twenty-one-year-old son means that Michael is probably in his late forties, maybe fifty. As we're led to a corner table in the discreetly elegant restaurant, I wonder, again, why he's having dinner with me, instead of a sophisticated divorcee closer to his age.

The waiter pulls out my chair, and I settle into place as if this is something I do every week. Michael eyes me across the table and lifts a crystal water glass. "To Savannah. And William Styron."

"In the same toast? I don't think so."

Michael breaks into a smile. It's a wonderful smile, in fact. "You're exactly as I remembered."

"Is that supposed to be a compliment?"

"Clearly. You knew that before you asked."

"Are we sparring?"

"It's what we do."

I smile back, reach for my own water glass. "Let's at least drink to Sophie."

Michael taps his glass against mine. "To Sophie."

Another waiter appears with a tray of olives and cornichons, while a third waiter hands us enormous leather menus and a wine list. "Would Madame like something to drink?"

Oh yes, Madame would. I could get used to this.

As if. Still, it's fun to pretend.

I learn a bit more about Michael Tate during the course of our meal. He does something corporate and financial that I don't really follow, though he's obviously good at it. In his free time, he likes to sail and play tennis. Of course he does. The pastimes of the rich.

He wants to know about me. I tell my lovely young widow story. I mention Leigh, but in a general way. No one gets to hear about Leigh unless they love her.

We talk about books, films, music. Michael has an eclectic taste and likes composers I've never heard of: Xenakis, Janacek, Granados. I don't bring up *Wolf Moon*.

The time passes quickly, yet there are things unsaid. As dessert shifts into after-dinner brandy, I move my glass to the side and meet his level, blue-eyed gaze. "Okay, time for the truth," I say. "Why did you go to the trouble of tracking down an insignificant English teacher?"

He gives me an amused look and moves his own glass, as if clearing the table. "There are a number of false assumptions in your statement, as I'm sure you know. First, there was no tracking down. I knew exactly where you were. And second, you're far from insignificant. Or were you fishing?"

"I wasn't fishing. It's a serious question."

He reaches across the table and picks up my hand. He turns it palm-up and regards it thoughtfully, as if my fate is written there. "You're right. It's a serious question. Too weighty for a first dinner."

"Now you're the one making assumptions." He arches an eyebrow, and I toss the dare back at him. "Will there be a second dinner?"

"That's up to you."

"Not until I've been invited."

He presses my hand to his chest. "I invite you to another dinner, Arden Rice."

His gallantry is either touching or presumptuous. I can't tell.

And I still can't tell why he's so taken with me. Then again, I'm enjoying myself. "All right," I say. "That would be nice."

"I'll be in Chicago all week," he tells me. "But let's have dinner on Saturday, if you're free." I nod, and he returns my hand to the table. "I can send a car to pick you, if you'd like."

"That's not necessary."

"I didn't ask if it was necessary. I asked if you'd like it."

"I've learned to make them the same."

"As the esteemed philosopher Stephen Stills advised: love the one you're with."

"Yes," I answer. "As he advised."

"It might be interesting to try unlearning that philosophy."

"You mean, not settle?"

"Your interpretation, not mine."

I shake my head. Michael Tate is quick and smart, but he has no idea what it's like to be me.

"In any case," he announces, "I'm putting you in a cab, and you can decide later about transportation for Saturday." Before I can respond, he adds, "I invited you to dinner. Getting you safely home is part of that invitation. Only a boor would leave you in front of the restaurant with a wave and a smile."

Putting me in a cab means he won't be inviting me to his place for a nightcap or wangling for an invitation to mine. I'm relieved, though a little disappointed that he didn't even try.

He hails a cab and presses several bills into the driver's hand. Then he kisses me on the cheek and holds the door as I climb inside. I give the driver my address. We pull away from the curb, and my dinner date ends.

Our second dinner is very different. For one thing, I'm looking forward to it. I've even bought a new dress, something I never do. It flows just below the knees, a swirl of rose-colored crepe with three-quarter sleeves and a cowl neck.

When I walk into the restaurant, I'm glad I dressed up. It's a beautiful venue, high above the city. Michael has reserved a table with a view of the harbor. And yes, I arrived in the car he sent.

We order aperitifs, hors d'oeuvres. A cellist plays Bach in the background. The notes rise from the strings and curl toward each other.

"So," Michael says, lifting his Negroni. The orange peel catches the light from a sconce on the textured wall. "If we plan to spend time together, as I hope we will, there should be no secrets. Do you agree?"

I don't, actually. Nor do I understand why he's making this leap, when we've hardly begun our second meal together.

Then Michael answers his own question. "I'm going to tell you your secret, Arden Rice, and then I'll tell you mine."

I tilt my head. "Sorry. I think I misheard you, or else you mixed up your pronouns. I think you meant that I would tell you *my* secret—if I have one—and then you would reciprocate."

"You didn't mishear," he replies. "I know your secret—because you do have one. I'm going to tell you, so you're clear that I know."

An ominous feeling crawls up my spine. Is something really creepy about to happen?

As if he's read my mind, Michael says, "It's nothing sinister. Simply, that it's important to know if we can trust each other. If we can't, we'll have an excellent dinner and then go our separate ways. I hope that won't happen. But if it does, better at the beginning."

"I don't understand," I say. Because I don't. It's too vague. What secrets is he talking about?

"I like you," he tells me. "I don't want to get my heart broken. Is that so terrible?"

No, of course not. It's exactly the right answer.

"I'll tell you your secret, first." He takes a sip of the Negroni, then sets it on the table. "You are not a widow, Arden Rice. You were married at City Hall three months before your daughter was born. Your husband didn't die, and you were never divorced."

I start to tremble. I feel exposed, as if my pretty new dress has been flung aside, revealing the scarred flesh beneath. "None of those things are crimes," I say.

"They're not," he agrees. "But I don't date married women. If we're going to see each other, you'll need to get a divorce. And I can help."

I'm still shaking, though it's not as bad as I feared. I understand that I need to get a divorce. I just haven't wanted to think about it. And yes, a man like Michael Tate could easily help me.

Then I remember the second part of his statement. *And then I'll tell you mine.*

"And your secret?" I'm already thinking: A convicted felon. In the Mafia. Still in love with Kira.

As he did at our first dinner, Michael reaches across the table and takes my hand. He wraps his palm around mine. His eyes are a deep blue, his bearing proud and unapologetic.

"I've had prostate cancer," he says. "I can, and will, satisfy you in every way you can imagine, and more. But you won't be able to return the favor. After my prostatectomy, I can't have intercourse. To be blunt: I can't get hard. While there are some promising treatments in development, there's nothing available right now, and it would be naïve to think of my condition as temporary."

My heart is thundering. I remember thinking that I didn't want to have sex ever again. And then worrying about how to handle it, if Michael Tate tried to open that door. And then feeling disappointed when he didn't. But never, never something like this. My impulse is to pity him, but his straight back and unflinching gaze make that impossible.

I look into his eyes. He's not asking for pity. He's telling me what he will do for me, if I can accept it. He is still in control.

Another thought crosses my mind. "Is that why you got divorced?" I hate Kira St. Cyr more than ever if she wouldn't stand by her man and love him no matter what.

"Ironically, no." Michael gives me a dry look. "That part of our marriage was always good. My diagnosis came after we separated. I wanted a life without her for unrelated—and well-justified—reasons."

I feel my hand in his. His palm is warm, firm. If I give any sign of pity or distaste, he will let my hand slip free. I am sure of it.

"She still doesn't know," he adds. "It's none of her business."

"Is it mine?"

"That's for you to decide."

I close my eyes, trying to take it all in. What he has told me, and what it must be like for him. What he is actually offering.

I breathe slowly, feeling the air go in and out. Then I open my eyes and ask my other question. "Am I the first woman you've told?"

"No," he answers. "The second."

"And the first?"

"It wasn't an arrangement that suited her. We parted amiably."

I want to cry now, picturing Michael with his steely pride as he accepted her reply. How can he possibly risk that again?

Whatever pity I may have felt turns to admiration for his courage. Then to the confusion I've felt from the beginning. "Why me?"

Michael smiles. It's lovely and open, without a drop of artifice. "You have the perfect combination of fierceness and charm. Perfect for me, in any case."

I blink away complicated tears. "Is that your final answer?"

"It's a commentary on my answer. My real answer is that you're smart and beautiful and unafraid. And I enjoy your company. I can't say that about many people."

"So you decided this just might work?"

"I did. I like you. Even though you lied about being a widow."

"But you can fix that."

"Easily." He pauses, deliberately. "I can do a lot of things."

There is no mistaking what he means, and I feel a surge of desire that shocks and embarrasses me. I am remembering an evening in Luxor, a restaurant strung with colored lights.

I look at Michael, and it's clear that he's seen what passed though me. I swallow. I like him too. What he's proposing seems bizarre, yet strangely possible.

If life were fair, it would be the other way around. After the men I've hurt, it should be me pleasuring Michael and getting nothing for myself. But the terms aren't mine to set. I can say yes or no. That's all.

If I say no, there will be no rancor, but I will never hear from Michael Tate again. If I say yes, I will be both generous and selfish, strange as that seems.

He is leaving it up to me. Like the dinner invitation.

I surprise myself again. I have said yes in my mind before I say it aloud. Yes, I will give Michael Tate the opportunity to be with a woman he genuinely enjoys being with, who knows the truth and accepts it, and with whom he can still be a man able to pleasure a woman. In return, I will receive that pleasure. Together, we will drink good wine and have good conversation.

I dip my head, almost shyly. He plucks a rose from the centerpiece and lays it across my napkin.

I can't afford to leave Leigh with a sitter very often, though I doubt that our unconventional arrangement will last more than a few months. During that time, I'm sure I can manage an occasional evening of childcare. Mrs. De Luca's granddaughter will appreciate the extra income, and the experience.

RIVER VIEW
1981

By mid-November, Michael has taken care of my divorce and set up a special room for Leigh at his apartment. He understands that I can't leave my child to be with him overnight, but he has a solution for that, the way he has a solution for everything. The room has apricot-colored walls with white trim, a soft washable rug. He lets Leigh choose the blanket and sheets.

Michael and I go to interesting restaurants and galleries, talk about books and history and art. Rarely about science, and never about medicine or emergent treatments. He brings us glasses of Armagnac to sip in bed, before we fall asleep. He surprises me by wanting to sleep entwined, my head on his chest, my legs across his; we are still lovers, even if we don't make love.

Just as Leigh has her own special room, I have a little spot in the study that is mine alone. Sometimes I slip out of bed in the middle of the night and go there to write down the words that come to me when I am languid and loose from Michael's expert attention. It is a habit I began when Leigh was an infant and I was with Jonah, a man I never talk about.

I have a rule for myself, about the lines I write. Every word has to be clean, real. Even if no one reads it but me.

A ripple, contracting
in the center of a bud

the precise place
where the cupped heartbeat
of an insect
thunders.

By early June, Leigh and I are preparing to move into Michael's luxurious apartment on Riverside Drive, not far from the building where Juliet and Stephen Montgomery lived or perhaps still live. I'm not taking much, only some clothes, books, and Leigh's favorite toys. I give the rest—dishes, linens, pots—to a local charity. I am aware that I have done this before, when I left the Tribeca apartment with the broken tiles, the place I lived with the man I am now divorced from. That time, too, I took almost nothing but my daughter and our clothes. Whether I will return to Brooklyn for a third sojourn if things don't work out, I can't say. I hope not; I am finally giving Leigh the life that I want for her. A bedroom of her own, with sheets and toys she has picked herself. An excellent preschool. A pediatrician who knows her name.

Classes end at the Brenner School, and we leave Brooklyn the following day. Leigh and I wait for the car that will bring us to our new home, and I hug each member of the De Luca family—three generations of mothers and daughters who helped me, individually, and as a family.

"You invite us to the wedding," Mrs. De Luca tells me, her expression stern. "Without a wedding, is no okay."

I don't disagree with her, in theory. Without marriage, my status in someone else's apartment is precarious, and Leigh and I could easily become homeless if Michael decides that he doesn't want us there. But I don't think that will happen. The move was his idea, not mine. Michael is a man who knows what he wants, and he will see it through.

A car is pulling up to the curb, the car that Michael has sent for us, and I give Mrs. De Luca another hug. She bends to kiss Leigh on both cheeks and presses a St. Christopher medal into her hands. "For safe travel," she says. "St. Christopher carried a child across the river. Now he carry you across the East River, to a new life."

I say goodbye yet again as the driver collects our suitcases. In less than an hour, we are at the elegant building that will be our new home.

Leigh is enthralled with the apartment. The view from the oversized windows, twenty stories below, and the tasseled cords that hold back the heavy drapes. The rosewood armoire with its row of tiny drawers, the buttons that make the recessed lighting grow brighter or dimmer.

I remember thinking, when I saw Juliet Montgomery's Central Park West apartment: *Someday I will live in a place like this.* Now I have a key to an apartment that is even larger and more beautiful. A man in a uniform opens the door for us. He admires Leigh's bunny and wishes her a fine day.

I lean toward my daughter, who is now three years old, and whisper, "We did it."

I don't need to teach summer school because Michael pays for everything. There is no rent, since he owns the apartment. The other expenses—utilities, maintenance, concierge—are unaf-

fected by my presence. He even insists on paying for the groceries. "It's just an extra potato," he tells me. "An extra egg."

I'm not entirely comfortable with his largesse, but I accept it.
I understand that I am providing something in return. It is
something he needs as much as I need the pediatrician and
preschool for Leigh—the knowledge that he is giving me, can
still give me, the pleasure that a man can give to a woman. It is
more important to him than it is to me, though I would never
tell him that.

Not teaching allows me to spend the whole summer being a
mother, a blissful freedom I haven't had since Leigh was an infant.
There are Mommy and Me music classes, walks in Riverside
Park, a puppet theatre production of *The Very Hungry Caterpillar*.
I don't ask Michael to join us. He is kind and attentive to Leigh,
but he is not her parent.

The Very Hungry Caterpillar is enchanting. Leigh knows the
story and is delighted by the sets and puppets and songs. She
doesn't want to leave her seat at intermission, afraid she will miss
something, but I show her that the stage is dark and we are all
meant to have a break, even the puppets. Her eyes light up. "To
go potty!" she exclaims, pleased with herself for figuring it out.
"The puppets have to go potty."

"Just like us." I stand, offer my hand, and we make our way
to the lobby where there are refreshments, souvenirs, and rest-
rooms. I am guiding us toward the women's restroom when I
hear a squeal of excitement. "Arden!"

I turn and find myself only inches from Juliet Montgomery.
My eyes dart to her side and yes, there is Zack, holding her hand
as tightly as Leigh is holding mine.

"Oh my God!" Juliet screams. "I can't believe I ran into you.
I always wondered how everything worked out."

I flush. In other words, I was too rude to let her know what became of me, after she opened her home so generously. But Juliet would never say that. There is no undercurrent of accusation in her joy.

I explain where I'm living now, and Juliet is thrilled. "You should have called to let me know. And a river view! How in the world did you end up in such a scrumptious place?"

I tell her about Michael, but not too much. "Michael *Tate*?" she says. "Are you *kidding* me? He's Stephen's hero. He's, like, the god of M and A. You know, mergers and acquisitions? He practically invented it."

I don't know how to respond. Michael's stature in the world of M and A has nothing to do with our relationship. The only reason I met him was because of the bullshit paper his daughter wrote and how he came to complain when lesser beings had failed to sway me. At the time, I thought he was an overconfident rich guy used to getting whatever he wanted—which, in a way, is true. If there are things he can't get, or get back, he has chosen not to want them.

I realize that Juliet is still talking.

"Maybe you'd like to come over for cocktails some time? Stephen would totally love it."

"I'll have to see," I tell her. "This is still pretty new for us. We're still figuring out how to be a couple without being a family."

Juliet makes a face. "I can't imagine how you can separate them. When you two get married, it will be simpler."

I glance at Leigh to see if she is listening, but she's poking at a potato chip on the carpet with her shoe. "We're not getting married," I say. It's not something we've discussed, no matter what Mrs. De Luca might hope.

"Whatever." Then Juliet gives me a mischievous grin. "Even so, you are one lucky devil to snare Michael Tate. Or do devils snare? What do they *do*, exactly, to hook such a big fish?"

"I didn't do anything. We just hit it off." I need to end this conversation. It's making me uncomfortable, and I don't know how much Leigh has understood. "I think they're about to flash the lights. We need to make a pit stop before intermission's over."

Juliet nods. "Call me," she says, and gives me air kisses on each cheek.

I ask Leigh if she needs to use the bathroom. She shakes her head no but I steer her there anyway. Three is not a reliable age.

I am not going to call Juliet Montgomery, although she has made an impression on me. She's sparked a question that troubles me in a way that Michael's infirmity does not. Can you be a couple without being a family?

A few days later, I get a phone call from my brother Hugh. I'm surprised, because we'd spoken only a week ago.

Then I register the tightness in his greeting. "I don't mean to alarm you," he says. "I just thought you should know." His voice catches on the word *know*.

"Know what?" I ask, though I'm already alarmed.

"Georgia. She found a lump in her armpit a couple of weeks ago. She was sure it was nothing, you know how she is."

I hear another sound, like a sob caught in a fist. I understand what he's going to say from the word *lump*.

"I made her go to the doctor," he says, "and they wanted to do a biopsy, send her to an oncologist. We got the results today."

The next words are so quiet I can barely hear them. As if he can barely say them. "It's breast cancer. Stage Three."

"Oh, Hugh." Georgia is so young. I know people get breast cancer at all ages, but doesn't seem possible. Not for Georgia, who is trim and athletic and grows organic vegetables in raised beds.

Hugh explains about the treatments that will start this week.

Surgery, chemo, radiation. The survival rate—meaning, alive after five years—is seventy-five percent. "That's not a bad average, right? It means there are people who live ten years, twenty years. Especially when they're young and strong, like Georgia."

I am flooded with emotion. Georgia is such a good soul. She would never want Hugh to see her terror. Because, surely, she is terrified.

I hate that I didn't go there for Christmas. They invited me two years in a row, but I always had a reason to turn them down. Money. Then Michael.

Hugh came through for me when I needed help. I will come through for them now.

"I'm coming out," I tell him. "You'll need another pair of hands after the surgery."

"I can take care of her. I just wanted you to know."

"Of course you can take care of her. But there are groceries and laundry and cooking. Changing the sheets. Picking up prescriptions and special pillows and whatever else she needs."

"Arden," he says. "I appreciate the offer. But it's not realistic. You have Leigh."

"She won't be in the way. I'll make it work."

I need to do this for him, after everything he did for me. I took from Juliet without giving anything in return, telling myself that Juliet had an extra room and an extra stroller. But Hugh is family. Ryżu.

"You're serious," he says.

"I'm completely serious. Give me a few hours to arrange it."

There isn't much to arrange. It's summer, and I'm not teaching. Michael can obviously manage without me. I have the urge to tell Hugh, "Be glad it's a breast. She can still make love without a breast." That would be a horrible thing to say to my anguished brother, and I don't. But I think it.

Leigh and I fly to Denver. It's her first time on an airplane. She clicks the little ashtray about forty times and wants to know what the vomit bag is for. When I tell her, she makes her bunny throw up his pretend carrots.

We take a taxi from the airport to Hugh and Georgia's house. Georgia is pale and weak, but glad to see us. "Hugh is driving me crazy," she confides while Hugh is outside with Leigh, showing her the garden with the owl decoys that are meant to keep the birds away. "He thinks he has to be strong and positive and perfect every single second, and if he says one imperfect thing, I'll die. I wish he would just be his usual irritating self. Then I could whine to my heart's content. This way, I feel like I have to be noble too."

Separately, Hugh tells me, "Georgia has been so incredible about all this, such an inspiration. I feel like I have to live up to her example."

I watch the two of them. How they are together, bringing out the best in each other. This is the way it's supposed to be. In sickness and in health. Why have I not understood this?

I think about how I've lived. I wanted to be free, unrestrained. To say and do and have whatever I wanted, right now. If I couldn't have it, I could still fling my anger at the uncooperative world, throw my underwear at the man who denied me.

Yet people have helped me, each time I needed it. Without them, I would have been lost.

It is a truth I haven't wanted to think about, yet it tells me that freedom, as I've defined it, is a child's notion. Yes, there are bonds that can hold you back. There are also bonds that connect you. It's not that I don't know this—because of Leigh. I just haven't thought it could apply to anyone but her.

I busy myself cooking, doing laundry, tending Georgia's garden. I read aloud to her while she rests. I tell myself that I am lucky. Happier with Michael than I deserve to be.

There is a conversation taking place in my head. It is loud and close, yet I hear it from far away, as if I am listening to people arguing in the street. One person repeats words like *lucky* and *appreciate*. The other person says *don't kid yourself, honey*.

The first voice isn't wrong. I do appreciate Michael. Enjoy being with him.

The second voice isn't wrong either. I know myself. I don't want to commit to a life where I will never feel a man inside me again.

I make Mrs. De Luca's special manicotti and serve it to Georgia on a tray with a salad of greens that Hugh has picked for her. She can only eat a bite at a time but smiles gratefully. Hugh wipes her forehead with a damp cloth. I watch him and tears fill my eyes.

I am not like Hugh. Good, the way Hugh is good.

But I could be.

I remember how I yearned for goodness in Deir el-Medina, a lifetime ago. I have never stopped yearning for it, despite everything.

Even if I'm not good, naturally, I can choose goodness. I can pledge myself—to Michael, a man who would wipe my forehead as carefully as Hugh wipes Georgia's.

Leigh and I remain in Denver for ten days. Georgia can't start chemo until a month after surgery, so there really isn't anything more I can do. I've stocked the pantry and freezer and bookshelves, cleaned the house, weeded the garden. "You've been a godsend," Georgia tells me. "We know you love us. Now go home."

I accept her frail hug and agree to go back to New York. When I return, I tell Michael, "I think we should get married."

He gives me a long, unreadable look. "Do you love me?"

"No," I tell him.

"Are you hoping there will be a miraculous cure for my impotence and I'll be able to fuck you?"

"No."

"Are you hoping I'll want to adopt Leigh and leave her a big chunk of my estate?"

"No."

"That's probably wise," he says. "I'm sure her actual father would have something to say about that."

"Her actual father has no idea she exists."

Michael raises an eyebrow. "Jonah Orenstein isn't her father?"

I shake my head. I've never lied about Leigh's parentage, but I've let him assume. I really don't want to get into this right now and am relieved when he doesn't ask, merely drawls, "The plot thickens."

I wait. I'm growing impatient with this quiz. If it's no, it's no.

Then Michael's expression shifts, and he gives me a lovely smile. He takes my hand and presses it to his chest, as he did at our first dinner. "Those are excellent answers. And yes, let's get married. I thought you'd never ask."

"I do like you," I tell him. "Very much."

"And I, you."

"It's a merger, not an acquisition."

He laughs, then lifts my hand and kisses my palm. "Of course."

It's a small wedding. Leigh is the flower girl. She thinks she is the one getting married because she is in charge of strewing the flowers wherever she likes.

WITH MY EYES
2013

The school question really had to be settled. The cocoon of home-tutoring had been good for a while, but Danielle needed to return to the world of her peers.

When Arden brought up the idea over breakfast, Danielle broke her carrot muffin in two and set the halves on the plate, facing each other. "Why can't I go on tour with Dad and have a tutor? Like Nora?"

Arden laid down her spoon. "Sweetheart," she began. There was no need to tell Danielle that her father didn't want her to go on tour with him; thankfully, there were other reasons. "That's only for child actors who can't go to a regular school while they're filming or performing. Not for children of the cast or crew."

"I could be a child actor," Danielle said. "I could play Anne Frank. That's the next play Dad's doing. He told me."

Arden lifted an eyebrow. Danielle had to know how ridiculous her idea was, without being told. "I'm sure they've already cast the part."

"They haven't. They're auditioning right now."

"Danielle." Enough. "You are not a child actor. You don't have training or experience or an Actors Equity card."

Danielle shoved her plate across the table. "I could *get* them. Dad could get them for me."

"People don't just—"

"He'd be *glad* to get them for me. So I could be with him."

"Danielle—"

"Nobody wants me to be anything." Danielle jumped to her feet, eyes pooling with angry tears. She grabbed one of the muffin halves and ran out of the room.

Arden sighed and let her go. Was this what Eleanor Cardoza meant by complicated grief? Was there any grief that wasn't complicated?

She had no idea what Danielle needed. A wide berth, a firm hand. Neither seemed right.

After she cleaned up from breakfast, Arden went to check her email. There were tire sales, vacation packages, edible arrangements. She was about to send everything to spam when she saw a message from an unfamiliar address. "So sorry about Leigh."

She was starting to dread those emails, but it seemed rude to ignore them. Grimacing, she opened the message. "Dear Arden," it began, "I hope this is you, and you still have the same email after all this time."

Arden froze as she read the next line. "This is Savannah Margolin. You knew me as Savannah Tate."

Her heart seized. It couldn't be.

"A ghost from the past, right? I read about the accident in the paper and recognized Leigh's name, and it was just so awful. I kept wanting to write, and finally I had to. You probably thought I was jealous of her, way back when, and maybe I was. But she was so cute and bright, and I always wanted a little sister. She was the closest I ever had."

Arden stopped reading as images leap-frogged across her memory. Savannah's speech about Miss Piggy, and her sullen presence at the wedding. Her patience as she read—and reread — *If You Give a Mouse a Cookie*, Leigh's favorite book.

They had never really connected, she and Savannah, except through Leigh. They were members of overlapping generations, competing for the role of Michael's favorite. And then, that terrible day, the last time they saw each other.

Savannah Tate. Margolin. She must be fifty now.

Arden bit her lip, returned to the screen.

"I just wanted to say how sorry I am," Savannah had written. "And to let you know that I never forgot the two of you, even though we—let's just say, lost touch."

A delicate way to put it. Arden wondered, as she had over the years, what Savannah had told her mother, and what Kira had done with that knowledge.

"You probably knew," Savannah went on, "but in case not, I thought you should know that my dad died a couple of years ago. He was seventy-nine, so it wasn't untimely or anything. Not like Leigh."

It struck Arden that Savannah didn't realize she had lost Connor in the same crash. Well, how could she? The name Connor McRae would have meant nothing to her. The last of Arden's husbands Savannah had known about was her father.

"I suppose it's always untimely for the person," the message continued, "and I'm sure my dad would have liked another decade or two. But I think he was more-or-less at peace, which is what matters, right? Anyway, I never forgot you, and I'm sure he never did either, and it's awful about Leigh. That's why I wrote. To say how sorry I am."

Arden stared at the screen. Maybe Savannah hadn't told Kira anything. There was nothing to imply that she had.

Sometimes people turned out to be kinder than you expected. Then again, the email had been written by a fifty-year-old woman, not the Savannah Tate she'd seen for the last time in a Vassar dormitory.

She'd have to answer, let the present-day Savannah Margolin know that she'd gotten her message. Carefully, Arden tapped the arrow for *reply*. "Thank you so much," she wrote. "For your thoughtful words, and the news about your dad, which I hadn't heard." She didn't know what else to say. They'd all moved on, lived their lives.

Still, she needed an ending, so she added, "I hope you're doing well and life has been good to you." She thought of asking about Michael's later years but didn't think she had the right. She inhaled, then clicked *send* and closed her laptop.

The email had shaken her. It stirred up a part of her life that she never thought about—and didn't have to, since there was no one who remembered except her. Connor had never really known about her previous marriages, only that they'd happened. They had agreed: whatever you'd lived through and done should be apparent in who you were now. If it wasn't, it hadn't really mattered.

The memory of those early conversations—walking among the apple trees, riding in the cab of his truck—pierced her anew. Everything rose up at once, filling her with grief.

Small things that hadn't seemed important until their absence made them large. How he never failed to greet the fruit vendors on the street, and the way he bunched his pillow like a child. His modesty about the papers he'd written, and how he always introduced himself as a farmer. After all those years away from the farm, he still liked to get up before everyone else and watch the sunrise.

Arden struggled to hold back her tears. Then she thought: Don't run from it. Tell about it.

Words were what she had. Her paint, her clay. She reached for her laptop, flipped it open again, and began to write.

I see you walking across the grass
in boxers, an old shirt:
a happy man.

A bubble of sun boils overhead,
erupts at your feet,
shoots spinning
threads of warm green laughter.

She dropped her hands as pain and loss swept through her. She had broken the hearts of her first two husbands. Now Connor McRae had broken hers.

She let Danielle pout for two hours, but the day needed to begin. Space was one thing, indulgence another.

Arden rapped on the door to Danielle's bedroom but didn't wait for an invitation. The rap was an announcement, not a request.

Danielle was sitting on the edge of the bed, watching the goldfish circle each other in the tank. She looked up as Arden entered. "Do you think they're going to die too?"

Arden winced. What had she been thinking, buying fragile tropical fish for a girl who had just lost her mother? There hardly seemed a stupider choice.

She'd wanted to get Danielle something, anything, to replace the cats she couldn't have, so she'd grabbed the first creatures her granddaughter seemed to want. Her relief about Tinkerbell and Tiger Lily—who had been given, finally, to Shelly Fremantle's sister—had been mixed-up with guilt at not finding a clever way to keep them. A girl who had lost her mother should get to keep everything else.

Arden eased down next to her granddaughter. "I don't know," she said. "Someday. But you're making their lives happy in the meantime."

Danielle shook her head. "I don't think fish feel happy or sad." She turned to Arden with an arch look. "We like to pretend they have feelings. But that's us, not them."

Arden's pulse jumped. Here it is, she thought. An opening. *Take it.*

"What about you, sweetheart? What feelings do you have?"

Danielle gave a snort. "At least that's an actual question. Eleanor just repeats what I say with a question mark at the end. Like, if I said I hated oatmeal, she'd say: 'You hate oatmeal?'"

Arden had to laugh. "I think that's a child therapist thing. You know, to let you know you've been heard. She doesn't do that with me."

"You talk to Eleanor?" Danielle's expression darkened. "About what? Me?"

Damn. Arden did her best to back-pedal. "I'm dealing with a lot, too, you know." It wasn't a lie, though the implication was. Still, it was better than letting Danielle know that they really *were* talking about her. Parrots, train wrecks, her mother appearing in a vision to retract what she'd said.

If Danielle was making things up, let Eleanor Cardoza figure out why. But if she wasn't, they needed to know. She, Arden, needed to know.

There were too many things she couldn't ignore. Leigh's irritation at her daughter, the affection she never seemed to show.

The things in her nightstand, and Danielle's matter-of-fact statement about her multiple partners. Arrows pointing to the same question. Who was Leigh, really?

Arden edged closer to her granddaughter. "You know," she said, "if there are things you're not comfortable saying to Eleanor, you can always say them to me. It's different because we're family."

Danielle gave her a deadpan look, then turned back the goldfish. "Maybe."

Arden watched them too. Wait, she told herself. If there was ever a moment to corral all those slivers of patience, this was it.

Danielle had said maybe. It meant there was something she needed to say. Otherwise, she would have made a snippy remark about Eleanor or changed the subject. She was deciding whether to tell. Or preparing to.

Arden felt a frisson of fear. Once you knew something, you couldn't unknow it.

"She was sloppy," Danielle said, finally. "If you're a mom, you're supposed to be careful around your kid. You're not supposed to let your kid see some guy's butt crack when she doesn't even know his name." Her eyes were fixed on the fish tank. "Or his gross thing. Swinging there. Whack, whack between his legs."

Arden turned pale.

"When he was walking to the bathroom," Danielle said. "Right past me. My mom knew I was there. She knew I saw, but she never said a word. Like sorry." She looked at her grandmother. "She was supposed to yell at him. Tell him to never do that again, my daughter lives here too."

Arden could hardly breathe. This wasn't polyamory. Not in front of a child, who couldn't do any of the respecting and consenting that Connor had explained to her, so long ago.

She struggled to save the daughter she still believed in, needed to believe in. "Maybe she didn't realize that you saw."

"She realized," Danielle said. "Because she looked straight at me. And then she winked. Like, *He's hot, right?*"

Bile rose in Arden's throat. She wanted to insist that Danielle must have misunderstood—only she knew, in every cell of her body, that Danielle was telling the truth.

Only a child would do what Leigh had done. A smirking, selfish child. Not a mother. Not someone who knew better.

It made no sense. If you'd known, growing up, how it felt to have a good mother—someone who always put you first—how could you *not* want to give your own child the same feeling of safety and trust?

Arden felt a blackness wrap itself around her, squeezing her tighter and tighter. She begin to plummet. A wingless bird, plunging through the darkness.

No, she couldn't go there, not now. Because *now* there was Danielle, who needed her.

She gathered the girl in her arms. "I'm so sorry, baby. You're right. She should have been more careful. She should have told him not to do that."

Danielle let herself be held, though her body was rigid. "It wasn't just that once. They all liked to show off. Walk around, let me hear them pee. No one cared if I was there."

Arden closed her eyes. Complicated grief, Eleanor had warned her. I hate you, go away, I never want to see you again. No, come back. Don't leave me.

She pressed her cheek to Danielle's hair, inhaling the scent of her clean shampoo. Then she pulled back and met Danielle's eyes. "You can tell me anything," she said. "As long as it's the truth. Something that really happened. Not just in your mind."

Danielle nodded, and Arden wondered if there was more. She thought there probably was but wasn't sure how to ask—or if she wanted to. Then Danielle broke free of her embrace and turned to the fish tank. "Look," she said. "I think that one gold-fish is kind of a bully." She pointed at the glass. "See how he's stalking the other guy?"

Arden followed the girl's finger. She was right. It was the small scrappy fish, chasing the bigger one.

Then Danielle spoke again. Her eyes were fixed on the goldfish. "My dad wanted me to take pictures," she said. "Like evidence."

A chill spread through Arden's body. "He knew?"

"I told him."

Arden could barely get the words out. "And did you take pictures?"

Danielle gave her a quick, sideways look. "He was being a moron. You can't just stick a camera up to someone's butt."

Yes, Ivan had to know that. But she was still furious with him. What the hell was he thinking?

"So you didn't take any pictures?" she asked, just to be sure.

Danielle turned to her again. Her expression was guileless, calm. "I did. With my eyes."

LEIGH
IN THE DIRT

1993

Whenever Leigh tried to go back and trace her path—from one slab of stone to the next, across the lawn of her life—there were always three stones that marked the beginning of the trail.

The first was the fall afternoon when a broad-shouldered, heavy-lidded senior named Blake Rasmussen singled her out for his attention. Only her, Leigh Orenstein, a mere freshman, among all the girls he could have chosen. How honored she had felt, as if she'd been dipped in glitter, anointed by his gaze, as he moved his eyes over her body.

How predictable it was, after that, when she let him take her hand and lead her to a place behind the gym that he told her was his "special spot." She thought it was the prelude to a pledge. She was still waiting for the class ring, the shy smile, when he pushed her against the building and jammed his knee between her legs. She tried to say *what* or *wait*, but he'd already pulled up the skirt she'd worn because it made her feel pretty, pale yellow cotton that twirled when she walked, and shoved his hard fat fingers inside her underwear.

Anyone with an ounce of self-respect would have screamed and run away, but she didn't. It was like she couldn't catch up. Her thoughts were from five minutes ago—*his special place, about to kiss me*—and she couldn't seem to move past them, couldn't seem to move at all. Everything was too fast, and she was frozen in the middle of it. A butterfly in her gauzy yellow skirt, pinned to the side of the building.

And then Blake did kiss her, but not her mouth—her breast, right through her shirt, and she thought her nipple would explode. Then the shock of pleasure between her legs as his fingers moved inside her, and the way he laughed as he opened his zipper.

The disbelief when he left her there, afterward. The slow realization, the humiliation, as she lay in the dirt behind the deserted gym—because of how stupid she had been to go with him, not just willingly, but eagerly. And shame, because of the moment when she'd been aroused, despite the hideous thing that was happening. He had seen and made sure she knew that he saw.

That was the worst of all. Worse than the way he'd spread her thighs with his thick fingers and pushed himself inside her, like she wasn't even a person.

She refused to cry. And didn't, not until the next day when she told her stepfather what had happened.

That was the second marker, after Blake.

Her mother wasn't home, she was teaching a night class, so it was just Leigh and Connor, sitting in the living room watching *Seinfeld*. She didn't especially like *Seinfeld*, but Connor loved it and she didn't want to be alone. Plus, Connor was easy to be with. He didn't crowd her, the way her mother did.

Leigh pulled the cranberry-colored shawl across her knees and fixed her eyes on the screen. She thought maybe she could just escape into the show, pretend she was Elaine, and stop her mind from reliving what had happened with Blake. But then Connor laughed at something Jerry said and turned to her with a delighted grin, welcoming her into his delight, and she couldn't bear his kindness. Before she could stop it, a strangled cry burst from her throat.

She liked Connor but never, ever imagined telling him. Yet there she was, shaking and ugly-crying as everything poured out. Not the part about wanting to scream when Blake took her nipple in his mouth. Everything else.

The sound of his zipper. The dirt. How he'd brushed off his jeans and walked away.

Connor listened without moving until she had finished. Then she said, "You can't tell Mom. You have to promise. It would make her feel awful, like she'd personally let it happen. You know how she is."

Connor had listened the way she needed him to, letting her talk and weep without taking over and turning it into a big macho war cry. But now, surprising her, he pushed back.

"I don't feel right keeping secrets from your mom," he said. "But it's not my place to tell her. It's yours. And you really need to, honey. For one thing, so she can take you to a doctor."

Leigh shook her head. "I'm not talking about it ever again. Not with some doctor, and not with my mother. I told one person. You. That's it."

She folded her arms, setting her mouth in a line. Connor had to know that about her. When she made up her mind, she was done.

In the background, she could hear Jerry and Elaine, a laugh track. Outside, the blare of a horn, the beep of a delivery truck backing into the alley. And beyond the sounds, a rimless silence.

Finally Connor spoke. "What happened to you was horrible, Leigh. There's no way to think about it or talk about it or see it as anything but horrible. But you can't let it define you as a woman."

His last sentence stopped her because she'd been sure he was going to turn it into another plea to tell her mother. Instead, Connor kept his eyes fixed on hers.

"There will be other boys for you, Leigh. A whole line of boys, who'll see how special you are. You don't need this jerk. Trust me, you can have all the guys you want."

She knew he was trying to tell her something because he was a good person and wanted to help. But all she heard was the last part. *Have all the guys you want.*

It was like a coin dropping into a slot. A second marker, an arrow pointing to a different path. A path of power, instead of shame.

She could have all the men she wanted. Not just one.

Connor McRae had told her so.

GIRL TRAPPED UNDER FALLEN CONCRETE

1983

'm sure that people, viewing us from the outside, think I married Michael for his money, and he married me so he could sleep with a younger woman.

Neither assumption is true, although neither is entirely false. I appreciate Michael's wealth, but mostly because of Leigh and the advantages it brings her. And Michael appreciates having a woman—who happens to be younger—who will let him pleasure her in the ways that he can. We also enjoy each other's company.

Most important, Leigh is happy. She goes to a wonderful preschool, full of bright colors and pretty teachers and attractive, well-bred children; soon she will start kindergarten. She loves her room, which has been redecorated in Barbie pink. She loves the doorman and pushing the buttons on the elevator and Riverside Park, especially the dogs. She is fond of Michael, but the person she truly adores is Savannah. To Leigh, Savannah is a life-sized Barbie, with her long legs and exotic wardrobe. Savannah is good with Leigh, though she's cool with me. I am the person, after all, who got her banned from those lacrosse games, made her redo an entire midterm assignment, and stole her father. We don't see Savannah very often, even though Vassar College, where she is now a junior, is only eighty miles away. She spends most of her vacations with her mother, her preferred parent; we see Michael's son even less. Charlie is in California, finishing a graduate degree. They are from another era, Charlie and Savannah. It's impossible for me to picture Michael as the father of toddlers, tossing them in the air and making them shriek with glee. Reading *Goodnight, Moon* and *The Runaway Bunny*. Singing the Pumpkin Song.

I only know Michael as he is now, and I'm certain that he is happier than he expected to be. Michael's happiness makes me happy too. If there are moments when I miss what I miss, I make sure he doesn't know.

I talk to my parents every Sunday. They have met Michael—he's flown them here to visit, several times—and are touched by everything he has done for Leigh, though they've never understood Jonah's complete absence. They asked for a while, but my answer was always: "Hey, people are who they are."

I am still lying to them, but I don't see another path. Or maybe I do, but I don't want to take it. I tell myself that I'm sparing my parents unnecessary distress. They are happy to see me settled and secure; isn't that enough?

I talk to Hugh and Georgia, who is doing well two years post-surgery. I talk to the new mommy-friends I made at the Mommy-and-Me classes. Juliet Montgomery is not among them. I tried, but her fan-girl obsession with Michael was more than I could handle.

Thanks to Michael, I am in the final semester of a master's program in English. When he asked if I wanted to continue at

Brenner or was there something else I'd rather do, I told him the truth, because the truth is what he prefers. "Get an advanced degree. Learn to write poetry."

Being Michael, he told me to do it. Money was no issue. It was one more check, like one more potato. I began with two classes. Then Leigh started preschool, and I became a full-time student. English Literature, with a specialty in Twentieth Century American Poetry.

I like my classes and am one of the top students. I work on my thesis in the library while a babysitter with impeccable references takes Leigh to the park or entertains her at home after preschool. Sometimes I lay down my pen and stare at whatever volume is open in front of me, astonished that I am actually getting to do this.

I've even made a new friend, a woman in my poetry seminar named Chloe Bernard. Chloe reminds me of Madonna—the singer, not the mother of Jesus—with her bubble skirts, neon leggings, and lacey tops under retro jackets. Multi-colored bracelets spiral up her arms.

Like me, Chloe is impatient for the instructor to get to the point, intolerant of classmates who waste time complaining about the assignments, and adamant that Denise Levertov has been seriously underrated—otherwise, why isn't her work in the syllabus? After our third class, Chloe asks if I want to get a cappuccino. I picture Leigh, happily eating ravioli with Veronica, the sitter with impeccable references, and say yes, sure.

We walk to a café near campus and exchange bios. I mention Leigh, my former jobs at the girls' school and the textbook company where I cross-referenced pages. When Chloe asks, I explain that I'm not working right now. My husband has done well financially and is paying my tuition.

I can tell by the arch of her eyebrow that Chloe thinks I

have found a rich man to take care of me. I try to tell her about Savannah and *Sophie's Choice*, but she is not interested. She wants to talk about herself: how she juggles three part-time jobs, waitressing at diners and bars, and takes double-doses of Ritalin so she can stay up till dawn to write her papers, then double-shots of Captain Morgan's Spiced Rum so she can reverse the Ritalin and get a few hours' sleep.

Chloe is fiercely committed to excelling. She needs a strong GPA to keep her scholarship, but it's more than that; her vision of herself allows nothing less than an A. She will be the best, the star. She is so sure of her eventual fame that it's impossible not to believe her.

When the barista hands us our coffee, Chloe makes no move to take out her wallet. I realize that she is waiting for me to pay. I am, after all, the one with money—which she knows, since I've just told her. I don't say, "I'll treat, you can pay next time." I simply pay, and we carry our cups to a table.

We talk about Wallace Stevens, Denise Levertov, and our dreams of literary greatness. Chloe confides that she has wanted to be a writer since she was seven years old. If it takes Ritalin and three jobs to get there, so be it.

Cappuccino after class becomes a Thursday ritual. It's understood that I will pay, and I don't mind; money is, ironically, something that is easy for me to give. In return, I am gifted with Chloe's friendship.

I am awed by her dedication and want her to know that I am equally dedicated. I tell her that I have a signed copy of Levertov's book, *The Poet in the World*. It's really Michael's, acquired before I met him, but Chloe doesn't need to know that. "It's too valuable to loan," I explain. "But come by some time, and I'll show it to you." I write our address on a piece of paper. She folds it into thirds and puts it in the Gatsby flapper bag she uses for a purse.

I have a burning need to win Chloe's approval. She seems free and alive, superior to me in all the ways that matter.

I am having a late, solitary breakfast before heading to campus for my seminar. Leigh is at preschool. Veronica will pick her up, feed her lunch, and entertain her until I return. It's one of those perfect mornings when the sky is a flawless dome of cornflower blue. A cartoon blue, as if a deity had declared: "Let there be blue."

I reach for the newspaper that Michael has left for me and skim the articles until a story at the bottom of the page catches my eye. *Girl Trapped Under Fallen Concrete.* I think, at first, that it's about a construction accident—until I see that it's a report from a journalist who has gone to the scene of a devastating earthquake.

As I begin to read, I realize that the reporter hasn't actually been there. He's describing something he saw on television. A video, taken by an ordinary person with a camera. Someone who left his house, needing to see what was left of his city.

I am assuming this is what happened, though the reporter doesn't say. He simply describes what the camera is recording.

Daylight is fading. There is only the grey of early evening, making the film appear to be in black-and-white. No streetlamps remain to illuminate what is left of the buildings. A layer of snow coats the rubble.

The man with the camera comes upon the girl suddenly. She is eleven or twelve, perhaps younger, pinned from the chest down by the collapsed concrete; only her pale frightened face is visible in the waning light. It's clear that they don't know each other, the man and the girl, and that his reaction to finding her —excited at first, to find a survivor—is turning to panic.

The camera moves closer, and he speaks to her. She answers. No, she can't move. Yes, she is cold, thirsty, and has been there since the previous day, when the building collapsed. It was too fast, there was no time to flee. No, she doesn't know where her family is.

Snow starts to fall. The image begins to waver, as if the man's hand is trembling, but he keeps filming. From the absence of other voices, it's evident that the two are alone.

"I'm going to get some help," he tells her. "You stay here." As if she can do anything but stay.

The girl's voice is low, barely a whisper. "Don't go."

"I'll be back, I promise. I'm just going to get help."

The girl's words grow fainter as she repeats, "Don't go."

The man is shouting now. "I'm going to get help. I told you— I'll be back." Then the film ends.

The story in the newspaper shifts to the long-term cost of the earthquake, which has destroyed most of the city. I drop the paper. I don't want to read a financial analysis of suffering. I want to find the man who wrote the article, grab him by the throat, and make him tell me how it ended. Surely, the man with the camera returned. He promised.

But there is nothing about that in the article. It is too obvious to mention. By the time the newspaper went to press, the girl was dead.

There is no way she hasn't died. Darkness came; snow fell.

I push away from the table. Quickly, I gather the sections of newspaper and stuff them in the trash.

When Chloe and I meet for coffee later that morning, I tell her about the story. She listens with interest. "Do you think the man, the one with the camera, was the first person the girl saw, after she got pinned under the rubble?"

I consider the question. "You'd think so, or she would have

said something. Like: oh, so-and-so already went to get help."

"Right. So now you have to stay here with me."

"But she didn't."

"No. It was almost like she didn't believe in help anymore." Chloe toys with the bracelets that line her arm. "Think about it. She'd been there since the night before, she couldn't move. She probably had to pee. What could she do, except pee down her trapped legs?"

I shudder. "You make it sound so real."

"It was real."

I remember how each of them, the man and the girl, kept repeating the same words: *Get help. Don't go.*

"Still," I say, "if he was the first person she saw, she had to feel a glimmer of hope. Finally, someone has come."

"Maybe not. Maybe she knew he was bullshitting her about getting help."

"That's a terrible thought."

"Hey, men are bullshit experts."

"Not all men," I say. Chloe shrugs. Then I have another thought. "You hear about people picking up whole cars, doing amazing things when they have to? Like their emotions give them super-strength." My voice gets louder. I'm excited now. "You think the man could have moved one of those concrete blocks, after he put the camera down? Just enough for her to roll out? Maybe that was why he stopped filming."

Chloe gives me a cynical look. "You really think some guy would do that? He didn't even know her. Why would he?"

An act of goodness, I think. Or maybe the girl asked him to. Did she say: "Can you get me out of here?" No, she said nothing. Just: "Don't leave me."

My heart begins to race. "Maybe he was afraid to try and fail. To get her hopes up."

Chloe shakes her head. "I don't think the girl had any hopes. Or she would have said: 'Hey, can you get this crap off of me?'"

"She knew he couldn't."

"Or wouldn't."

That isn't the way the story was related in the newspaper. The man had been frightened too.

We aren't talking about the newspaper story, not anymore. Chloe's eyes burn into mine.

"Sometimes it really is *wouldn't*," she says. Her face hardens. "A person could maybe lift one of those blocks, but he won't. Maybe he likes having the other person a little bit trapped." She uses her fingers to separate the bracelets that have slid into a tangled heap at her wrist. "We're all the same, you know. Trapped under a big mess of concrete that fell from nowhere. A thousand pounds of something, pinning us down." She lets go of the bracelets. They clatter down her arm. "Could be we put it there ourselves, just to see what would happen. Or maybe we saw it coming and just watched it fall."

She's talking about herself, but I feel stupid because I don't understand.

Chloe gives another shrug. "You just have to kick the rocks away. One rock for each shitty thing."

"Shitty thing done to you?" My voice catches. "Or by you?"

I remember everything now. Syrup made of oranges, and a lie that ruined a man's life. A truth that broke another man's heart. There was no earthquake. I did it.

But that wasn't the end of the story. I changed my life. Rolled free, my daughter in my arms.

I meet Chloe's eyes. "I got myself out."

She leans back, her expression cool. "Good for you. Not everyone can do that."

It's true. Sometimes there is no opening, no benevolence. Darkness spreads; snow falls.

Chloe flicks her hair. "And hey, who knows if any of it really happened? Maybe the reporter made the whole thing up. You know, a human interest angle."

"You really think someone would do that?"

"Either way, it worked. I mean, here we are, talking about it." She reaches for her coffee cup, blows along the rim.

I lift mine, too, blow in a circle the way she does. "I'd like to think he came back with six guys, and they got her free."

"Six guys and one tired girl? Ha. Easy to picture what happened next."

"Chloe. You can't mean that."

"Arden. I can mean whatever I want."

I set my cup down. "The story is awful enough. She died alone."

"Probably. Truth is, we don't know."

I echo her words. "We don't know."

There is nothing more to say; we move on. We talk about movies. *Return of the Jedi*, *Tootsie*, *Sophie's Choice*. Chloe hates *Sophie's Choice*. She thinks it shows women as victims, defined by men. "The whole thing was just so Stingo could get laid and have something interesting to write about? Fuck that."

I busy myself with the coffee spoon. They made a movie out of the Styron novel. Michael and I went to see it, homage to the way we met. A regular couple would have had anniversary sex afterward. We are not a regular couple.

I think of how Michael saved me. It was Michael who lifted the concrete block, because Michael Tate can take care of anything. I lied to Chloe when I said that I did it myself.

I remember what I thought, when I decided we should get married. How I pictured Michael wiping my forehead, as Hugh wiped Georgia's. I didn't picture myself wiping his. I didn't picture myself doing anything, except being there, pretending there was no concrete block pinning Michael down.

It pins him below the waist, just as the girl was pinned. I can't lift it, but I can pretend it isn't there. That's my job.

Chloe pushes her cup toward the center of the table. "I have a meeting with my advisor," she says. "Time for me to hit the road."

"Me too," I say, though it's Leigh who awaits me. We are going to Story Hour at the library.

I gather my belongings, say goodbye to Chloe, and hail a taxi. I stare out the window as the driver careens through the park. Trees, cars, a line of cyclists in neon vests.

My own reflection, startling me. I don't know if I'm on the inside looking out, or on the outside looking in.

LEIGH
THE HORSES
1994

You can have all the guys you want.

Leigh took Connor's words as a manifesto. She knew he meant there would be other boys in her future—but, really, there was no reason to confine his words to a future Leigh. *All the guys she wanted* could happen right now.

It didn't mean she was a slut. A slut fucked anyone who would have her—to get attention, please others, whatever. Leigh fucked to please herself. She was the one who decided yes, no, or maybe later. Deciding felt good, even better than sex. When she passed Blake in the hall, she looked right through him. He was nothing, like a telephone pole or a mailbox. She'd screw every other boy in the school before she let Blake near her again.

Leigh was sure her mother would have a fit if she knew because her mother was a one-at-a-time person. She remembered the years before Connor, when her mother had one boyfriend after another. Always someone, rummaging in the kitchen for a corkscrew or sitting at the breakfast table in a tee shirt.

Most of them ignored her, but there was one who really did like her. Devin, who introduced her to the joy of riding. He had a tattoo of a hummingbird on his left shoulder and a blond ponytail and, most of all, a horse named Annie Oakley that he kept at the Claremont Stables in Central Park. At eight, Leigh had been in love with horses, the idea of horses. She'd never actually ridden one, not until Devin, whose entrance into her life felt like the most amazing gift. Then her mother broke up with him, for no reason that Leigh could see, and she was furious because it meant the end of her Thursday afternoons with Annie Oakley.

Her mother had seemed surprised that riding meant so much to her and, in one of the grandest gestures of Leigh's childhood, said of course she could take lessons, real lessons, money was no issue. Leigh understood, then, that someone had given them a lot of money. Her mother asked if she remembered a man with blue eyes named Michael, and she said, "A little," which seemed closer to what her mother wanted to hear than, "Not really."

She'd been eight when Devin showed her how to mount and dismount, how to shift her weight and let Annie Oakley know when she wanted to break into a canter. She was twice that age now—tossing her commands at boys, who were stupider than horses, and not as nice—but she still rode whenever she could. Riding was the best way to forget herself. To become pure movement, pure air, free from the rage that seethed beneath her skin.

After Blake, she'd thought that the power to pick and discard her partners would get rid of the anger, but it didn't. She was angry at stupid things instead, things that didn't even matter. Zippers that got stuck, shampoo bottles that slipped from her fingers.

Not at Connor, whom she liked, though she wished they had moved to his farm instead of him moving down here. She would never have met Blake if she lived on the farm. Just a kid on a tractor, suntanned and sweet. Her mother thought she was doing Leigh a great big favor by getting her into one of those swanky private schools, but she was wrong. Those schools were full of assholes like Blake.

She was never angry at the horses, though she was angry *for* them. Anyone could tell that they wanted to be free. She always whispered *sorry* and *thank you* when she put her foot in the stirrup. Because no one ever asked, or even wondered, if they were willing to carry those great big humans on their backs. The horses were more powerful than the people, but they didn't act like they were. They just stood there, letting people throw big heavy saddles on their beautiful bodies and climb on top. They never even tried to shake them off.

Leigh talked to them, thanked them, but it wasn't enough because she was still doing the exact same thing that everyone else was doing. That summer, eleven months after Blake Rasmussen raped her behind the gym, Leigh decided that she was a hypocrite for feeling the way she did, but continuing to ride. Maybe she couldn't set the horses free, but she could stop being someone who used them.

She gave up the horses. Told them goodbye, as tears ran down her cheeks and she didn't even try to stop them. Because every living thing, even a horse, ought to be able to say what it wanted to carry and what it didn't.

The horses were the third marker. The loss of the horses.

Those were the first stones on the path.

BABY BELUGA

1984

Chloe Bernard shows up at the apartment on a rainy April afternoon. It's too wet to go to the park, so I'm coloring with Leigh at the kitchen table while a roast slow-cooks in the oven. There's a cassette player on the counter made of child-friendly red and yellow plastic, and the cheerful sounds of Raffi singing "Baby Beluga" fill the room.

Baby Beluga in the deep blue sea / Swim so wild and you swim so free.

There's a buzz from the intercom that connects us with the doorman. I hold up a finger, signaling to Leigh that I'll only be a moment.

I press a button on the wall. "Yes? Is there a package for us?"

"No, ma'am," the doorman replies. His voice, usually so polite, is guarded. "There's a young lady here to see you. A Miss Bernard."

Chloe, here? Then I remember the signed Levertov and my offer to stop by. I'm surprised that she has simply appeared, without calling first, though it seems like the sort of thing Chloe would do. "Right," I tell him. "Send her up, please. It's fine."

"Very well." I can hear him warning me to be careful. It's probably Chloe's outlandish attire, and I feel a dart of annoyance. *She's a graduate student, you know.* But I say nothing. There is no upside to pissing off a New York City doorman.

"Mommy has a friend coming up," I tell Leigh. "We might go in the living room to talk. Do you remember how to rewind and hit *play*? Or do you need me to show you?"

Leigh gives me a haughty look. "I can do it myself."

"That's wonderful," I say. "I'll be right in the living room, just in case."

The doorbell rings, and I hurry to answer. Chloe storms past me. "Thank God," she says, her voice loud. "I need to borrow your car. You do have a car, right?"

I step back, startled by her brusqueness. "Hey, catch me up." I close the door and motion her toward the living room, away from Leigh.

Chloe is too hyped-up to realize that I'm steering her down the hall, slowing her down. "I need it right now," she announces. "It's an emergency. A fucking cluster-fuck, to be exact."

She rakes her fingers through her hair, which is already wild. I'm aware of an odd smell, like vinegar. Then I realize it's coming from Chloe. Because she's drunk.

I lower my voice, hoping Chloe will follow my lead. Leigh is two rooms away, but she has an uncanny ability to pick up words I'd rather she didn't hear, like *fucking cluster-fuck.* "What's going on?"

Chloe whirls around, registers the size and décor of the living room. "Whoa. You've been holding out on me, girlfriend. I knew you had a Sugar-Daddy, but this is *mega.*" She gives me an arch look. "Your car must be, like, a Beamer, right?"

"Chloe," I repeat. "What is going on?"

Finally, she focuses on me. "I need to get out to Montclair to catch Travis with that bitch, and I need to do it right now. I need your Beamer."

"Chloe." I feel like a parent. "Who is Travis?"

Her eyes are slits. "My supposed boyfriend."

Enough pieces are coming together for me to know that Chloe behind a wheel is not a good idea. The smell of alcohol has gotten stronger. Then I frown, confused. I thought Captain Morgan was just for the nighttime, so she could sleep after her three jobs.

"I'm in a hurry," she says. "Just give me the keys. I'll bring it back before Sugar Daddy gets home."

She's pacing around the room now, touching one object after another. I'm starting to feel nervous. We do have a car, but it's Michael's, not mine. And I'm not about to loan it to a woman who's clearly had too much to drink.

"It's not my car," I tell her. "It's not mine to loan."

"Oh for Chrissakes. What's mine is thine. Isn't that the marriage vow?"

She sweeps her hand toward the suede couch, the paintings, the jade statues of Kwan Yin and Ganesha at either end of a polished credenza. Her face turns hard. "It's just a car. I didn't ask you for your signed *Levertov*."

I'm shocked by the ugliness in her voice. I tell myself that her hostility is just a projection onto me, her friend, of the hurt and anger she feels toward this Travis person. That part is okay, sort of. But it's not okay for her to think I'm some kind of coddled rich girl who doesn't know what it is to work for a living.

Her lip curls. "Just lift the damn rock, Arden. It's not that big. Ask your servants to help."

"You're drunk," I tell her. "I'm not giving Michael's car keys to a person who's drunk. I don't care who Travis is screwing."

We lock eyes. She is daring me to refuse her.

"Whose side are you on?"

"That's not the point."

"You need to give me those keys, Arden."

"I don't *need* to give you anything." This is not a cappuccino. "And it's not a Beamer."

"I thought you were my friend." She's still angry, but there is something else there too. Panic. Fear. Then she lashes out again. "Why are you so fucking selfish? What the hell is your problem?"

The two of us are only inches apart, locked in a tableau that seems both artificial and hyper-real. I feel the blood moving through my body, beneath my skin.

I think of all the people who have helped me. My brother Hugh. The De Lucas. Juliet Montgomery. Michael.

I want to repay that generosity. I want to be a person who gives, helps, saves her friends, when no one else will. Moves the fallen concrete. But what Chloe is asking is impossible. I have no doubt about the disaster that would ensue if I let her drive Michael's car out of the underground garage. I won't do it.

But I'm not selfish. That part isn't fair.

There are two, equally impossible options: helping and refusing to help. Yet I need to do something. Something else, a third thing.

Chloe's eyes glisten with angry, reproachful tears. "You have everything. Just look at you." She gestures at the living room again, the piano and paintings and expensive rugs. "Who the fuck do you think you are to say no, when you have everything?"

I do, I have so much, and it fills me with shame. There's no reason for me to have all this, while Chloe has to wipe tables and smile for tips at a Village bar.

I can't give her Michael's Audi. But I can balance the scale. Let her know that my life isn't as perfect as she imagines. That way, she won't feel so bitter. She won't hate me. She will stay my friend.

"I don't have everything," I say.

She eyes the rugs and piano with distaste. "Could have fooled me."

"I don't," I repeat. There is a moment when I can stop, before saying what I am about to say. When I haven't yet seized on the idea that her compassion will mitigate my refusal to help. When I can spare Michael, instead of throwing him at Chloe like a worthless card in a competition for who was dealt the worst hand.

Then the moment is gone. It's too fast, the stop-and-reconsider option zips past, because I am too impatient to get this done.

"I really don't," I tell her. She gives me a disbelieving look, and then I say it. "Michael isn't my Sugar Daddy. He can't get it up."

As soon as the words are out, I am filled with horror.

We stare at each other. "Whoa," Chloe says. "Travis might fuck other women, but at least he fucks me too." Then she starts to laugh. It's not an amused laugh. It's mean. "Just like the Beatles said. *Can't buy me love.* Thank goodness he's got a great big *car.*" She cracks up, delighted by her joke.

"Stop it, Chloe." I can't believe that I've betrayed Michael. I didn't even explain the reason. There's no time now. I just need Chloe to shut up.

"It's too hilarious." She can barely contain herself.

"You can't tell anyone," I hiss. "I mean it."

"I can't? Because why? Did we make some kind of deal that I missed?"

"Chloe. Please." If this is a ploy to get me to buy her silence with the car keys, I can't do it. I can only beg her, for the sake of our friendship. The irony isn't lost on me. It's the same friendship she invoked as a reason to help her, though I wouldn't. "This isn't about me. It's about someone's dignity. His privacy."

"That you violated." Her voice is cold. All signs of drunkenness have vanished. "It was your idea, girlfriend. I didn't make you tell me."

My heart is beating so loudly that it's drowning out the sound of Raffi's voice in the kitchen, a thousand miles away.

Baby Beluga in the deep blue sea / Swim so wild and you swim so free.

"Hate me, if you want," I tell her. "But leave Michael alone. He hasn't done anything to you."

Chloe lifts a shoulder. "I'll think about it."

I search desperately for something to offer, threaten, implore. But I have nothing except a fading hope for her mercy. And money. I have money.

"I can give you taxi fare to Montclair," I say. "Round trip."

There's no mistaking Chloe's disgust. "Why not have your chauffeur drive me?" Then she flicks her hair, pushes it away from her face. "I don't even care anymore. Let the two of them fuck their brains out."

She glances at the open doorway, toward the kitchen, where music is playing and Leigh is happily coloring. "Your little girl?"

I want to cry, "Don't hurt her!" But that's crazy. Chloe hasn't threatened my child. The only person in danger of getting hurt is Michael, and whose fault is that?

I nod, terrified of saying the wrong thing. Then Chloe waves her hand, dismissing me. "Whatever. I have to go." Before I can react, she's crossed the room, flung open the door. Left.

I wipe my face, realizing that I'm drenched with sweat. Raffi's voice fills the apartment.

I have no idea what ensues with the faithless Travis because there are no more Thursday cappuccino dates. Chloe and I avoid each other for the rest of the semester. I dare to hope that she has let the whole thing go.

For a while, it seems that she has. Then the spring semester grades are posted. I receive an A in our poetry class. Chloe Bernard, a B.

Ten days later, the postcards start arriving. They are handmade rectangles, each a split-screen. On the left, there are photos of phallic-looking objects, cacti and zucchini. On the right, wilted stalks. Across the left-hand photo, in bold black letters: *Not You.* Across the right: *You.*

The postcards are addressed to Michael Rice at our address because Chloe doesn't know that we have different last names. When I pull the first postcard from the little cubicle, I give a thank-you to the gods, the universe, that I was the one to get the mail and not Michael.

My relief is short-lived. I know, somehow, that there will be more postcards, and I can't be sure that I'll always be the one to unlock the glass door to the cubicle that holds our mail. If Michael gets there first, it will be unbearable.

I ask the doorman if he can hold our mail behind the desk, or change the lock for the little glass door, or buzz me when the mailman comes. He explains, sternly, that it's illegal to interfere with US Mail. Only the mailman has a master key, not him.

I understand, apologize. I just have to get there first every single day until Chloe tires of her game. Michael can't know about this.

There is something else he can't know. I have another secret, and it is just as brutal and unshareable as this one.

I pretend. My pleasure is false.

It wasn't, at first. But we have been together for three years, and now it is.

A chill passes through me. Maybe the two things Michael can't know are connected.

I am a model wife all summer. I find exhibits of experimental art and off-Broadway plays for us to attend. I am enthusiastic in bed. I get the mail every morning while Michael is in the shower. Sometimes there are handmade postcards, sometimes not.

Leigh learns to swim. In September, she will enter kindergarten. In November, I will turn thirty. Michael will be fifty-three. Technically, he could be my father, although my actual father is fifty-nine and playing golf in Tucson. I have no idea where Leigh's actual father is.

Savannah turns twenty-one. She's preparing to enter her senior year at Vassar and has a summer job interning at a literary agency in Manhattan. She stays with Kira for the eight weeks of the internship but comes to visit us at the end of August. The plan, as in past years, is that we will drive her back to Vassar for the first day of class.

This year, however, Michael has to go to Chicago on business; it's a last-minute trip and can't be changed. I offer to drive Savannah myself.

It's not a difficult drive—the Taconic is easy, bucolic, with its greenery and gentle curves. I don't want to bring Leigh, though. Three hours is too long for her to be content with coloring books and Connect-the-Dots and no mother to entertain her in the back seat. I arrange for Veronica, the babysitter, to watch her while I'm gone.

When Leigh hears of the plan, she starts to cry. She doesn't want Savannah to leave. Somehow, during Savannah's four-day visit, she has concluded that Savannah is finished with college and will be moving in with us.

Savannah kneels and puts her arms around my little girl. "I have to go to school," she says, "just like you. Only my school is starting first. But hey, we can send each other pictures, whenever we want. Like pen pals, only drawings, until you learn to write."

"I can write," Leigh says. She means: her name, and a few words.

Savannah feigns amazement. "You're kidding, right?" Leigh shakes her head, and Savannah says, "That is *awesome.*"

Leigh's chin is still quivering, but there's a hint of a smile. Then she breaks free and runs to her room. I'm worried that she's truly upset, but she returns a moment later with the stuffed whale she got at the aquarium. "Here," she tells Savannah. "It's Baby Beluga. You take him. He'll keep you company."

Savannah accepts the stuffed animal and gives Leigh a kiss on the forehead. "He'll go right on my pillow," she says. "As long as he doesn't snore?"

"He doesn't snore," Leigh promises.

I like Savannah so much right now, and I can't help thinking that some kind of truce might be possible after all. Leigh hugs her tightly, and then, finally, we are ready to leave.

Savannah and I carry her belongings to the elevator and descend to the lobby. There, we will switch to the service elevator that will take us to the underground garage where Michael's Audi is parked.

As we're about to pass the reception desk and the wall of brass-trimmed mailboxes, a couple enters from the street, shaking out their umbrellas. "Is it raining?" I ask.

"Just started," the man says.

"Damn." I turn to Savannah. "I'll run back and get an umbrella."

"Want me to go?"

"No, better not," I tell her. "Leigh will get all worked up again. You stay here with your stuff. I'll be right back."

I return with an umbrella for each of us. We retrieve the Audi and head north.

We've just passed the exit for Carmel and Cold Spring when Savannah turns to me and says, "Oh, wait. I forgot to give you the mail."

A stone drops in my chest. "The mail?"

"The mailman came while you were upstairs getting the umbrellas. The old guy, the one who used to give me the supermarket flyers and Chinese takeout menus? I guess you didn't know me then, but he still remembered me, can you believe it? I told him, hey, just give the stuff to me, you'll be back in a second. Only, duh, I forgot all about it." She reaches into her tote bag, pulls out a stack of mail, and begins flipping through the bills and magazines.

"It's fine," I say, though fear is inching its way up my spine. "Just throw everything in the back seat."

Savannah isn't listening. "Dad's old prep school, looking for a nice long drink from the money faucet—after, like, thirty years? I mean, *really.*"

I pray there's no postcard from Chloe. "Thanks for getting it," I say. My throat constricts, but I force the words out because I need her to do what I say. "Just toss it in the back, like I said."

Savannah doesn't answer. She's still looking through the papers. Then she says, "What the hell?"

And I know. My heart plummets. It seems so unfair, after a whole summer when I've tried so hard.

She holds up the postcard. "What's this supposed to be? It looks like a limp dick."

I try not to panic. I can still save this. It's just a picture.

"And why is it addressed to Dad as Michael *Rice*? He's not Rice. You are."

I tell myself that I am the teacher and she is the student. *I can handle this.*

"Just someone being stupid, I guess."

"But why?" she insists. "Why would someone call Dad a limp prick? It's like, really hostile."

I desperately want to wave her question away, but my hands are clenching the steering wheel and won't let go.

Then her eyes widen. "Shit. What if Dad tried to cheat on you, and she got pissed off because he couldn't perform?"

I begin to tremble. Why is this conversation happening while I'm driving at sixty miles an hour? "No," I manage. "It's nothing like that."

Savannah pounces on my reply. "How do you know?"

"Trust me. It's not."

"Then what is it? Why would a person send him that?" She eyes me suspiciously. "You're covering for him. He cheated on you, didn't he?"

I can feel her outrage spiral. In her fantasy, Michael has betrayed not only me, but her mother Kira—spurned her again, for a nameless woman Savannah has invented.

The steering wheel is jiggling like crazy now. I'm terrified that we're going to crash. I need to focus on the road, and I need to focus on this conversation which is entering a collision course of its own. The fork ahead comes into focus: Michael Tate, who cheats on his wife, or Michael Tate, who can no longer have an erection. I need to choose, quickly. Philandering seems worse than impotent. It's selfish and cruel. Michael isn't like that.

I choose victim for Michael Tate, not villain. I choose the truth, which is what he always wants. I think I am taking the kinder path, but I am not.

I tighten my grip on the wheel. "Because I told her."

Savannah doesn't understand. "Told her that Dad was fucking around?"

"Told her that Dad can't fuck around."

"What do you mean, *can't*?" Savannah is growing angry with me. "No man is too pure and noble for *can't*. Even Dad. Sorry."

She is going to make me say this. I feel the words form in my mouth. I tell myself it's the only way.

"*Can't*, Savannah. Even with me."

It takes her a moment to process what I've said. And when she does, she is furious.

"You told some woman, some *friend* of yours, that Dad can't get it up? You gossiped about Dad's penis like it was some kind of *topic of conversation*?"

I try to explain about the prostate cancer, but Savannah slams her hands over her ears. "Just shut up!" she yells. "I don't want to hear about your sex life. Leave me alone."

"Savannah. There's more to the—"

But she shouts, "I said *shut up!*" and flings the mail into the back seat. It scatters everywhere. Then she yanks her headphones out of the tote bag and jams them on her head. I try to talk to her when we arrive at Vassar, but she won't take the headphones off, won't even look at me. She walks fast, pulling a suitcase with each arm. I follow, carrying the typewriter and hair dryer. The soft little body of the stuffed whale is pressed under my arm.

When we get to Savannah's room, I set the typewriter and hair dryer on the desk and lay Baby Beluga between them. Savannah's back is still turned, but the headphones are off—she had to remove them when she checked in—so I try once more. "You don't want to talk to me, okay. But give your dad the courtesy of asking for the whole story."

I wait, but she won't answer. Finally, I leave, drive home.

That's the last time I see her.

I don't know if Savannah will actually talk with Michael or whether I want her to. One minute I tell myself that she is twenty-one years old, not a child, and needs to understand that this has nothing to do with her father's innate virility. Then, the next minute, I just want her to forget that the horrible conversation ever took place.

But Michael makes an unplanned stop to see her on his way back from Chicago, three days later. Regretting that he didn't get to send his daughter off for her senior year, he reroutes into Stewart Airport, rents a car, and takes her out for dinner at a scenic restaurant on the Hudson, where she tells him how his replacement wife has mocked and betrayed him to her friends.

Savannah is the lacrosse star in the school cafeteria, in charge of the narrative; her father is her audience. She spares him nothing.

When Michael comes home and confronts me, I can't stop crying. I try to explain about Chloe and how angry she was at her boyfriend—and at me, for the big expensive apartment—but none of it makes sense and it doesn't change what I did.

I hate myself, and I want Michael to hate me too. With wrath comes punishment, and with punishment the possibility of atonement. But that is not Michael's style. He listens to my weeping confession and says, "I knew it was a risk, the first time I asked you to dinner." His voice is flat. "Realistically, something was bound to happen, sooner or later. A secret lover, a chain of one-night stands."

"Never." I'm sobbing now. "I never did any of those things."

He is unmoved. "It took a different form. The point is the same."

I don't understand how he can be so cold and rational. I thought he cared about me. I thought our life together mattered to him. And then I do understand—because this is Michael Tate, who needs to stay in control.

"It's fortunate," he says, "that your so-called friend didn't know my actual name. If she had, the fallout would have been difficult to contain."

He means in the business world. I nod, grateful that he's been spared that particular humiliation.

But there is still Savannah. It's hard to imagine that she didn't run to Kira with her fury, her gift.

Michael doesn't mention Kira, but we both know what Kira can do with a grenade like this. Perhaps she will wait, saving the weapon for when she needs it most. As long as she waits, makes him wonder, she has the power to hurt him.

Pride, power, control—the pillars of Michael's manhood. I have handed Kira the means to castrate him more surely than the disease ever could. I'm sure it's a greater victory than she ever hoped for.

I don't say any of this. I don't have to.

I think we have passed through the worst of the conversation, but Michael is not finished.

"Whatever your friend—"

I cringe at his use of that word for Chloe Bernard. I want to tell him that she is not a friend, but he doesn't let me interrupt.

"—decides to hurl at a fictitious Michael Rice won't land anywhere. There is no Michael Rice. But there is us. You and me."

He pauses. It's not a hesitation; it's a space, to underscore what he will say next.

"We had an understanding," he says. "Trust, respect, privacy. A foundation on which everything rested."

Yes, of course. I can't seem to stop nodding, like a bobble-head doll. "We did. Do."

"Did."

"Please." I start to beg. It's all mixed up now. My feeling for Michael, my fear of losing him, my terror at what I've done and who I am. My teeth are chattering. I want to throw up.

Michael's eyes are the icy blue of a fjord. "It's over, Arden. There's no going back. You know it too."

I shake my head. *No.* I am sobbing so hard I can scarcely breathe. But Michael is a businessman. When a trust has been broken, it can't be restored. The merger is dissolved.

We divorce. We have a pre-marital agreement, but Michael gives me far more than I am entitled to, or deserve. He gives me the apartment as well, explaining that he doesn't want to evict Leigh from her home, her neighborhood, her school. When I object, he says that he prefers not to live there anymore.

I agree to his offer; how can I not? I want my daughter to have this apartment, this life. She has lost her third father, so I will give her the room with the apricot-colored walls, the matching pillows and comforter that she chose herself.

I am aware of how painful it will be for me to live in the apartment without Michael. I agree to that pain.

I have to say something to my parents. I can't tell them what I did to ruin our marriage because that would mean telling them about Michael's condition. Instead, I choose the other road, the one I didn't take with Savannah. I make Michael the villain, a rich SOB who grew tired of me. I am certain he would prefer their rage to their pity. I do it for him.

My misery allows my parents to feel needed, to comfort their daughter, though for the wrong reason. It's a solace I haven't earned but I accept because it makes them happy to be needed.

I do these things privately; unlike Savanah, I have no audience. It is a thin, bitter consolation to know that I have finally done something for the good of others, even if none of them know it.

After Michael and I divorce, I embark on the chain of meaningless affairs that he predicted. It lasts for a surprisingly long time.

I abandon my plan to get a PhD and take a job teaching literacy and creative writing to incarcerated women. They are not sweet like the girls at my first school nor clever and ambitious like the girls at Brenner, but they need me. I need them too. I don't feel like a bad person while I'm helping them with their sentences and stories.

It is through one of the women, in fact, that I learn that Jonah Orenstein has become a successful musician. His band released an album that was named one of the best, and best-selling, albums of the year. Delilah and her sister just love his songs. She wants to write lyrics like his when she gets out.

I am glad for Jonah but say nothing about knowing him— not to Delilah and not to Leigh. Leigh is too young for his kind of music. Even if she weren't and happened to come across his album, there seems little chance that she would make the connection between their last names.

Then Leigh turns eleven, and I decide that I am done with men forever. I turn my fervor to teaching and writing. Eighteen months later, I take my daughter to the Southwest for the summer. I want her to see the stark beauty of Bryce Canyon, the

Vermilion Cliffs, Ghost Ranch—a different kind of beauty that makes me feel clean and strong. We return to New York, and she begins eighth grade. She chooses sustainable farming for a class project. We visit a farm near Red Hook. A man gives us a basket of apples.

Some years later, a number of treatments are approved by the FDA for prostate-related impotence. There are injections, pumps, and medications, all with a high success rate. Michael is in excellent health, so it's reasonable to expect that they would have worked for him. I like to think that they did.

There is a pattern, clearly. Is it my fault, for not being able to wait?

Then again, if I had waited, there would have been no visit to the McRae farm, no basket of apples, and no marriage to Connor—with whom, at last, I stop measuring the size of the dung ball I am pushing, and let myself be happy.

PART THREE

AIR INTO LIGHT

CALL ME

2013

Just when Arden had given up, there it was: a response from Robert Altschuler.

"Of course I remember you," he had written. "It was a long time ago, but we had some great adventures. I don't think people can do that sort of thing anymore, Europe on ten dollars a day. When my twins went to Spain for three weeks, they could hardly get lunch for ten dollars. And that was per person."

Arden had to stop reading to let his words register. Their chattiness astounded her. Didn't he hate her for ruining his life—unless, somehow, she hadn't? There were twins, for one thing. That, presumably, meant a partner who didn't think he liked to have sex with boys.

She adjusted the angle of the screen, then returned to his message. "Sorry it took me so long to answer," Robert continued, "but we were up at our cabin, and there's no internet. Quentin and Caleb, my twins, came up too, so it got pretty hectic, as you can imagine."

No, Arden couldn't imagine. Who *was* this person? He was

nothing like she had pictured. A family man, with a regular house and a cabin. Not a miserable pariah who could never get another job. She was glad for him but confused.

"Anyway," he wrote, "it's nice to hear from you and I hope you're doing well. I wonder if there's a particular reason you contacted me, since you didn't say. Or were you interested in ordering some of the photos and wondered if it was the same person you knew from way back when?"

Arden remembered the images on his Facebook page, close-ups of water and reeds and insect wings. Robert must be some kind of photographer. Not a librarian. Not someone whose life was ruined by a reckless young woman who had thought, at twenty-four, that she had the right to do whatever she wanted.

She sat back, staring at his message, as everything came back to her. The train to Istanbul, and the boy with all of Castaneda's books in his backpack. The rolling sea and a sky filled with stars, on the journey from Piraeus to Alexandria. Mangos and flies in Cairo. And, yes, Luxor. A restaurant by the Nile, strung with red and blue lights. She wondered what Robert remembered from that time. Different things, certainly. He would have no memory of the underwear she had thrown on the ground, the call to room service. Their wild erotic coupling—yes, he would remember that, because it was so unlike them.

It had, of course, led to Leigh. And now that he had responded, she needed to tell him about Leigh. And Danielle. That was the reason she had reached out, not to hear about his cabin and his twins.

"I'm really glad you answered," she wrote. "There are some things I need to tell you, so I'd like to move this conversation to the phone, if that's okay? Here's my number. Call any time." Then she hit the little blue arrow for *send*.

She gazed at the iPad and wondered, suddenly, if telling

Robert about Leigh even mattered. It had seemed so important when Leigh died, a way to restore something she had taken from both of them. Now, she wasn't sure. Did she really want to tell Robert Altschuler that the daughter he never knew had grown up to be a careless and selfish parent? Why not leave him in peace with his new children? Quentin. Caleb.

Still, she would do it for Danielle. Robert needed to know about Danielle. For that, he needed to know about Leigh.

Meanwhile, she had to talk to another absent father, that imbecile Ivan Chernowski.

Just thinking about Ivan made her livid. Why hadn't he simply claimed Danielle, rescued her, instead of asking a ten-year-old to gather *evidence* by taking pictures of naked men? It felt cowardly and exploitive. Pornographic.

It was one thing to relinquish custody because he, quote, wasn't in a position to take care of a child, another thing to use that child to get revenge on her mother. Clenching her teeth, Arden left Ivan a not-nice message saying that they needed to talk.

It struck her that she ought to get in touch with Eleanor Cardoza too. The therapist needed to know what Danielle had told her about the naked men—who had been real, not like Leigh speaking from the grave. Another answering machine. Another voicemail.

This was impossible—especially when the person Arden really wanted to talk to, Leigh Alexandra Orenstein, was no longer available to answer the questions that were pounding in her brain.

Did you ever think about Danielle, instead of yourself? The messages you were sending, how they were affecting her?

Were you a bad mother?

You were, weren't you? But why?

It felt unfair, almost spiteful, after all the things she had done for Leigh. The flight from Jonah Orenstein. The move to Riverside Drive. The museums and lessons and unwavering devotion—none of it had made Leigh into someone who wanted to give her daughter the care and consideration that she herself had received.

Arden pushed the iPad across the desk. She rose, stormed into the kitchen, and flung open the refrigerator, as if the answers she needed were hidden inside.

The perishables were neatly arranged on the transparent shelves. Milk and freshly squeezed orange juice on the tallest shelf. A plate of cheese, covered with plastic wrap. A bowl of clementines and organic grapes.

She wanted to knock all of it to the floor. What good did it do, to be so diligent? She might as well have fed her daughter chips and candy—because she didn't, didn't understand how a girl who had been so carefully tended could have turned into someone who let her sexual playmates walk around naked in front of her daughter.

Leigh had marched for voting rights and the ethical treatment of animals. At thirteen, she already believed in the elimination of fossil fuels and eco-conscious farming. It was Leigh who had insisted on the visit to the McRae farm.

Arden slammed the refrigerator door as hard as she could. Thinking about Leigh hurt. Remembering that day at the McRae farm hurt too. It all hurt.

Connor, alive. Leaning against the side of the farmhouse with his long legs and suntanned arms, talking so casually about being celibate. He had seemed both arrogant and naïve.

The same way he'd looked, later, when he explained the virtues of polyamory. No one left out, everyone equal.

Arden froze, as one thought followed the next.

If Connor had been capable of that kind of arrogant naïveté back then, when he was already a grown man, who could say that he wasn't capable of a similar arrogance, a few years later? Perhaps not as something to act on, but as a way to impress Leigh, who looked up to him.

Connor would have liked impressing Leigh with his knowledge of polyamory; it was just the sort of boundary-pushing behavior that appealed to her. And he loved the thrill of admiration. Maybe he thought he'd outgrown it, but no one really outgrew something like that. All it needed was the right set of circumstances.

Just look at her. Every time she felt trapped, when she couldn't sit still a second longer, she had done the same kind of rash, hurtful thing that she swore she would never do again.

Danielle was watching a movie in her room, supposedly for a history project, so Arden opened the cherrywood cabinet where Connor kept his best selection of spirits and poured herself a shot of Glen Fiddich.

It was an evening for Scotch, that was for sure. Arden wasn't really a drinker, but she yearned for something to quiet her roiling thoughts. Connor. Robert. And Leigh, at the center of everything.

She took a sip of the Glen Fiddich, then set the glass on top of the cabinet and pulled an album from one of the shelves.

Leigh's high school years. Arden was happily married to Connor, who loved her as madly as she loved him; Leigh was busy with tennis, snowboarding, championing the rights of animals and the disabled. She had stopped riding, something Arden had never imagined Leigh would do, but her new passions seemed equally absorbing. There were family vacations, holidays, pizza and a Blockbuster video on Fridays.

Arden flipped through the album, looking for a sign she had missed. But there was nothing. Whatever had tipped Leigh onto a different path must have happened later. Or earlier. Arden pulled another album from the shelf. Leigh at twelve, when they were in the Southwest. The photos she had taken at Slot Canyon and the Vermilion Cliffs, a landscape sculpted in russet and crimson.

There were no answers in that album either, nor in the earlier albums. Arden turned the pages from back to front, watching Leigh get younger. In front of the Christmas tree in Rockefeller Plaza. Perched on the Alice in Wonderland statue in Central Park with a tutu on her head. At the beach, with a yellow bucket and shovel.

Leigh had liked to pour water on the sand and watch it disappear. "But where is it *now*?" she would ask. "Where did it *go*?"

Like a person's life. You poured your acts, good and bad, onto the sand. Then they were gone. Attempts to be good, failures to be good.

The albums were strewn across the carpet when Danielle burst into the room, complaining loudly. "That was such a dumb movie. They didn't—" She stopped, frowning at the open pages. "That's Mom."

"It is." Arden felt a ping, like the sound of a bell. *Pay attention. Mark this.*

She watched as Danielle toed one of the albums. It was open to a page with pictures of Leigh at ten or eleven, at the height of her obsession with horses. Leigh was standing with her arm around a chestnut-colored horse, in a round helmet and a bright blue jersey with CLAREMONT 175 W89 stitched on the front pocket.

"What's Claremont 175?" Danielle asked.

Arden peered at the photo. "Claremont was the stable where

your mom used to ride. 175 is part of the address. See? 175 West Eighty-Ninth Street."

Danielle nodded. "That's how Mom looked when she talked to me last night."

Arden gave her a careful look. "You mean, that's how you saw her in your mind, when you thought about her last night."

"No. It's how she really looked."

"Sweetheart." Arden let out her breath. "You know your mom is dead. And when she died, she was a full-grown woman."

"Well, duh. That was when she died. I'm talking about how she looks now."

Arden prayed that Eleanor Cardoza would choose this moment to return her call so she could put Danielle on the phone and let Eleanor handle it. But Eleanor didn't. It was only her.

"Danielle," she said. "How could your mother be ten years old again?"

She meant the question as a nudge toward rationality, but Danielle seemed to take it as a request for more information. "I think she wanted us to be the same age when she talked to me."

"When she talked to you."

Danielle gave another nod. Arden fought to stay calm. "And what did she say?"

"That she was sorry. She didn't mean it."

Complicated grief, Arden thought. The naked men in the hallway. Whack, whack, swinging between his legs. *No one cared if I was there.*

The real Leigh never said: *I'm so sorry, honey.* Or: *Hey, cover up, my daughter lives here too.* Then she died, and Danielle created an imaginary Leigh who came back from her green grave to apologize and explain that she hadn't really meant it.

It was brilliant and heart-breaking, like the magical thinking that Eleanor Cardoza had described. Danielle would fix what her mother had broken, replace the indifferent mother she'd had with the remorseful mother she'd needed.

Arden looked at her granddaughter. "Didn't mean what?"

Danielle folded her arms. "She did mean it, though. You can tell when someone means what they're saying."

Saying? The way Danielle had related the story of the naked man, Leigh hadn't said anything at all. That was the point. All the things Leigh hadn't said, like *sorry* and *you can't do that* and *my child comes first.*

Arden had been certain that Danielle was talking about what Leigh actually *did.* Smirked, winked. That was why she had to bring her mother back. To undo it.

And yet, Danielle was literal, precise. If she used the word *say,* it was because she was referring to something her mother had actually said. Arden wished, again, that Eleanor was there to rescue her. At the very least, to tell her what to do.

She cleared her throat. "Sometimes," she told Danielle, "*I didn't mean it* is a way of saying that you really wish you hadn't said something because you only felt it for one tiny second."

Danielle gave a skeptical look. "But that one tiny second counts. You can't say that you never meant it."

"Only for a second. And then she was so, so sorry."

Arden had no idea what they were talking about. She was inventing a story about what Leigh had said to her daughter, hoping it would somehow lead to the truth. Or, if not the truth, to some kind of solace.

"Maybe." Danielle shrugged. "She said she was sorry, but I don't think she was." Then she gave the album a little kick. "Anyway, I just wanted to let you know that I watched the whole documentary and that counts as an hour of history. I already did my math, so I'm done."

Before Arden could decide how to reply, Danielle spoke

again. "Can I play *The Sims* now? They have a new houseboat."

Arden blinked. "Yes, of course."

A moment later, Danielle was gone. Slowly, Arden pushed the photos into a pile. So many versions of Leigh, strewn across the carpet, and no way to fit them together.

She checked her messages one more time. No one had called back.

WAIT AGAIN TILL NEVER

2013

The therapist, social worker, and court-appointed guardian ad litem, whose job was to represent the best interests of the child, were in agreement: Danielle would stay with her grandmother for the next six months, subject to home visits to monitor her mental and physical wellbeing, with permanent custody to be determined at the end of that period. Therapy needed to continue. A suitable school near her grandmother's residence needed to be found.

Arden contacted an educational consultant, who arranged visits to three well-regarded schools that were willing to consider a midyear applicant. Danielle seemed to accept her fate and stopped talking about being a child star while she went on tour with her father.

Ivan himself had faded back into his role as absentee parent. Yes, the arrangement was fine. Arden was better than Leigh, who'd been a hedonist bitch. And yes, he had maybe, sort of, not seriously, suggested that Danielle collect photos as evidence. Sorry.

Robert texted that he'd be glad to talk, but could it wait a week or two? Things were kind of crazy right now, with Caleb's wife about to give birth, which meant he was about to be a grandfather.

Arden had to stop herself from typing, "You already are a grandfather." "Of course," she replied. It seemed like a small accommodation, given the way she had dismissed him without an ounce of kindness all those years ago.

The goldfish were still alive.

The only one who wasn't all right was Arden herself. She was holding herself together for Danielle, but inside she was struggling not to spiral into despair.

At the center there was grief, so dark and thick that she thought it would squeeze the life out of her too. Around it, anguish at what she had learned about her daughter. And now, winding through all of it, doubt about her husband.

Connor McRae, the man she had loved and trusted. Giving Leigh a noble-sounding name for her promiscuity—because that was what Leigh did, put pretty frames around second-rate photos to make them seem better than they were. Telling her that he'd gone there, too, knowing that would make it seem cool. Showing off.

Arden could see it, hear it. She knew Connor so well.

And then, the worst part. Because she did know him.

Connor wasn't someone who talked one way and acted another. If he praised polyamory, he'd start to think that he ought to practice what he preached. Otherwise, he'd be all talk, a sham.

Connor McRae, putting his ideas into practice, just as he'd done with sustainable farming. But secretly, so she wouldn't know. Lying to her, even about how he spent the last night of his life, in a hotel in Albany. It was possible. Anything was possible.

Arden felt sick. It was the same feeling of a double-loss

that she'd had with Leigh. First, the loss of the flesh-and-blood husband she had known. Then a second loss, of the person in her mind and heart and memory. If that was gone too, she had nothing.

Thanks to the educational consultant, Danielle was spending the morning at Emerson-Alcott, a private school only sixteen blocks away that seemed like an excellent fit. If everything went well, she would enroll.

The half-day at Emerson-Alcott meant that Arden had the apartment to herself for the first time since the train crash. She knew how she wanted to spend those hours.

Connor had a study in the small room off the kitchen that had probably been meant as a maid's room, back when people had live-in maids. Arden had rarely gone in there while he was alive and definitely not since accident. But she went in there now, closing the door tightly behind her, as if to contain whatever she might find: evidence that Connor had encouraged Leigh in the name of polyamory, maybe returned to polyamory himself, or something to prove that he hadn't. She needed to know, one way or another.

The study could have belonged to no one but Connor. An ergonomic desk chair, modern and high tech, paired with a battered wooden desk that was simply old, not antique. Books on every subject, filling the shelves and stacked on top of other books. A reading lamp next to a deep leather chair. Two of the walls were covered with photographs. Some were black-and-white prints: close-ups of jazz musicians, orchids, egrets in flight. Others were brightly-colored compositions: people waiting in a salmon-colored bus shelter, a girl in a blue doorway. There was a Chagall-like rug, a flannel shirt dropped on the back of the leather chair, a Mexican mug half-filled with cold coffee that nearly made Arden burst into tears.

She lifted the shirt and held it in front of her, staring at the red-and-gray plaid. Then she pulled it close to her heart, fingers spread across the flannel, and shut her eyes. The gesture felt melodramatic, but she didn't care. After a minute she opened her eyes and tied the shirt around her shoulders. Then she sat down in the ergonomic chair to do what she had come there to do.

The desk had five drawers: a wide middle drawer and two deep drawers on either side. It seemed like the obvious place to look. Arden rested her hands on the scarred wood, remembering her search of Leigh's bedroom. She had found things in Leigh's nightstand that she hadn't expected and wasn't meant to see. And now, sitting in her husband's chair, about to look through his desk, the tightness in her throat told her that she was about to find something equally private.

She started with the center drawer. There were pens, a checkbook, a valet key for the car. She pulled the drawer all the way out, but its recesses revealed nothing of interest. No surprise. Who kept incriminating evidence in the same drawer as a checkbook, Post-its, and extra staples?

She moved to the side drawers. In the top drawer on the left, there was a folder called "Arden" that made her heart race. But no, it was just the latest W-2 from the university and some bills from the dentist. She rifled through the papers, flipping quickly through the insurance claims and receipts. Then she felt something made of stiffer paper and pulled it free.

It was a poem she had written for Connor, right after the glass of Glen Fiddich in Tarrytown, when everything between them was about to change. So much seemed to be at stake, and she needed him to understand how important it was for her.

A simple turning,
the way a blade of grass,
having barred the light,
can turn, permitting hue.

This woman I more wholly am
might dare a fuller sail this time—
could turn to you, at once,
or wait again till never.

The lines were pasted onto the back of a photo of the Hudson River. Behind it, there were a dozen other cards, valentine and anniversary, some silly and risqué, others tender.

He had saved everything. A man who saved poems and valentines from his wife couldn't possibly have something to hide. This is insane, Arden told herself. She truly didn't think Connor had been unfaithful; if he had, she would have felt it. And yet, the reference to polyamory was too much of a coincidence.

Or maybe it was all vicarious, and Connor had encouraged Leigh to do what he himself hadn't? Maybe he was hoping, through her, to find out what he had missed. It made perfect sense, and it made no sense at all.

There had to be answer—here, in one of the desk drawers. She jerked open the lower drawer, eager to get this over with. Then she had to laugh at herself. It held a flashlight, a pair of wool socks, and a set of old-fashioned metal bookends.

There were papers and folders in the right-hand drawers, but no diary, correspondence with Leigh, or anything remotely related to polyamory. Only manuals for the appliances, copies of his papers on biodiversity, a map of Tuscany from the trip they'd taken last year, along with an English-Italian and Italian-English phrase book.

Arden's amusement turned to annoyance; why was he making this so difficult? Then it struck her: People didn't keep printed copies of things they wanted to hide. It had to be digital. Links, messages, emails.

Connor's phone had been taken by the police, in case it yielded clues to what had happened. Telltale sounds, warnings from the conductor. Evidence that could be used by one of the lawyers in the case against the engineer or in his defense.

She hadn't gotten it back yet, but his laptop was right there, on a green felt pad in the center of the desk. Whatever was on the phone would be on the computer too. She didn't have the password, but it had to be something logical, intuitive.

She pulled the laptop toward her, hit the power button, and waited for it to boot up. After a few moments, the screen filled with the wallpaper Connor had chosen, a photo of the Brooklyn Bridge surrounded by fog. In the center, there was a circle with his face, name, and a blinking bar for the password.

Arden bit her lip and tried to think of what it might be. She tried his birthday, their anniversary, the zip code for the McRae farm. Then she thought: Aha, I know the perfect password for Connor McRae. It was so perfect that she laughed out loud. Apple, of course. She was stunned when it didn't work. She dropped her hands into her lap. If it wasn't apple or his birthday, it could be anything.

There had to be a way to access her husband's secret digital life. What if she needed essential information about subscriptions or donations, or something the estate lawyer hadn't asked about yet, but might?

From a corner of her mind, Arden remembered that Apple—the computer company—had started something that let people store information from their phones and computers in some kind of ethereal library called the Cloud. She didn't understand how it worked, but it meant that the information was somewhere. All she had to do was convince the cable company, or just a tech-savvy someone, to give her access to this Cloud. Like an angel.

She stood, ripped the flannel shirt off her shoulders and threw it on the chair in a gesture of defiance. She could do this. Make some phone calls, get what she needed.

Her fists tightened. She wanted it *now*, while Danielle was at Emerson-Alcott. It wasn't fair to have to wait. A surge of anger shot through her. The goddamn laptop. She wanted to bang it on the desk until it spit out its secrets. If it wouldn't, she'd throw it at the wall, out the window, until it crashed on the sidewalk. Why not? Everything else had been smashed on the rocks.

Then, all at once, the mania that had propelled her mad search dropped away. She stood in the middle of Connor's study and let her clenched hands fall to her sides.

Angels and clouds. A stupid way to pretend that someone wasn't dead. The angel fish that had died, for no apparent reason. Her yellow bird, so long ago, because of a Teflon pan. Connor McRae, because of a stranger's sleep apnea.

Her baby girl. The child she hadn't kept from harm after all.

Arden snatched the shirt from the chair, taking it back, and pressed it to her face as sobs wracked her body. Grief, helplessness—and horror, as understanding crested like a wave and broke over her.

She had wanted to blame Connor for Leigh's behavior, so there would be someone to blame. But she'd picked the wrong person.

There was only one person it could be. Her. Mary Arden Rice. The one who had been there for Leigh's entire life.

Had she really not seen it till now?

Leigh had been careless with men in front of her child. She'd never expressed any concern, as if it didn't matter. It was only a step beyond Arden's own carelessness, when she'd had that string of affairs. Serial partners, with hardly a gap between the end of one and the beginning of the next. Luke had morphed into Devin, Devin into Ryan or Jay. Was it such a big leap, really, to the idea of simultaneous partners?

Leigh had been seven, eight, nine years old. Watching. Aware. Arden had been a fool to imagine that her daughter hadn't noticed or cared. Yet she had said nothing, as if not talking about the chain of lovers meant that it was of no consequence.

Don't look here. Look at all the wonderful things in your life. Your beautiful room with the apricot walls. Your riding lessons.

There had been nothing inappropriate, though. That part was on Leigh's shoulders, not hers.

And then, suddenly, Arden remembered something. A moment.

One of the boyfriends—it was Luke, because she could still see the fine blond hair on his arms—had put his hand inside the kimono she was wearing, as she sat on his lap at the kitchen table. She'd been naked underneath, and the kimono had fallen open. Leigh had walked in, carrying a stuffed panda, as Luke's hand slid across her breast.

It was just an instant. Arden had jumped up, twisted the ends of the belt into the world's fastest knot, and pretended that nothing had happened. She could remember what she'd thought. *Maybe Leigh didn't see. If I say nothing, it means that she didn't.*

A single moment—and yet, if it had happened once, it had probably happened more than once. Breadcrumbs, a trail for Leigh to follow.

Arden, lifted her face from the flannel. No. That wasn't right.

Leigh wasn't someone who followed a path that others had dug or copied what she saw. She did what she wanted.

Plus, she was an adult, a mother. Whatever she had or hadn't glimpsed when she was small, she still had choices. She still had to take responsibility for her acts, like everyone else.

Not everyone. Not Arden Rice.

A second wave swept over her. Not icy this time but hot, scorching her.

She had done things that she'd never had to be responsible for. Harmed good men who had done nothing wrong. Walked away without paying. Mary Arden Rice, gold medalist in selfish and thoughtless acts.

Maybe the train crash wasn't a literal punishment. But she had still done those things, caused that pain. She'd been staring so hard at Leigh that she hadn't paid attention to the person who had strapped Leigh to her chest.

The shirt dropped from her hands, onto the floor. How could she be angry at the daughter she had raised to be just like her?

Arden met Danielle at the entrance to Emerson-Alcott and exchanged pleasantries with Regina Elias, the admissions person who had shepherded Danielle through the morning. Regina's smile was gracious but revealed nothing.

"Enjoy the rest of your day," she said. "I'll be in touch."

"Very good." Arden restrained herself from blurting the questions that Regina had to know she was bursting to ask. *Did you like her? Do you want her?*

She needed to ask Danielle, too. If Danielle disliked the school, it would be a hard sell. And the people at Emerson-Alcott would have felt it.

She waited until they were back at the apartment, though barely. "So, Nellie," she asked, reaching for a coat hanger. "How did it go?"

Danielle took the coat hanger without meeting her grand-mother's eyes. "I want to go back to my old school."

Arden wet her lip, exhaled. "I understand, sweetheart. I wish we could all go back to the way things were."

"Not everything. Just my old school."

No, not everything. Not the brush of naked buttocks in the hall. Not the sound of men urinating.

Or was there something more? Something Danielle hadn't talked about, but needed to.

She did mean it. You can tell when someone means what they're saying.

"Not everything," Arden echoed. She made her voice as gentle as she could. "What did your mom say to you, sweetheart? That she was sorry about."

Danielle set the coat hanger on the back of the couch. She tilted her head and looked at the floor, tracing the parquet slats with her toe. Then her shoulders sagged, as if she had resigned herself to the inevitability of telling her grandmother what she wanted to know.

"It was just before you picked me up. To go to the museum."

The day before Leigh died. The last time Danielle saw her mother.

Danielle's gaze was still on the parquet slats. "I knew we were going to walk around the museum so I put on my Wallabees. You know, the ones we got for the Vermont trip? But I couldn't wear them, the edges were all bent. I told her we had to go to the store and get new ones, but she said she was too busy. I kept asking and asking, but she wouldn't."

Arden nodded. Danielle was hyper-sensitive to seams and labels and straps. Her mother knew that, yet the request was last-minute, ill-timed—and, no doubt, issued in the kind of needy, petulant voice that Leigh hated. Her refusal didn't seem unreasonable. Maybe this wouldn't be so bad after all.

"Then she got mad at me." Danielle raised her eyes to meet Arden's. "Because I'm a great big burden. Something she never wanted."

"Nellie—" Arden began.

"She told me." Danielle's voice sharpened. "*Why did I have to get saddled with you?*" She burst into heart-wrenching tears.

Arden gathered Danielle into her arms, willing herself to embody the warmth and softness her granddaughter desperately needed. Below the softness, she was raging.

She had worked so hard to unspool the thread, even when it led back to her, so she could forgive Leigh for her unforgivable carelessness. If she had been careless with men, first, then it wasn't Leigh's fault. She was the source and bore the responsibility.

But not for this, Leigh's rejection of her own child. That wasn't something she had modeled. She was back where she started, sickened by her daughter.

Arden felt the darkness spread through her body. A cold black despair, like a tunnel descending forever.

LEIGH
SADDLED
2013

She should have known better. That was what Leigh told herself, later. But when she met Ivan Chernowski, she ignored all the rules she had made for herself and fell crazy in love. Before she knew it, there she was, faithful to one man.

And then, naturally, Ivan did the very thing she had given up for him. Not caring enough to hide it or lie about it, even when she was pregnant with his child. Fucking some woman in New Haven while she was giving birth to their daughter. Humiliating her in front of her mother, who had to drive her to the hospital when Ivan didn't even answer his damn phone.

She had thought, stupidly, that he would just *know* and show up, but he didn't. Not when an orderly wheeled her down a hall into the delivery room. Not when she began to shake with the terrified certainty that she would die or the baby would die. Not when she was howling and splitting open.

The doctor had to cut the cord, even though Ivan had sworn

he would do it. Well, screw him. She didn't put down his name as the father.

Then, ten days later, there he was—full of excuses and apologies and promises that Leigh wasn't sure she wanted to hear, since she already knew they were bullshit. But she let him talk, partly because of the baby, and partly because of herself. Ivan was charming, contrite. She was filled with postpartum hormones and didn't have the energy to resist.

For a while, it seemed like it might actually work. Ivan got a grant for a cycle of one-act plays—two whole years of work that kept him in New York, with her. And with Danielle, the solemn little girl who looked just like him. He was happy, they were happy. Until the whole fucking circus started up again with a twenty-two-year-old twat who thought that banging the director would get her the lead in the edgy new play he was about to cast.

Leigh wasn't someone who sat around waiting for a man to slink back home. Once, maybe. Not a second time. Guys lined up to be with her. She could have all the guys she wanted.

She needed to reclaim her power. As long as Ivan knew about it; that was the point. She made sure to pick actors—and actresses—in his tight little circle, and was stunned when it didn't work. He got disgusted instead of jealous.

Leigh didn't understand. Ivan was supposed to plead with her to stop. He didn't plead. So she didn't stop.

Five years of back-and-forth, each of them trying to prove that they didn't care. Or maybe Ivan really *didn't* care, except for his pride. When he finally gave her the ultimatum that she thought would make her feel like he couldn't bear to lose her, it was more like he was screaming at her for being trashy and embarrassing.

Fuck him. She'd do what she wanted.

It was Connor who got wise to what was going on. He stopped to see her on the way back from one of his farming conferences, and it took him about two minutes to pick up on the clues her mother had totally missed. Being Connor, he tried to talk her out of it, as if telling her about his own sorry attempt at polyamory was supposed to be some kind of deterrent. It didn't make her quit, but it did give her a pretty way to frame it.

No possessions, like Lennon said. Equal love for all. Whatever.

She didn't say that to Connor. He liked to feel helpful, and why hurt his feelings? She knew he wasn't her father, though it would have been nice if he were. Her mother used to tell her that her father had died. She kept wanting to see his grave until her mother finally said no, he hadn't actually died, he was just gone. That was worse. She had no father, just some anonymous jerk who hadn't even bothered to see how she turned out.

It still hurt, if she let herself think about it, which she didn't. Except sometimes, when she looked at her own child and saw Ivan's face.

As if Ivan had played a mean joke on her—stamping himself on the one person she had to look at, day after day. Each time she looked at Danielle, it was like Ivan hit her in the chest with a rock.

It made her angry at Danielle, too, because she got to look across the dinner table and see a father who looked like her. It was another rock, sharp and cruel.

Day after day, stone after stone. A path that led, finally, to the words she flung at her daughter, twenty years after Blake Rasmussen left her in the dirt.

Leigh regretted them immediately. She hadn't meant it, not

the way it sounded. She'd meant having to raise her child alone, without a husband, just like her mother predicted when Ivan didn't show up at the hospital—especially when Arden herself had three of them, so greedy and unfair. It was the unfairness and her mother being right and no Ivan to take Danielle to the shoe store. The unfairness, not the child herself.

Saddled was just horse language, an old habit. There was nothing wrong with a saddle. The opposite was so much worse, when someone didn't want to carry you at all.

She needed to explain that to Danielle, the quirky little girl who had nothing to do with Ivan deserting her. He was never going to be a forever partner, anyway; she'd known that from the start, even if she hadn't wanted to admit it. If anything, Danielle—the fact of Danielle, and how she looked like him— kept him around for a while.

There was no time to explain any of that because her mother was already knocking at the front door. Arden wasn't supposed to pick Danielle up until ten o'clock; she was bringing her to Manhattan for an art exhibit and lunch. But, being Arden, she'd gotten impatient and arrived early.

Leigh promised herself that she would talk to Danielle the first chance she had, after the art museum. Fix the horrible thing she had said. Words rose up in her chest, like a prayer someone had whispered to her, long ago. *Let me be good.*

Her own plea had always been, *Let me be happy.* She knew it was a stupid plea, since it never worked. But now, suddenly, she realized that she had it backward. You couldn't be happy unless you were good. Not someone else's definition of good. Your own.

If it was your own definition, no one could tell you that you weren't good.

This is how it feels to be good. And this goodness makes me happy.

A wondrous new feeling moved through her—as if her heart had released, opened, expanded. It was so big that it almost hurt.

She could start over. Take the worst thing she had done to her child and turn it into the best thing. Share her beloved horses with Danielle, the horses she had given up. Give *to*, instead of give *up*. She looked at her daughter, her face lit with love and joy.

She caught her mother's eye, just for an instant, though she wasn't sure if Arden saw. It didn't matter; she'd tell her later, for her birthday.

She stepped off the old path, because there was another one. It was so simple, and so easy.

SOME OF THIS IS TRUE

2013

Arden held her granddaughter as Leigh's words echoed in the living room. *Why did I have to get saddled with you?* Leigh had thrown the words at her daughter and walked away. Not even wondering how they affected Danielle, no more than she'd wondered how any of the things she did affected Danielle.

Arden had no words of her own that could undo them. *She was sorry, she didn't really mean it.* How could she know what Leigh did or didn't mean?

All she had were the wordless forms of comfort she had offered in the days and weeks after Leigh's death. Hot cocoa, a mound of pillows, the cream-colored shawl that Danielle liked to wrap around herself while they watched an inspiring movie where no one died. Tonight it was *The Sound of Music*, three hours of Alpine scenery and happy cooperative children. They watched in silence until the von Trapp family arrived safely in Switzerland. Then Danielle said she was tired and wanted to go to bed. Arden kissed her forehead and let her go.

Alone now, Arden stared at the darkened screen. What was she supposed to do? Scream at her dead daughter, take back the things she had done for her? The lies she told her brother, her parents. Those painful months in an apartment where Michael Tate's ghost lingered in every room—a pain Arden had accepted, so Leigh could keep her happy, privileged life.

If this was who Leigh turned out to be, then her own choices had been wrong and it was all for nothing. She might as well have stayed with Jonah Orenstein. Spared him—and Michael— the pain she had caused.

Arden wrapped her arms around one of the pillows that Danielle had discarded, pulling it close. She was sixty years old, and there was no way to rewind a life. You could face it; that was all.

She sat for a long time in the dark, holding the pillow to her chest the way she'd held her infant daughter in the Snugli, all those years ago.

Arden rose, finally, and went to the bedroom where her phone was charging, hoping that Regina Elias had left a message while Julie Andrews was twirling across the meadow.

Amazingly, she had. Yes, they'd liked Danielle. Everyone understood that she was dealing with a terrible loss. They felt certain that she would warm up and fit in well. Might Arden phone tomorrow so they could speak about the next steps?

Arden let out her breath. Her relief was so intense that she nearly missed the second message.

"It's Robert. Got your text. I can talk tonight if you want. Any time until ten or so is fine."

Another message Arden had been hoping for—but instead of relief, it filled her with alarm. Did she really want to confront

Robert—now, tonight, when she wasn't sure how she felt about their daughter? After thirty-five years of silence?

You have to, she told herself. For Danielle.

She looked at the clock on the nightstand. Nine forty-seven. Squaring her shoulders, she tapped on the blue circle. *Call.*

As soon as she heard the first ring, she thought: It's too late, he won't answer. She hoped he wouldn't. Then she could say she'd tried and let it go.

But Robert had already picked up. "Ah," he said. "Caller ID tells me that it's the one-and-only Mary Arden Rice."

Arden lowered herself onto the edge of the bed. How strange to hear his voice. It was still slow and deliberate, but there was a hint of mirth that she didn't remember. Or maybe the mirth was new, acquired since she told him to go away, don't follow me, leave me alone. "I don't know about one-and-only, but it's me, yes."

Robert gave a soft chuckle. "Ghost of Millennia Past."

Millennia? Arden frowned, then realized he meant before Y2K, when years began with a one instead of a two. "I hadn't thought of that," she said, "but yes, you're right. Though it makes me feel ancient, when you put it that way."

"I prefer to think of myself as well-marinated."

Arden closed her eyes. It felt bizarre to be bantering like this, as if they were old high school classmates. She remembered how mean she had been, the last time Robert tried to call. He had phoned again and again, left a stuffed bear with a red bow outside her door.

It all came back, an assault of memory. Her irritation with him in Istanbul. The orange sauce from room service. If the handsome Egyptian, Nabil, hadn't turned her down, what would have happened? Maybe she would have abandoned Robert in Luxor, instead of later.

If she hadn't pretended that Robert was Nabil, they wouldn't have had sex that night and there would have been no Leigh. No reason to contact him now.

No Leigh meant no Danielle, asleep in the room down the hall. A different family. A different life.

Arden shivered, then opened her eyes. What did it matter? She had the life she had, and she needed to set it right.

"Thanks for getting back to me," she said. "I'm sure it was a surprise to hear from me, after all this time."

Again, she thought: It's not too late. I could back out, invent a different reason. Buy some photos. She didn't understand her reluctance. This was the call she'd been waiting for.

"There's a reason I got in touch," she said, forcing herself to go on. "Something I never told you, back when we knew each other."

"Back in the prior millennium? It can't have been all that important, if it didn't surface until now."

"It is, though." Her heart was banging so loudly that she was sure he could hear it. She pushed each syllable, one at a time, from the dry tight hollow of her throat. "It's the most important thing there is."

For an awful moment, she was afraid he would turn it into something clever and wry. But his voice was grave. "What is it you never told me, Arden?"

She tightened her fingers around the phone. "I'm sure this is going to be a shock. There's no excuse for waiting so long, but—well, I just couldn't."

"This is starting to sound ominous."

"Not ominous. Serious."

Arden had no idea how she was going to get through the conversation. Yet again, she wondered if she should just hang up—because, really, why do that to him? *Hey, I wanted you to know what you missed, now that it's too late?*

Even so, he had the right to know—well, not everything, not how she had made Jonah believe that Leigh was his and hurt him so terribly. Not the orange sauce she had ordered for him in Luxor. If she needed to cleanse her conscience, she could talk to Eleanor Cardoza. But Robert had the right to know about his firstborn child.

She steeled herself. No more preambles.

"When we left each other in Rome, I was pregnant, though I didn't know it. I didn't even know later, when we broke up. In America." She said *broke up*, to give it some dignity. "By the time I realized, I had no idea where you were."

That part was true. After the stuffed bear and the evil thing she had done to make him stop wanting her, he had disappeared.

Robert's voice was guarded. "You had an abortion?"

Yes, that would have been a reasonable assumption. Instead, she'd had the baby, who turned out to be Leigh.

Arden understood, before she spoke, that Robert had already intuited her answer. An abortion wouldn't have warranted a phone call, thirty-five years later.

"No," she said. "We had a daughter."

There was a beat of silence. And then Robert's question— because he was literal and had to clarify what she'd meant. "You said *had*. Did you mean the event, when you gave birth to a daughter?"

Arden felt sick to her stomach now. "Had. Used to have." Tears filled her eyes. "She died. It was a freak accident. The train should have had automatic brakes, if they were going to go around such a dangerous curve. I mean, anyone would have known that." Arden knew she was babbling but couldn't seem to stop. "She was in the front car. Five people were killed. It doesn't seem fair, if there were only five. Because Leigh didn't do any-thing, except sit up front. For my birthday."

There was no point pretending to be in control anymore. She could feel Robert struggling to grasp what she was saying.

Finally, in a burst of despair, she told him, "I thought you should know. Because you were her father."

More silence, long and dark and empty. Then the question she hadn't been ready for.

"Did she know that? Did you tell her about me?"

Arden squeezed the phone against her ear. No, she hadn't. She'd acted as if Leigh had no father. Only a mother.

Jonah Orenstein was the father on her birth certificate, but Leigh had no memory of him, and Arden had let him disappear too. Michael Tate had provided for Leigh, but she'd always been Arden's child, not his. And Connor McRae had come into her life too late to pretend he was the father she longed for.

"No," Arden said. She wanted to explain that she hadn't let anyone else claim Leigh either, but the words were frozen inside, and it wasn't what Robert had asked.

"So she never knew."

"Neither of you knew."

His words were flat, the mirth gone. "Why tell me now?"

Because of Danielle, Arden thought. First, though, Robert had to know about Leigh. Had to love Leigh, so he would love Danielle. "It just seemed—I don't know, respectful of her life."

"What about respectful of my life?"

She tried to hold back the tears but there were too many now. "Yes. You're right." She'd dismissed Robert's life, as if it were less important than her own.

Remorse swept through her—flooding her, the way the Nile flooded the desert. She remembered a younger self, proclaiming with such certainty, "I have nothing to apologize for. I did what I had to do."

Her voice broke. "I'm so very sorry."

She waited for Robert's anger, but there was nothing, just a deathly quiet that was worse than rage. She wanted him to shout at her, hate her.

Then, as the seconds passed and Robert said nothing, she dared to hope that she would slip through, contrite but whole, the way she always had. Wasn't that what people said to each other? *I'm sorry.* And the other person said, *Hey, it's okay.*

Not this time. She'd known that before he answered. That was why she'd been so afraid.

It wasn't okay. It would never be okay because Leigh was dead.

Remorse sliced through her. It wasn't enough to be contrite. "What can I do?" she whispered.

An absurd question. It was too late to do anything.

Still, not trying was worse. "Can I tell you about her? What she was like?"

Leigh. She realized that she hadn't told Robert their daughter's name.

"Leigh," she said. "Her name was Leigh."

"Leigh," he repeated. There was a small, cracked sound. Then he said, "Yes. All right."

Arden sagged against the edge of the bed. She wanted to cry *thank you, thank you* for his acceptance of her tiny inadequate offering. She searched for how to begin, for something that would help him feel that Leigh Alexandra Orenstein had really been his child.

But there was nothing. Because Leigh was so different from Robert. She was extravagant, rebellious, while her father was cautious and deliberate. She liked to defy convention, flaunt her singularity in how she dressed, decorated, embraced causes and careers—and yes, explored her sexuality. Robert liked to follow the rules.

Arden could feel him waiting for her to speak, but everything felt too complicated and abstract. Leigh herself seemed to be receding—the living, vibrant Leigh, with her flawed impossible charm. Arden struggled for something to grab onto. For the essence of Leigh, that she could offer to Robert.

She remembered how she'd spread the albums on the floor, all the stages of Leigh's life. Toddler, school girl, adolescent, with that glorious auburn hair. Like his.

That was it. *Little red cabbage.* She'd send photos, and he would see.

She began to talk rapidly, as if Robert might try to stop her. "I can send you pictures. I have baby pictures. School pictures, birthdays."

The words caught in her throat. Her excitement seemed inane, offensive. Photos were no better than words. Souvenirs of a past he hadn't known.

Fresh tears stung her eyes. "It's too little. Too late."

"Arden," he said. His voice was firm now. "Don't do that. I'm sure you tried your best to find me. It's not your fault that you couldn't. There was no social media back then, no LinkedIn. I wasn't findable."

Arden was glad he couldn't see her face. She hadn't tried her best. She hadn't tried at all. Instead, she'd given the happy news to Jonah Orenstein, a sweet, loving man who never questioned the paternity of the little girl who arrived after a seven-month pregnancy. She wouldn't have gotten away with that if Robert had still been around, aware of her pregnancy and doing the math, the way he did.

He wasn't around because she'd made sure that he wasn't, launching the rumor that assured his banishment.

She began to tremble. A quiver at first, starting in her jaw and spreading to her shoulders, her arms. Leigh's existence was the easy part. Robert himself had given her a story that almost absolved her. *It wasn't your fault that you couldn't find me. There was no social media back then.*

There was no story that made the other parts worthy of absolution. The way she'd treated him in Luxor, like a thing to shove out of her way. The lie she'd told, back in New York, telling herself that it was only to make him stop liking her—but knowing, surely, where it would lead. She taught in a private school, too, understood the power of perception.

Knowing, and doing it anyway.

The trembling grew stronger, rattling her teeth. Surely Robert could hear it. Surely he was remembering how he came to be unfindable, why he had fled. And what he must have understood about the source of that malicious lie.

Then she thought: Wait.

If Robert knew she had uttered the words that ruined his life, why wasn't he furious at her? Why had he even responded to her message—so he could scream at her, berate her? But he hadn't. It didn't make sense.

Arden switched the phone to her other ear. She had to hear the story from him. What had happened. What she was missing.

"Why weren't you findable?" she asked.

Robert let out a sigh. "You remember where I was working, back then? That ultra-preppy boys' school?"

He was waiting for her to answer, so she said, "Yes. Right." As if she could forget.

"Well," he began, "I'll skip the unpleasant details, but the short version is that there was this aggressive group of parents—big donors, naturally—that went totally nuts. Seeing perversion, or the threat of it, in every corner. They had to quote, *protect*, their kids. They wanted the faculty to *report potential issues*. To rat on each other, in other words. Without evidence of any harm, even if someone was quietly gay in his own private life. Can you believe it? A few rich, bigoted zealots. And the administration allowed it because of their money."

Arden shut her eyes again. She remembered Michael Tate, offering to use his influence with the head of the Brenner School.

"The whole place was becoming completely toxic," Robert went on. "When I got back from Europe and walked in for the first day of orientation, it really hit me. I wasn't the only one who felt it. So a bunch of us quit. Walked out."

Her eyes flew open. "You quit? You weren't forced to leave?"

"The opposite. They tried to scare us out of leaving. Said we'd be blacklisted if we broke our contracts. But we did it anyway."

Her mind was reeling. This was a different story. Not the one she'd told herself all these years. "You quit," she repeated.

"Five of us quit. Sometimes you have to take a stand, right?"

Arden thought of Savannah Tate's paper on *Sophie's Choice*. She had taken a stand too. In her case, it had turned out well. A beautiful apartment, riding lessons for Leigh.

"I have to tell you," Robert said, "it felt pretty damn good."

"To walk away?"

"To walk away, and watch their mouths drop open."

Arden was still trying to catch up, to align the pieces in an order that made sense.

If Robert hadn't been fired, it meant that her lie hadn't made its way to the school administration. She'd told that friend of theirs, whose name she'd forgotten, so the friend would tell someone else, and it would get back to Robert. She was like that, Arden remembered. A gossip. And then, when Robert disappeared, she had assumed that she knew the reason. But she had been wrong.

"The blacklisting wasn't an empty threat," Robert said. "One of the teachers who walked out tried to get another job later, but they told her she was on a permanent shit list, even though they were desperate for chemistry teachers."

"What did you do, then?"

"Hey, it was the seventies." Arden was amazed to hear him laugh. "I followed my bliss. Took up photography. And here I am."

Here he was. A cabin, a family. Not ruined.

She was struggling to take it in, to accept the mercy she had just been granted. As if the arrow had withdrawn from the flesh it had pierced and returned to the bow. Never released after all. "An artist," she said, needing to say something.

"Not an artist. More of a computer geek. Photography's all about computers these days." Another laugh. "I'm the least artistic member of the family. I can't even carry a tune. My sons barely tolerate me when they have their bluegrass evenings."

"Bluegrass?"

"My wife grew up in Kentucky. That's where the boys got it."

"Kentucky," she repeated. Nothing was what she'd imagined. Then she said, "What's her name? Your wife."

"Jennifer," he told her. "We got lucky. Twenty-eight years last month."

Arden nodded, as his words settled. Maybe Robert *was* lucky. Who could say how luck really worked? Her rejection of Robert had led to his luck with Jennifer.

"I'm glad," she said, and she was. It meant that her mark hadn't been as deep as she'd thought. Better for him—and yet, strangely, a loss.

Of what? Her starring role in the story of Robert Altschuler's life?

It was a made-up story. Not the real one.

For decades, she'd clung to the idea of her own importance. But there was no scandal, no ruined reputation, because of her. None of it had happened.

No, that wasn't true. Some of it happened. Robert might not have known what she'd said about him, but she'd still said it.

She heard Robert clear his throat. "Well, then," he said, his voice turning brisk. "Your news was a big shock, as you can imagine, but I appreciate your tracking me down, I really do. And I look forward to the photos, when you have time."

He was ending the conversation. She could hardly blame him. It was a lot to take in.

But she wasn't finished. She hadn't told him the whole truth. She'd left out the worst parts. Spared herself. Rolled away.

She wouldn't let herself do that, not this time. She had to tell him right now, before he hung up.

She opened her mouth to speak—then stopped. Because that wasn't right either.

If she burdened Robert with a confession that he didn't want or need, just to ease her own conscience, it would be one more selfish act. For her benefit, not his.

Why mar the happy story he'd made of his life? For the drama, the release of the weight she carried?

That wasn't the brave and good thing to do.

And what was?

There was only one answer. Silence. The willingness to carry the memory of her meanness, just as it was, without hoping that someone else's forgiveness would transform it. Restraint, not avoidance. A harder path.

For the good of Jennifer. Quentin. Caleb. For the good of all.

"I'll scan the photos first thing tomorrow," she told him. "You'll see how beautiful she was."

"I look forward to it," he repeated. "Take care of yourself."

"You too." She heard the buzz of a dial tone.

Arden set the phone on the nightstand and let her hands drop to her lap. The conversation had been nothing like she'd imagined. A strange end to a strange day, beginning with Danielle's visit to Emerson-Alcott, where she'd be enrolling, as soon as—again, Arden stopped.

Had she really forgotten to tell Robert that he had a granddaughter, Leigh's child, who was very much alive? There had been too many other things to talk about. Well, next time. Surely there would be a next time.

Maybe they could even meet. Maybe one of his sons was a literal thinker, too, who insisted that grass couldn't really be blue.

Her eyes darted to the clock. Ten thirty-five. They'd talked for forty-five minutes while Danielle, their grandchild, slept in a nearby room. Arden was seized with the urge to look at her granddaughter, to study her face to see if there was anything of Robert Altschuler in it.

She would be quiet. Just a look, after the day Danielle had been through. A visit to a new school—and then saying aloud, at last, the words she had carried since her mother's death.

Arden made her way down the hall to the guest room that was now Danielle's. The fluted sconces, scalloped shells of palest pink, cast cones of light on the hardwood floor. She heard the ticking of the clock in the living room, the hum of the kitchen fan.

The bathroom door was ajar; next to it, Danielle's door was closed, the way she liked it. Arden turned the handle and stepped inside. The room was dark. She waited for her eyes to adjust. She could make out the organdy curtains, the mound of the dresser. The empty bed.

"Danielle?" In the bathroom, then. But no; there had been no one inside. Nor had Danielle crept into Arden's bedroom so she wouldn't be alone, as she sometimes did; Arden had just come from there. "Danielle!" she cried, louder this time. She flung open the closet. Stupidly, she yanked open the dresser drawers, as if Danielle could be hiding inside.

Not under the bed. Not curled in the back of a closet. Not anywhere.

Frantic, she raced through the apartment, shouting Danielle's name as she ran from room to room, opening cupboards, shoving aside curtains and furniture. Danielle had to be somewhere. No one could have kidnapped her, not in a doorman building where you needed a code for the elevator. Not through a twentieth-floor window that wouldn't even open.

Danielle wasn't peacefully asleep. It meant she had left, on her own, while Arden was talking to Robert.

Run away.

MASTER OF THE WORD

2013

The plastic case for *The Sound of Music* was still open on the coffee table, next to the remote. The ivory shawl lay in a heap where Danielle had dropped it on her way to bed. Everything was just as it had been when Arden went to check her messages—except Danielle was gone.

Do not panic, Arden told herself, though she already had; fear was crawling up her arms, her neck, into her scalp. Danielle had to be somewhere. Maybe in the lobby, telling Samuel, the kindly doorman, that she couldn't sleep. Leigh used to do that sort of thing, though it had driven Arden crazy. Why not Danielle?

She grabbed the phone on the wall and buzzed the doorman's station. "Samuel?"

"No, ma'am. Samuel is out sick. This is Wallace. How can I help you?"

Damn. She had no idea who Wallace was, nor would he know Danielle. Even so, she asked, "I was wondering if my granddaughter was there, in the lobby. She's ten, with long dark hair. Or if you saw her leave the building?"

"There's no girl here," he said. "And I can't say if a girl left. There was a lot of commotion, you know. They were delivering a couch to the Crenshaws in 8B, one of those big sleeper couches? And there was all that trouble with the elevator that I had to sort out, though it beats me why someone would deliver furniture at this hour."

Arden didn't give a crap about the Crenshaws and their couch. Samuel would never have let Danielle leave the building in the middle of the night. But Samuel wasn't there. She was sure now that Danielle had seen the substitute doorman's preoccupation and seized it as a chance to slip away.

But why? Where did she go? Danielle wasn't a child who wandered impulsively, without a destination. If she left, it was to go to a particular place.

Or person. To Ivan, her remaining parent. Who else could it be?

Danielle had given voice, at last, to her mother's rejection. Leigh had spurned her twice: first by her words, and then by her death. That left Ivan as the only one who could make it right, by wanting her. Being with an imperfect father would be better than being with no parent at all.

Running to Ivan made a sad and awful kind of sense—but where? He was in New Haven, or maybe it was Princeton or Cambridge. Arden couldn't remember. Somewhere that wasn't New York, preparing for his new production. Could Danielle really have made her way to Penn Station and bought herself a train ticket to an unfamiliar city?

Leigh might have done that, but not Danielle. And not without calling first, to be sure her father was actually there.

Yet she couldn't have called, because Arden had been on the phone the whole time. With Robert. Danielle had no cell phone. Would she have simply left?

Arden's head was spinning. She should probably call Ivan, alert him, though she didn't want to. If he knew she'd let this happen, he would use it against her. He didn't want custody, but he wouldn't mind making her suffer.

And what if she was wrong, and Danielle was somewhere else? She'd look like an incompetent fool.

She slammed down the in-house phone, not caring if Wallace-the-doorman thought she was rude. Her gaze flew from one object to another. The umbrella stand, the copper teakettle. She needed Connor desperately. Or Leigh. It wasn't fair that the two people who could help had both deserted her. She shouted Danielle's name again, as if she might be in the apartment after all. Or in the elevator. On the sidewalk, right outside the building.

She could run into the street, shouting *Danielle, Danielle.* Surely, Danielle hadn't gone very far. Or she could call the police, though the notion filled her with dread. It would mean that Danielle was truly missing. And when she was found, they might take her away because her worthless grandmother hadn't kept her safe.

No, not the police. Not yet.

But who could help her? Not Ivan. Not Eleanor Cardoza. Only someone who was like Danielle would know how her step-by-step mind had led her from the guest bedroom to—somewhere.

She had to think like Danielle, but how? They were so different.

Arden froze. She knew who could help her.

The person who was connected to Danielle by blood and DNA, even if he didn't know it yet. The only person who might care enough to help, once he understood.

She raced back to her bedroom and grabbed the phone from the nightstand. Her hand shook as she found the last number she had called. She wanted to cry *I'm sorry, I'm sorry.* She was disturbing people she didn't even know, in the middle of the night. Another thoughtless act—only it wasn't, because it was for Danielle.

The phone rang and rang. Finally, she heard a woman's voice. Sleepy, with a Kentucky twang. "Hello?"

Arden squeezed the phone. Jennifer, that was her name. "Please. I need to talk to Robert. It's an emergency."

"Excuse me? You do realize what time it is? Who *is* this, anyway?"

"Please." Her voice quavered, broke. "I'm so sorry to wake you, but a child is missing. Robert is the only one who can help."

"Who is this?" Jennifer repeated.

Arden began to sob, and Jennifer said, "Oh, for heaven's sake." Then, to Arden's relief, she heard a man's voice. "Let me take it."

"Robert." She was shaking now. "It's Arden. I need your help." The words came in ragged spurts. "A girl is missing. I need you to help me think like her, so I can find her."

She heard him take a deep breath, and then he said, "Are you having some kind of nervous breakdown?" His words were careful, though not unkind. "I understand that you've been through a horrible shock. A tragedy. You're mourning your child, and you want to set things right. But Arden, you can't fixate on me as—"

"No, no," she interrupted. "A child really *is* missing. Leigh's daughter. She's ten, and she—she's so much like you."

"A daughter?"

"Danielle." There was no time to explain. "I need you to show me how to think like her. Because you do. You think the same way."

"Slow down, Arden. Back up a few steps."

"You'll help?"

"Walk me through this. Then we'll see if I can." She heard him murmur, "It's all right. Go back to bed. I'll be along shortly."

Then he returned to the phone. "You're sure she's really missing and not just hiding?"

"Missing. I've looked everywhere."

"A friend's house?"

Arden tried not to weep. There were no friends in Manhattan. Just a huge city with a thousand places a girl might be. "I'm certain she ran away."

"Is there a reason she would do that?"

Too many reasons. Her mother was dead, her father didn't want her to play Anne Frank, and she was stuck with an old lady in a place she didn't want to be, with no pets except a dead angel fish and a school where she didn't know anyone.

And worse. Her mother had let men walk around with no clothes and pee with the door open. She hadn't cared that Danielle could hear. Then her mother had flung cruel, loveless words at her, even though she'd come back in a vision to say she was sorry.

It would take too long to explain, and Arden didn't want to because she was afraid it would make Robert hate Leigh. "Her mother was killed in a freak accident. Isn't that enough?"

"I don't know. Were they on good terms before the accident?"

Arden winced. "Not really."

"What happened?"

Arden made her answer as vague as she could. She couldn't let Robert think badly of the daughter he had never known. "As far as I can understand, Leigh was irritated because Danielle was pestering her about some shoes, and she said something nasty that I'm sure she didn't mean."

"What did she say?"

"I wasn't there. It's only what Danielle told me." She could feel Robert waiting. She closed her eyes and readied herself to repeat the ugly words. "'Why did I have to get saddled with you?'"

"It's a curious way to put it," Robert said. "Most people would have said *stuck* with you. Did the word *saddle* have any special meaning for either of them?"

Arden felt a flare of annoyance. Why were they talking about linguistics when Danielle was missing and every moment counted? "I suppose," she said. "Leigh used to ride. She loved it, until she decided that she didn't."

And then, in a burst of clarity, she remembered.

How Danielle had come into the living room, where she had spread the photos on the carpet, the photos she'd promised to scan for Robert. How Danielle's eyes had widened at the photo of Leigh with a chestnut-colored horse. How she had announced, with absolute confidence, "That's how Mom looked when she talked to me and told me she was sorry."

Sorry for saying she'd been saddled with her. Made to carry the burden of a sensitive, quirky child who was hard for her to understand or enjoy.

And then Leigh returned to her, ten years old again, just like Danielle, ready to saddle and be saddled in her jodhpurs and helmet.

The words matched. But it didn't explain where Danielle had gone.

"Did Danielle ride too?" Robert asked.

"No." Danielle arranged things by size and color, divided recipes into fractions. "But she'd just seen a photo of her mother with the horse she used to ride. It made a strong impression on her."

There was no need to get into Danielle's fantasies. She needed Robert to focus on the real clues that Danielle might have left.

"Where? Where did she ride?"

Arden searched her memory. "There was a place in Central Park, but it closed down a few years ago. I think it was bought by a school. Anyway, she'd stopped riding long before that."

She remembered her daughter's excitement when she got to ride or simply spend time with the horses, grooming them, talking to them. It was because of Leigh's insistence on seeing the barn, when they went to the McRae Farm, that they'd ended up in the urgent care place in Rhinebeck and stayed for dinner and brought home a basket of apples. It was because of Leigh wanting to see the horses that she'd found Connor.

Tears welled up again, hot and sharp. She'd lost Leigh. She couldn't lose Danielle too.

Then the crazy thought: If she rescued Danielle, she would rescue Leigh. Find and restore her.

"You said there was a photo?"

Arden shuddered, returned to the present, to Robert's voice on the phone. "Yes. Of Leigh, in her riding gear."

"Get the photo." He sounded different now. In charge. This wasn't the Robert she remembered, who had waited for her to tell him what to do and who to be. "Look at it, as Danielle would. See what she saw."

"Yes. Right."

The phone in her hand, Arden ran to the living room, knelt, and flipped through the photos that were still strewn across the floor. Quickly, she tossed the pictures aside that weren't the one she needed. Leigh, dressed as Glinda the Good Witch for Halloween. Doing a handstand. Holding up a steaming pizza on a wooden platter, with a silly chef's hat and missing front teeth.

Arden could hardly bear it. Yes, Leigh had done some terrible things, but so had she. What was she supposed to do, reject herself too? Chop herself into pieces so she could throw out the unacceptable parts and keep the others?

She wiped her eyes with the back of her hand. Of course not. You couldn't wander through the garden of a person's life, even your own, picking only the flowers you liked. You had to accept the whole person. Flawed, and yet, maybe, stumbling through the dirt toward grace.

And then, there it was. The photo of Leigh that Danielle had been staring at. A big happy grin and a blue jersey. With an address. "Oh my god," she whispered.

Pay attention. Don't miss this.

"Arden?"

"I know where Danielle is."

"You're sure?"

"I'm sure. It's the place where the horse got saddled."

"Then go there," Robert said. "But if she's not there, you have to call the police right away. You can't be a Lone Ranger."

"Yes. I know. I understand."

"Find her," he said. "Find my granddaughter."

Arden shoved her wallet and phone in a coat pocket, buttoning her coat in the elevator as it made its unbearably slow descent to the lobby. She barely glanced at Wallace, the substitute doorman, as she flung open the door and ran toward Broadway, where there would be taxis. She was sixty years old but felt thirty. Or a hundred.

She hailed a taxi and yelled, "Eighty-ninth and Columbus." It hardly made sense to take a taxi for such a short distance, but every minute was another minute that Danielle was alone, waiting to be found.

The driver pulled up to the curb, asking which corner she wanted. She didn't care about corners. She threw a twenty-dollar bill at him, slammed the door, and sprinted toward the address she had burned into her brain. She already knew that the Clare-mont Stables wouldn't be there. The Romanesque building that used to house a riding academy had been repurposed and taken over by a special-education school. As she ran toward a building that looked nothing like a stable, Arden began to panic again. Surely Danielle had been confused too. Not finding what she pictured, she could have gone anywhere.

And yet, instinct told Arden to go to the address on the blue jersey, because that was what Danielle would have done. A spark of certainty glinted in her brain. She was thinking like Danielle now. She ran faster.

It was nearly midnight. The sky was huge and starless; whatever stars might have glittered overhead were obscured by the ambient light of the streetlamps, cars, the city that never slept. A sliver of moon shone through a gap in the buildings.

Arden sensed Danielle before she saw her. Knew, somehow, that the curled figure on the granite steps was her granddaughter. She slowed her pace, gave Danielle time to take in her approach. Then slowly, carefully, she eased onto the step, beside Danielle.

Danielle stiffened but didn't move away. After a minute, Arden said, "Looks like it's a school now. Places can change over the years, become something different."

Like people, she thought. If they have enough time.

"I wanted to see the horses," Danielle whispered. "Without their saddles."

"We can do that," Arden told her. "Up at the McRae Farm."

Danielle didn't answer, though she inched closer. Arden put an arm around her shoulders. "We could even stay overnight. Finn said we could do that any time we wanted."

Arden hadn't known what she would say when she found Danielle—but the words found her, just as she had found her granddaughter. They were simply there, for her to use.

"The horses are beautiful," she said, "but saddles are good too. They let people stay on, without falling."

She could feel Danielle listening, taking it in. "I think," she went on, "that your mom was telling you that you could stay on, no matter what. That she would carry you, wherever you needed to go."

Danielle bit her lip, blinked hard. "I didn't think of it like that."

"Words can mean a lot of things. Sometimes they need a little time to come into focus, like one of those old-fashioned photos. What you see at first—or think you see—might not be the actual, final thing."

Danielle turned to face her. "Then how do you know what they really mean?"

Arden's heart tightened. She had hurt so many people with her words. Afterward, she had wanted to snatch them back and stuff them in the gunny sack of the unsaid. But words, once released, didn't belong to you anymore. They landed somewhere and were fixed there forever, like flies in amber.

Maybe that was why she'd been drawn to poetry, a language that kept circling back and becoming something new. She smoothed her granddaughter's hair. "Sometimes you just have to decide what they mean. It's up to you."

"Like Humpty Dumpty." When Arden lifted an eyebrow, Danielle quoted: "'The question is,' said Alice, 'whether you can make words mean so many different things.' And then Humpty Dumpty says, 'The question is, which is to be master—that's all.'"

Arden had to laugh. "Perfectly stated, my darling. It's exactly the kind of thing your mom would have said."

Danielle shook her head. "I'm not like my mom."

"Of course you are. You can have bits of a lot of people. But mostly, you're *you*. Your own unique person."

She thought of Robert Altschuler, whom Danielle really did resemble—or maybe she only resembled Arden's image of Robert, from long-ago. Meanwhile, it was getting late and the real Robert was waiting for her call. She needed to call him, and then they needed to go home.

"You know what," she told Danielle. "If we walk along Broadway, I'm pretty sure we could arrange to walk past that all-night chocolate chip cookie place on our way home. What do you think?"

Danielle's lips curved into a smile, though Arden could see her trying to hide it.

"I have to call someone first," she said. "Someone I promised to call when I found you."

The smile dimmed. "Eleanor?"

"No, no. A relative. You'll meet him—soon, I hope. He's a photographer."

"Like Mom."

Arden eyed her carefully. "Your mom didn't actually take the photos, sweetheart. She just made special frames for them."

"She did take them. With her camera. She showed me."

Arden stared at her granddaughter. Somehow, she had assumed that Leigh used photos she found on public sites. It had never occurred to her that Leigh had taken the pictures herself. Like Robert.

"She told me that a person's eyes were a camera," Danielle said. "You could take a picture with your eyes, and it would be yours for always. In your brain. And if you tried really, really hard, you could even take pictures of things you weren't actually seeing. You could feel it, and then you'd see it."

Arden's breath caught. What was Danielle saying?

"Is that what you meant by your pictures? When you saw your mom, even though you weren't with her?"

Danielle looked away. "Kind of."

Oh no you don't, Arden thought. The girl had extended a

hand, and she wasn't going to let her pull it back. "What does *kind of* mean?"

Sheepish was the only word for the expression on Danielle's face. "I tried to do what she said. Most of the time I got it wrong. But once in a while I got it right, and she liked that."

Arden narrowed her eyes. "What did you actually do, to get it right?"

"Mostly, I kind of guessed," Danielle admitted. "From what I sort of knew. Like, if it seemed like something that maybe *could* be real. But I didn't always see it, like she was telling me to. That's why I was so bad at it."

Arden gathered all of Danielle's words and let them come together in an answer to the question that had been troubling her. The parrot, the girl in riding clothes, even the fall on the ice—clues, scraps, and lucky guesses, repackaged to win her mother's elusive attention.

Then she remembered the morning of the train wreck, when Danielle had bolted upright in bed, screaming. That was different. Not a guess.

The pieces moved apart again; the picture unformed. Arden struggled to hold both true things at the same time—Danielle pretending, and Danielle screaming in terror at a real event that was taking place miles away—but there was no way to make them touch.

Yet she understood, there on the steps of what had once been a riding stable, that nobody was just one thing. She had put her granddaughter in a box called *literal, methodical.* Whatever didn't belong in that box couldn't be true. It was a ridiculous way to think about a human being.

"I know for a fact," she told Danielle, "that it made your mom really proud and happy to have a daughter who was so sensitive and attuned to her."

It was an interpretation of what Leigh had said, a shading of her words. But that didn't make it untrue.

Arden remembered Leigh's insistence that her daughter had a special kind of emotional intelligence, while Arden herself had worried that it was a ploy to get attention. Perhaps it really was both. Perhaps everyone was both. Sensitive and selfish. Worthy and unworthy.

Even her. Even Leigh.

Arden had no idea if Leigh had meant *saddled* in the way she'd just framed it for Danielle, but she might have. Why not?

Danielle nodded, and Arden said, "I just need to make that phone call but I'll be quick, I promise. And then we'll be on our way to warm chocolate chip cookies."

She dug her phone out of the coat pocket. She prayed that Robert was still awake and would answer so she wouldn't have to disturb his family.

He did answer; he'd been waiting. "She's fine," Arden said. "I'm sorry I didn't call sooner. We've been sitting here talking."

"Was she where you thought she would be?"

"She was."

"Aha. Well done."

"You're the one who showed me how to look."

"You're the one who figured it out. I just fed you the lines. *You* found her, Arden."

"*We* found her."

The sentence hung in the air between them, like a benediction. For a long moment, neither of them spoke. Then Danielle announced, loudly, "You *said* it would be a quick call."

"Indeed I did." Arden gave her a thumbs-up and told Robert, "We'll speak again. Soon, I hope. And please tell Jennifer that I'm so sorry for disturbing her."

"No worries. She's pretty forgiving."

Arden gave a wistful smile, then ended the call. "That cold has crept right into my bones," she told Danielle. "I believe the doctor is prescribing warm chocolate chips, ASAP."

Danielle, already standing, put out a hand to help her grandmother. "Technically," she said, "I don't think you should be rewarding me for sneaking out in the middle of the night. But I'm going to give you a pass, this one time."

"A wise decision. As Ralph Waldo Emerson said, 'A foolish consistency is the hobgoblin of little minds.'" Danielle smiled, and Arden gave her a smug look. "You're not the only one with a quote or two up her sleeve." Then she linked her arm through her granddaughter's and they headed west, toward the bakery— and home.

When she had tucked Danielle back into bed—for the second time that evening—Arden went into Connor's study and closed the door. She eased herself into his ergonomic chair and laid her palms on the wooden desk. She sat quietly for a few minutes and then slowly moved her fingers over the landscape of dents and scars. Then she reached into her pocket for the pen she had brought with her, a blue ballpoint that Regina Elias had given her with Emerson-Alcott's logo. She found a sheet of blank paper in the center drawer and wrote what would become the title poem in her first published collection.

> Rain falling into river,
> river lifting into rain.
>
> One water, offering itself
> in endless translation,
>
> Irrigating the arid land
> equally, for the good of all

DRINKING FROM THE SKY

2014

Danielle was finishing the year with good grades, a fascination with the Japanese game of Go, and a small part in the school play. She even had a best friend named Waverly who, like her, loved to unravel questions like the difference between *et cetera* and *infinity*. Eleanor Cardoza had reduced their sessions to twice a month. The permanent custody hearing was scheduled for July. Ivan had visited a few times, but the eight-city tour made it difficult for him to stay longer than an afternoon. Still, Arden had to concede that he was trying.

She'd sent Robert the promised photos, though he and Danielle hadn't actually met. There were a series of late winter storms, and then Waverly invited Danielle to come to Montana with her family for Easter break, and of course Arden said yes. There was no point in visiting Robert without Danielle, so she put it off again.

While Danielle was in Montana, Arden went to visit her sister-in-law Georgia who, ironically, had outlived her husband. The surgery Hugh had undergone for a blocked artery—the reason he couldn't come to Connor's funeral—hadn't gone as they'd hoped, and Georgia had become a widow too.

As Arden sat on Georgia's patio, gazing at the snow-capped Rockies, a plan began to form in her mind: to join households. She'd always liked Georgia. They were more alike than different now, women over sixty who weren't sure what came next. She thought the idea might appeal to Georgia, who was too friendly and generous to enjoy living alone.

It would be good for Danielle too. The more Arden thought about it, the surer she was that raising Danielle in yet another insulated dyad wasn't a great idea. Custody was important, but it wasn't everything. Danielle needed more than one influence in her life.

If Georgia was willing to come to New York, as Arden hoped, she'd introduce her to the Whitney, the Guggenheim, the High Line—the garden walkway that had been built on the tracks of the old West Side elevated train. It was one of Arden's favorite places: a train line reclaimed, transformed.

She'd sell the apartment, find a brownstone in Chelsea or a big airy loft. Georgia or no Georgia, it was time.

A second plan was simmering too: a trip she wanted to make with Danielle and Waverly—to Egypt, during their next winter break. The pyramids, Karnak, the Sphinx. It would be the right season this time.

Arden remembered the mangoes and water buffalos, the heat. The feluccas with their big white sails, and the paintings on the underground tombs. Clumps of purple grapes, sheaves of corn. Creatures with bird heads, jackal heads, cobra heads. Processions of baboons and white-robed maidens. A café by the water, strung with glittering lights.

She thought of the scarab beetle, revered by the ancient Egyptians, and how its eggs lay buried in dung until new life was

ready to emerge, nourished by the dung itself, slowly transform-
ing, until it was time to wake up, walk out.

Survivors, like her.

It wasn't until Arden was sure Danielle was going to be happy at
Emerson-Alcott that she allowed herself to let go of what she
thought Leigh had owed Danielle—or her.

In truth, she had been just as selfish as Leigh. The only difference was that she'd had time to set things right—or to discover
that they'd already been set right, if not by her, then by what
came later and seemed more important.

Leigh, in contrast, hadn't been given the time she needed.
That unfairness let Arden be angry at fate, or time, but not at
Leigh. It wasn't forgiveness, exactly, but almost.

And then there was Connor. Arden had spoken to someone
at the phone company about the Cloud thing and how she could
get access to Connor's messages. Apparently, it wasn't as simple
as being a bereft widow. If it wasn't your own data, you needed
some kind of emergency or official order. At first, Arden had
been upset at being thwarted. And then, whatever had been fuel-
ing her determination to know Connor's secrets—if there were
any—seemed to fade away. She either trusted and believed him,
or she didn't.

She remembered deciding, long ago, when they met over a
glass of Glen Fiddich, that she would be someone worth trusting. It meant that she would trust him, too, and she always had.
Why would that change, just because he had died?

Strangely, as the months passed, it almost seemed as if she
could see Connor more clearly than ever. Not just memories of
times they had shared but how he must have looked when he
gave one of his talks in Albany or helped Finn crate apples at the

farm. She hadn't actually seen him do those things, yet they were just as real to her as the things she had seen for herself.

There were real memories too. How Connor looked when they were taking the train through Alaska, and he leaned forward to catch a glimpse of Denali. His inability to carry a tune, his delight when he found a perfect peach.

The summer they rented a house on the beach with an outdoor shower and two kitchen doors, a tiny front yard filled with white stones, and a roof deck instead of a backyard. The night the fog turned into rain, and they drank from the sky.

Connor's plan had been to open the special bottle of Château Lafite Rothschild that he'd been saving for a "no-occasion occasion."

"It's a 1986," he explained. "The best vintage they've ever had, and now is the perfect time to open it. I say: let's drink it tonight."

Arden remembered being dismayed at the extravagance. She had no idea when he'd bought the wine—before they met, certainly—but it seemed like something you ought to save for a bona fide "special moment," not a random evening on a summer vacation.

When she tried to say that, he gave her one of his wonderful smiles. "Every moment is a special moment, my ardent Arden, because it might be your last. You never know."

His declaration made her remember the girl with braids and the tomato elves. He'd told the girl that every day was your birthday and every moment was the first moment you'd been alive. It seemed like the same thing. Your first moment, your last.

Besides, there was no point arguing with Connor. She waved a hand—*As you wish, it's your bottle*—and waited while he took two glasses from the cabinet and made a great ceremony of removing the cork. She watched as he filled their glasses. Then she took one and lifted it for a toast. But he said, "Not yet. Let's take it up to the roof."

"All right." She followed him up a spiral of metal slats that ended in a gable with a blue door. Connor pushed the door open with his shoulder, holding his wine glass aloft. Arden eased past him, cradling her own glass, and looked around.

It really was a spectacular view, even swathed in fog. Dunes, rocks, and an expanse of ocean. They'd gone up there before to sunbathe but never in the evening. Arden tilted her head, looking for the moon. Then she felt the ping of drops. "It's raining."

"Just a drizzle," Connor said. He gave her a look that made her heart catch. She wasn't the only ardent one; he had a plan for the wine and the dark rooftop. "We're not going to let it stop us, are we?"

Arden met his eyes. No. She wasn't going to stop.

"Open your mouth," he said. "Taste the rain."

Like an obedient child, she lifted her face and inhaled the smell of brand-new rain. Petrichor, it was called. The Greek word for the earthy scent when rain falls on dry soil.

She felt the water on her face. Let it run down her skin.

Then she turned and met Connor's gaze. He took their glasses and set them on the ground, under a little table made of white rattan. The wine didn't matter. She did. They did. He took her face in his hands and opened her mouth with his. Her arms slid around his back.

There was a chaise lounge on the roof deck, next to the rattan table. He led her to it, pulled her on top of him. The rain covered them like a blanket.

It seemed extraordinary to Arden that she had become a happily married woman at last. It could so easily have not happened. She could have been too angry or too proud to meet him at the little place on the river, in Tarrytown. She could have met him, just so she could reject him back. Or they could have just been one more partner in each other's chain. But it did happen.

It struck her that without Connor's experiment with polyamory, they wouldn't have come together. It had humbled and opened him, and he had invited her into that open place.

Maybe that was why he had told Leigh about polyamory. If he even had.

Arden no longer cared. There were too many pieces that made up a life. You couldn't pull them apart, no more than you could pull the rain into separate drops.

You could only lift your face and let it get wet.

Drink what the sky offered, as it spun air into light.

Discussion Questions

1) Arden is certain that there is a "payment" she owes for her past acts. Do you think she is right? Why, or why not? Was there a point in the story when you felt that she really did "pay?" If so, how?

2) Money plays a recurring role in Arden's life: the need for money; the power and freedom that money can offer; the credit card that makes her feel that she isn't helpless. Robert's meticulous accounting of expenses is contrasted with Jonah's disregard for money; Michael's money can solve some problems but not all of them.

Do you think Arden places too much importance on money?

What role does money play in our lives? Does it play different roles for different people?

3) On the first page of the book, Arden says that she did what she had to do, "no matter what kind of rock slide was threatening to bury her." Later, a girl is buried under fallen rock, Connor and Leigh are killed on the rocks, and Leigh talks about the stones that have marked her path.

A rock (or stone) calls to mind something hard, inanimate, that can't move or change. In contrast, there are things in the book that *do* change—even the old West Side Train Line transforms into the High Line, a pedestrian walkway filled with plants and trees.

Are there things in your life that can't be changed? Other things that, perhaps, could be?

Is it up to us to push the dung ball across the ground so new life can emerge—to roll ourselves free? Or, like Arden, do we need the help of others?

4) Arden hurts people with her words, yet words are also her tool, as a poet. As she says on page 198: "Words were what she had. Her paint, her clay."

In one of the book's final scenes, Danielle finds a new meaning for her mother's hurtful words, along with a new freedom. She quotes Lewis Carroll about how words can mean so many different things: "The question is, which is to be master—that's all."

Did words help Arden and Danielle, in the end? Or was it something other than words? Have words been helpful in your own life, or do you think that only actions really count?

5) Do you think Arden was a good mother? Why, or why not?

Acknowledgments

Profound thanks to all who helped on the journey from first draft to final book:

~ Lidija Hilje, smart and generous developmental editor, for her keen insights as I was finding my way to tell the story.

~ Beta readers Joan Fernandez, Judith Turner-Yamamoto, Kay Scott, and Gretchen Gold for their thoughtful reflections that were so vital in lifting that first rough manuscript to the next level.

~ Writing bestie Maggie Smith for her unwavering support at every turn—for believing in this story from the very beginning and being there through thick and thin.

~ The fabulous team at She Writes Press: visionary publisher Brooke Warner; gracious, impeccable, and ever-patient project manager Lauren Wise Wait; and brilliant cover designer Julie Metz, who outdid herself with a cover that's even more glorious than my first three.

~ Anne-Marie Nieves of GetRed PR, my wonderful publicist, whose advice was always spot-on and whose thoughtful response provided the spark for a slightly different ending to Leigh's story—one that I think Leigh deserved!

~ Renee Weiss Weingarten, founder of Renee's Reading Club, whose support of my work, and the work of so many other authors, has meant the world to me

Special thanks to painter and friend Thierry Guillemin for providing the words used in the epigraph. Thierry wrote those words to convey the theme of his 2024 show, *The Promise of Dawn*, yet they also capture the essence of *Roll the Sun Across the Sky* so beautifully.

Author's Note

The train accident that upends Arden's life is based on a real event that took place in December of 2013 on the Hudson Line of Metro North, New York's commuter railroad. I've changed some of the details, but the essential facts are true.

Similarly, I've taken a small liberty with the date for the last time the Orient Express made its way from Venice to Istanbul. It was, indeed, in 1977, but on May 20 of that year, not in the late summer. I shifted the date for the sake of the story since, as a teacher and school librarian, Arden and Robert couldn't have made an extended trip to Europe during the spring.

About the Author

BARBARA LINN PROBST is an award-winning author of contemporary women's fiction living in New York's Hudson Valley. Her acclaimed debut, *Queen of the Owls*, is the story of a woman's search for wholeness, framed around the art and life of iconic American painter Georgia O'Keeffe. Her second novel, *The Sound Between the Notes*, chosen by Kirkus Reviews as one of the best independent press books of 2021, explores timeless questions of identity and belonging through the unique perspective of a musician. Her third novel, *The Color of Ice*, finalist for the Hawthorne Prize, is framed around the magical art of glassblowing and set in Iceland.

Each of Barbara's books has been a medalist for prestigious national awards, including the Nautilus Award for Fiction, the Independent Book Publishers Association Award in both literary and popular fiction, and the Sarton Award for Contemporary Fiction, for which she was the 2022 gold medalist.

Barbara has a PhD in clinical social work and is a former researcher, teacher, advocate, and therapist. She has given numerous workshops and presentations for organizations including the Author Learning Center, the Women's Fiction Writers Association, and the Kauai Writers Conference online. She has also published over 75 essays on the craft of writing and the writing life. *Roll the Sun Across the Sky* is her fourth novel.

Looking for your next great read?

We can help!

Visit www.shewritespress.com/next-read
or scan the QR code below for a list
of our recommended titles.

She Writes Press is an award-winning
independent publishing company founded to
serve women writers everywhere.